I WON'T CRY
FOR
YESTERDAY

I WON'T CRY FOR YESTERDAY

Paul B. Spence

Asura Press

I WON'T CRY FOR YESTERDAY

An Asura Press Book

PRINTING HISTORY
Paperback Edition / 2020

ISBN: 978-1-929928-12-5

www.paulbspence.com
author@paulbspence.com

For all those lost in memory.

CHAPTER ONE

I've been told that if you die in a dream, you'll never see the light of dawn.

I've seen enough dawns to know that isn't true. Many times in dreams have I died, over and over, only to be resurrected in a cold sweat the next morning. The dreams are never *exactly* the same, but they all share a common theme: I'm a child, and horrible things are happening to me and to the other children.

Day after day, I wake up screaming. You'd think that a person would become inured to dreams of pain and the fear of death, but it always hits me the same way when I wake up. The terror and the poignant sense of loss are the worst. I feel as if the nightmares are my only link to something important. I feel a connection to something I don't understand.

The dreams are always with me, even when I'm awake.

The cold darkness is forever lurking in the back of my mind, waiting to pounce. I dread things that trigger those memories. I fear thinking too much about them.

I've never gone to a therapist about the nightmares; I know they'd say my parents had abused me, or some bullshit like that. They wouldn't understand. I saw a therapist once before, for... something that happened in college. I thought then that the answers the therapist gave were, at best, educated guesses.

Hell, *I* can guess. I can do better than that. It's my head, after all.

Maybe the nightmares are just how I face the horror of my job. I'm surrounded by the reality of death all the time. Dead hopes, dead dreams, and dead bodies: a smorgasbord of fear and frustration to feed my subconscious paranoid delusions. I can't lie to myself that way, though; I've had the nightmares much longer that I've had my job.

My job? I'll get to that.

I'd never told anyone about my nightmares. People think I'm strange enough as it is. I *have* sometimes thought the nightmares might be some sort of repressed memories, and *that* is truly frightening. I usually have a very clear memory, but I do have some dark, foggy places. That's where the dreams lurk, on the tattered frontiers of my own personal psychosis.

I've tried a few times to conjure up those memories, but my head begins to pound, and I find myself facing another migraine. It's easier to pretend that I'm normal. As if anyone would ever think that, if they got to know me.

I'd had a particularly bad night and slept the morning that things really started to happen. Maria picked me up for lunch. She wanted to talk about the River case, and all I could think about were my nightmares. They had a chilling sense of premonition, despite me being a child in them. I suspected then that something was going to happen soon, something that would change my life. I didn't realize how right I was. Or how sorry I would be to have that burden of knowledge.

Maria was saying something about the police.

"I'm sorry, what did you say?" We were finishing a business lunch while waiting for the police to give us the clearance to visit the latest crime scene. I was, as usual, lost in thought.

"Are you doing okay today, Michelle? You seem distracted. I mean, more than usual. This serial killer stuff boring you?"

I toyed with the remains of my salad. "I just had a rough night. You were saying…?"

"Right." She paused, as if to collect her thoughts. Maria Delgotti liked to have plans and outlines of everything she talked about. She was very organized. I'm not, and I think it drives her crazy. "The Cincinnati police are dragging their feet about getting involved in this. I talked to Agent Taggart about the FBI submitting a formal request for information, but that takes time. You know how I hate these murder cases." She took a long drink of coffee. "I don't know how you handle it."

I shrugged. "I try not to think too much about the victims when I'm not on the job." Maria was the public relations liaison for the consulting company I worked for. We often worked together on jobs. I did the actual work; she kept the press at bay. That was fine by me.

"Still...," she said.

"Have they identified the last victim?" I interrupted.

"I don't think so."

I didn't reply, being lost in thought again.

"You know, Michelle, if you're having anxiety, your health insurance will pay for you to see someone."

"I'm fine, Maria."

She wouldn't give up, though. "Sleep disorders are often anxiety-related. Do you have bad dreams?"

I gave her a sharp look. "That's none of your damn business."

"Right," Maria said with a sigh. She checked her phone. "I'm ready to go when you are." She paid the tab, and we left together to walk out to Maria's silver BMW. She didn't say anything, but I knew she was still worried about me. In a way, I was the core of the company we worked for. I was certainly the most profitable part.

On the books, I'm a consultant who specializes in occult crimes. The reality is a little more muddled. Isn't that the way it always is with reality?

I rode with Maria in silence and tried not to think about what I was going to have to do when we reached the murder site. The sky was clear and bright, but my thoughts were dark and turbulent. Traffic was heavy through Covington. I tried to watch the cars and concentrate on blocking out the feelings of despair rising from the city.

The emanations flowed through the streets in waves. Certain parts of the city are worse than others, and all roads carry echoes of tragedy along them. Pain and terror beat at me for a moment as we passed a burnt-out building. I closed my eyes and sank deeper into the leather seat. It's always worse in the poorer parts of a city, where people are desperate and emotions run high.

The psychic pressure eased up as we neared the river. Water carries away all of our filth.

I clipped on my identification badge as Maria parked. Stepping out of the car, I saw a narrow footbridge in the distance. I felt myself drawn to it by something dark and terrible. I knew that whatever it was, it had nothing to do with my case for the day. I also knew that something terrible would happen there in the future, something that would involve me directly.

I forcibly shoved the feeling out of my mind and walked down to the line of yellow police tape.

CHAPTER TWO

The body was down the hill from me, on the bank of the Licking River a few hundred yards from where it flowed into the Ohio River. I stood there feeling ill and listening to Maria retching loudly, somewhere behind me. That didn't help with my queasiness. I made a note to myself not to accept lunch from Maria before going to work anymore.

I didn't actually get sick, though. I never do.

I looked around the scene of the crime, anywhere but at the bloated, rotting *thing* they had pulled from the river. Most of the police officers weren't looking too good, either. That, perversely, made me feel better. Back along the crest of the hill, a few reporters were starting to gather. It had been a slow month for local news, and the possibility of another grisly murder here in town had the news vans circling like buzzards. I turned my head and closed my eyes, horrified. I hate the media. I think of the glee with which they report others' suffering, and I feel suddenly violent.

I felt like making some news of my own.

"Ms. Fredericks?"

I opened my eyes to meet the bright blue ones of a police officer not much taller than me. "Yes, officer?" I said.

He swallowed convulsively, eyes darting down at the body and back. "Here are some gloves and a mask, ma'am." I hated being called *ma'am*. That had started in my late thirties. The officer was looking pale and far too young to be on a crime scene like this, so I guess *ma'am* made sense. He looked like a scared high school student. Barely had peach-fuzz on his cheeks.

I took the items from him with nodded thanks and let him beat a fast retreat. I keep forgetting the police don't like you to touch their evidence with your bare hands. That usually makes my job much harder. I was thankful today, though. I hadn't wanted to touch rotting flesh without a layer of latex in between... I closed my eyes again and fought down the inevitable reaction that thought provoked.

Hell, I didn't want to touch the body even *with* latex gloves on.

The mask had a strong menthol scent. Someone had thoughtfully smeared Vicks VapoRub on the inside. That would help hide the putrid smell, or at least numb my senses. I pulled on the mask and gloves, and forced myself to look at the body again.

One of the pathologists from the Kenton County coroner's office was currently examining the body, dictating notes into a handheld recorder. I stepped up to where I could hear him. His assistant scowled at me but didn't say anything. I was there at the request of the local office of the FBI, after all.

The body had belonged to a young male, probably in his early teens. It looked to me as if he had been beaten badly, maybe tortured, before being dumped into the river. If so, that would make him the fourth murdered child found in the river this year: two girls, two boys. With each consecutive body, the clues were getting harder to find. The killer was learning, getting good at covering his tracks. I hadn't found any useful clues on the last body. Maybe it had been in the river too long.

Clues might be the wrong word. I'm not a detective – not in the normal sense of the word, anyway. Officially, I'm a consultant in criminal anthropology. I wrote my dissertation on ritual cult murder, after having had a close-up view of it as an undergrad. In reality, I'm mostly a psychic investigator. I've always been psychic to some degree. I grew up in a haunted house, which will help speed along the development of psychism faster than just about anything else. You can think what you want about that. I know there are fakes and frauds out there; I've met them. If it makes you feel better, think of what I have as really good intuition.

I'm not much of a people person. My talents tend to make me stay away from people as much as I can. Three years ago, though, a friend contacted me about an unusual job. He'd been approached through certain channels by the local police. They needed an occult expert to help them with a case they were working on. He wasn't interested himself, but he wanted to know if I wanted the job. I was curious, and essentially unemployed, so I decided to try it.

It was a nasty case involving a string of violent murders. I'd heard about it on the news, so the chance to help find the killer was irresistible. The Cincinnati Police Department hired me as a consultant. It took some time for me to get enough evidence, but I helped catch the bastard. I think that first case solidified my reputation, more than any I've done since. I have a good reputation as being easy to work with and a decent record of providing useful information that closes cases.

I have a lot of minor psychic abilities, but the one of most interest to my current employer and indirectly, the police, was that I'm a psychometrist: I can touch an object and get some kind of feeling about things that have happened with it. This ability used to give me a lot of grief, until I learned to control it. I get little flashes, like pictures or memories, from strong emotional events in an area or on an object. That's what makes me good to have around when trying to solve a crime. If the victim saw the killer when they were killed, I can sometimes catch a glimpse of the killer in my flashes. It's called a residual, a psychic trace left on a place or thing. Put that together with good old-fashioned crime solving, and you sometimes get lucky enough to make an arrest.

I work with various police departments, in three states, on two or three murder cases a year that have some form of ritual component. Unsolved occult murders are common enough to keep me working for many years. I rarely work with the FBI, but serial killers get a lot of media attention. That produces pressure on the police to find the murderer quickly.

I don't always help catch the killer; I don't always get a glimpse or anything else useful. It can be really frustrating. But the ones I do help catch make it well worth it to keep trying. I usually have spectacularly horrible dreams during and after a case. You can only see so much before it really gets to you. Maybe having the abilities I do sets me up for nightmares. I'll probably have them my whole life.

I started working for the Criminological Research Institute in Dayton, Ohio about two years ago. They were the ones who had referred the police to my friend Mark. They contact me when they need me to check out a report of something odd, or give a lecture on cults. I hate public speaking, but they pay well enough to keep me doing it. The non-police cases that I work for them are usually poltergeist and demonic-possession related. Most of them are bogus. There isn't much of that sort of thing actually going on.

The ones that are real get scary very quickly, though.

Did you know that Louisville, Kentucky, has more reported demonic possession cases than the whole rest of North America? I never had liked that city, so when I found out about the demonic possession reports, it didn't surprise me. I try to avoid going through Louisville if at all possible, and I never accept work there. To be honest, I try to avoid entering most of Kentucky except the part I live in, but that doesn't have anything to do with demons.

CHAPTER THREE

Okay, enough procrastinating, I thought to myself.

I squatted down next to the coroner and lightly touched the body, ignoring the foul physical sensations. I couldn't sense anything, not even the usual death echoes. I closed my eyes and concentrated, letting my awareness spread out from my hand. My head started to pound like a spike was being driven through it. My stomach wasn't doing so well, either.

Still nothing.

"Right," I said, swallowing a sudden buildup of saliva. I walked carefully around the edges of the mess. My head started pounding worse. It was the kind of headache that comes on suddenly, like a storm. I get sinus headaches quite often when the barometer drops and a storm rolls in, but the weather that day was fantastic, a clear blue sky with no clouds in sight. It was one of those times in my life I look back on and realize that I should have known instantly what was happening, but I had no clue at the time. You'd think that after years of being subjected to psychic attacks while growing up, I'd recognize an attack as it was happening. They always catch me off guard, though. I keep stumbling through the mundane world and letting the supernatural one slip away.

Supernatural is a strange term, don't you think? Beyond or above the natural. More than natural? It's used to explain things that don't seem natural at all. Most people use the term to describe ghosts, the Loch Ness Monster, and even UFOs. I can't imagine anything more natural than psychism. It isn't magic.

I opened my senses wide, forcing the ability to work, and I felt...*fear*. Something bad was going to happen soon. The feeling didn't come from the body. Someone was *angry*. I felt something rushing toward me; something screamed in the darkness in my mind. I shook myself and opened my eyes.

Maria was standing next to me, looking concerned. I must have looked awful, for Maria to come down to the crime scene. She never did that. She was... *squeamish*.

I struggled to my feet and walked away from the body, carefully pulling off the gloves and mask, wiping the smeared Vicks from my face. Maria followed me, and we walked until the trees cut us off from the crime scene. I breathed deeply and tried focus my thoughts, but my mind was spinning. I couldn't steady my thoughts on anything.

I couldn't quite understand.

Maybe... I lost the feeling.

It was then that my head began to throb harder. Something was wrong with me. I couldn't concentrate. I shivered, although I wasn't cold. I felt like I had the flu, but I knew I didn't.

"Did you get anything from the body?" asked Maria. "Michelle? Are you okay?"

"No. No, I didn't. I'm having trouble sensing anything," I admitted. "No evidence of anything ritual or occult, either. I'll have to wait till the autopsy to see if this body has the same marks as the last ones. If the pattern of abuse is the same, it could be cult related."

I'd been called in to work this case because of the occult symbols that had been found carved into the backs of the first two children. Personally, I thought the marks were red herrings. They were poorly executed designs that sort of matched known occult symbols. The problem was they didn't go together. I'd told the FBI I thought someone was trying to make it look like occult murders, but that they weren't.

I don't think anyone believed me.

Maria looked at me strangely. "We've known each other, what, two years? I've never known you not to be able to sense *something*. What else is wrong? You haven't been on your game today. Is it those nightmares?"

Good old Maria, nosey as ever. Bitch. "I have a headache from hell. I don't know what's wrong." I leaned against a tree. I was starting to feel weak and dizzy. It had nothing to do with the body. This feeling wasn't from what I'd seen but from what I'd felt.

As I leaned against the tree, I felt something else. I felt my head suddenly drawn to the right by a strong sense of unease. The trees blocked the view of where the police were keeping the media back, but whatever was bothering me, it was coming from that direction. My eyes had these little flashes, like the precursor to a migraine. I hoped *that* wasn't what was happening. A migraine would ruin my entire weekend.

I rubbed my eyes. Maybe I'd had too much sun today or something. Heat exhaustion is always a serious problem at this time of year. The feeling of unease got stronger; the hair on the back of my neck rose up. I knew something else was wrong. This wasn't heat exhaustion; it was much, much worse.

I shook my head to clear it. Maria asked me again if I was okay, but I ignored her. I pushed away from the tree. I needed to focus. Psychism is a very delicate thing; even the moods of people around you can affect it. I'd felt this feeling before, though. Somebody wanted my attention, and not in a good way.

They had it. There's nothing like an attack on a person's mind as a way to say hello.

That happens fairly frequently when you study psychism. You start trying to understand the world around you, and someone takes notice and decides to slap you down. I guess that isn't any different from the mundane world, now that I think about it. There was always some jerk ready to knock you down a few pegs just for asking why something is the way it is.

What was odd about this attack was that I hadn't been doing anything to attract notice recently. I'm laid-back and practice psychism in a slow, careful manner. I'm quiet about it. Most of my abilities are passive senses anyway. Psychism is like any branch of specialized knowledge, though: some people just don't want other people to know anything about it.

I've never attacked new people I noticed, but I have been attacked many times before. There was this one case I had worked on last year that... It doesn't matter. Let's just say that I lead a dangerous life sometimes.

I started back toward the car. There was nothing else I could do at the crime scene. The sense of menace grew stronger, though, and the pain in my head got so intense that I gasped and doubled over. Whoever was attacking me was strong and had a lot of built-up anger. I couldn't imagine anyone hating me that much. What could I have possibly done? I'm not saying I'm an innocent little wallflower, but I have a live-and-let-live attitude toward most people. I mostly just stay at home.

Who could I have pissed off?

CHAPTER FOUR

The next few minutes sort of blurred Then Maria was tugging on my arm, and I realized I'd fallen to my knees. My shoulders were so tight, I felt as if I couldn't even turn my head. I was suddenly hypersensitive to everything. The damp ground hurt my knees. My clothes were too tight and constricting. I struggled just to take a breath.

It's weird, really. I've had this theory for a long time about psychic attacks. I think people who are sensitive to psychism, who have abilities themselves, are more vulnerable than people who don't have any abilities at all. I know that seems a bit counterintuitive, but here is how my theory goes: *Disbelief is a powerful shield.* Of course, there's no way to test my theory. If you don't have any abilities, how would you know if you'd been attacked that way?

Who knows how many migraine sufferers are actually just being attacked psychically? It kind of gives me cold chills, thinking about it. A correctly timed attack could cause a person to swerve off the road and wreck. How many crimes have been committed that left no physical traces?

I still vividly remember the first time I experienced a psychic attack. Back when I was in college the first time, I was up late in my dorm room, reading some books on psychism I'd found in the university library. I was practicing a channeling technique that was supposed to get you in touch with your higher self. In hindsight, I was probably generating a psychic beacon that could be felt for miles. As the evening drew closer to the middle of the night, I felt something odd at the end of the room and looked up just in time to see a phantasm coming through my wall.

Now, I didn't know what a phantasm was back then, and I stared at it in shock for a little too long. I mean, this *thing* had just walked out of a wall. If that seems odd to you, think about how *I* felt. It was man-sized, naked and apparently sexless. It had pale, grayish, dead-looking skin that hung in folds off a bony, emaciated body. There wasn't a head, just a mouth, a large slit on the end of a flexible neck, filled with hundreds of translucent, needle-like teeth. The arms ended in long, thin hands; the spidery fingers ended in fleshy knobs. It didn't have any fingernails. It moved toward me with quick, birdlike movements.

It abruptly leapt across the room and tried to bite my throat out. The funny thing is, it was my shock that saved me. *It wasn't really there.* Phantasms are only real in your head. They're thought-forms, nightmares projected into your mind as part of a psychic attack. My disbelief that such a thing could exist was almost certainly what stopped it.

That night almost scared me out of the study of psychism. It wasn't until a few years later that I found out what had actually attacked me. I never did know why. I'm glad, though. All in my head or not, it might have been able to kill me, or at least scare me to death. What was happening by the river was not as bad as that thing had been, but it was still trouble. I was hurting so bad, I didn't know if I could defend myself.

What I needed to do was prepare a mental defense before whoever was attacking me decided to take it to the next level. I needed to build a barrier before something tried to eat me. At least, that's what I was thinking. Funny how pain can make you panic. My mind was racing through the steps required for the barrier when Maria grabbed my arm again, shocking my mind out of the proper state. The pain almost doubled then.

"Damn it, Michelle! Are you okay? You're scaring me!"

"Just shut up for a minute!"

I picked up a stick and carefully drew a circle around us in the dirt. The circle isn't necessary, but it helps to have a focus. I began preparing the mental barrier again. This time Maria had the sense to leave me alone.

I was almost finished when the pain suddenly eased off. Whoever attacked me had decided to stop. I sent out a few mental feelers, but the feeling was definitely gone.

"Michelle? What's going on?"

I stood up slowly and tried to ease my tense muscles. "Psychic attack. Somebody just tried to put a whammy on me. Pretty much succeeded."

"You stopped them?"

I just held up my hand and reached out with my senses. Not a trace of any residual negative energy. "I didn't have anything to do with it, Maria," I said.

"What? But you were..." She trailed off in confusion, then gestured at the circle.

"I didn't have time to finish. The attack just stopped on its own."

"Do you think it was related to who killed the boy?" she asked.

I shook my head. "No, whoever attacked me either wasn't serious or was just warning me about something. A killer wouldn't have backed off. Whoever killed the boy was something worse. That boy," I said, walking back toward the body and the police, "was murdered by a psychopath."

CHAPTER FIVE

Maria stayed to talk to the police, and I went and sat in her car and thought about what just happened. The attack had jarred me out of my preoccupation with my dreams. Whoever sent it had wanted to send me a message. The fact that they dispelled it was interesting. They seemed to want to scare me; it worked.

I hate not having anything to report to the police when they ask me to help with a case. Four murders now, and I hadn't found a thing. This was going to leave a mark on my reputation, and not a good one. Most of the police officers don't believe I could really help anyway. The ones who do believe what I say don't always believe that it has anything to do with a cult. They'd believe it even less if they knew I got my information from psychism. Some of the police seem to think I just guess or make stuff up. Some have thought I was an accomplice of the murderer.

I was even accused of *being* the murderer once.

It took about half an hour for Maria to free herself and come back to the car. She got in but didn't start the engine. She just gripped the wheel in silence.

"What's up?" I asked.

She gave me an odd look. "Everything is fine. One of the officers told me something strange, though."

"Something strange?"

"Yes. He said a woman had been there asking about you. Maybe an hour ago," Maria added.

"So, just about at the time of the attack."

"Do you think she could have anything to do with the murder?"

"Did he get a name, or give you a description?"

"Only that she was chubby, pale, and blond."

"Oh, that should narrow it down," I said cynically. Since most of the people in the Cincinnati area have some German blood, blond hair is fairly common. My brown hair actually makes me stand out. "I'm not sure about anything with this case. If it's just a serial killer, there may not be much I can do. If it's some kind of a cult, then the woman might have been very important. I just don't know."

"Is there anything at all you can tell me?" asked Maria.

"I'm sorry. Maybe if you get me the autopsy results, I can think of something."

"I'll see what I can do."

Maria dropped me off at my house with a promise to call if there were any developments in the case. I wasn't going to hold my breath, though. I checked the mail and sorted it as I walked to my door. My head still hurt, and I ached all over from the mental abuse I'd taken.

I live in Latonia, only a few miles from the Ohio River. It's a bit shabby in places, but fairly quiet – mentally quiet as well as mundanely. I could have bought a house somewhere else, but this was my mother's house, and she had left it to me when she died. I'm not sentimental about it; it's just that the mortgage is paid off, and I don't want a house payment.

Besides, I have the advantages of being near a big city but get to live out closer to the wilderness. I need to drive out into the country sometimes just to clear my brain. The psychic noise of a city can be overwhelming.

It was a little after seven, according to the clock in the living room. Samson, my cat, greeted me by trying to trip me in the hall. I scooped him up and carried him with me, purring, while I made sure my home was secure against intrusion, natural or otherwise. Then I dumped him on the bed and got out of my clothes to take a long, hot shower. I was shaken by what happened at the crime scene but trying not to think about it too much.

These things happen in my business.

After my prolonged scalding, I went into the kitchen and made myself a nice hot chocolate with a dash of whiskey. Given my background, I don't drink alcohol all that often, but I do drink a bit. I just make sure that I never get drunk. I don't want to end up like my mother and drink myself to death.

The chocolate and liqueur worked their magic on my mind and body as I worked my way through the clutter in my living room to my desk and checked my email. In case you haven't noticed, I'm not exactly a normal kind of gal. I do what I want to do when I want to do it. I usually don't feel like cleaning. I straighten the place up regularly, and sweep and such, but why clean constantly when you live alone? I'd never find anything if I put it all away. I don't have guests over very often anyway.

I opened my personal case file for the River murders. I logged my notes for the day and looked over the information on the other four victims. I couldn't concentrate on it, though. I kept thinking about the psychic attack. That led me to call my friend Mark. He wasn't home, so I left a brief message about my problem. Mark knows more about psychism than anyone else I know. Maybe he would have some answers, or at least some ideas. Until then, I was going to have to try to ignore the problem and keep myself protected.

Easier said than done.

I tried to watch the local news, but all they wanted to talk about was the brutal murder of an elderly man in Covington. I was a little shocked, because it was only a few blocks from where I live. Home invasions scare the crap out of me. They weren't going into many details, but given how enthusiastic the reporters seemed, it must has been a horrific murder.

I sat up late in the night, thinking about that and the psychic attack I'd experienced. My brain kept wanting to link everything together: the River murders, the psychic attack, the old man, the feeling I'd had about the bridge. I knew there was no connection, but at least it kept me from worrying about the dreams that sleep would bring.

Mostly, anyway.

INTERLUDE ONE

I know that I'm dreaming, and I can't wake up.

I'm running along a seemingly endless corridor.

I'm wearing a loose gown that billows as I run. The back is open, like a hospital gown. I slow down, stumbling. I'm so tired. I can't keep running. Someone is holding my arm, pulling me forward, urging me to run. I can feel his fear as well as my own.

There's blood on the floor behind me.

My feet are bare. I'm cold and frightened. I pull my arm away from the person in front of me. He is a young boy, thirteen or so, the same age as I am in the dream. He has the most incredible green eyes I have ever seen. I see his mouth moving, but I don't hear him. The alarms drown out his words.

There is a body on the floor behind me. That's where the blood came from: the blood on the floor, my hands, my gown. The body's throat has been ripped out, and somehow I know I had done it. I don't need to be goaded along now.

We run.

The corridors are wide. I don't know where we are. It looks like some kind of hospital, but it isn't. The doors all have electronic locks. The colors are all wrong, not soothing but stark and antiseptic.

I wonder if I've gone mad.

We slow as we come to a corner. He motions me still. He's taller than I am. That seems strange to me, because I'm fairly tall, aren't I? I'm not so sure – not here, not now. His hair is dark brown like mine, maybe with a touch of red, but that could be blood. There's blood covering him as well.

He looks familiar, but then, they all do.

Who? The other kids here, in this place.

I'm confused but willing to believe the rules of the dream.

I have some other memory trying to break through, but it fades. My thoughts are like the surf. Memories wash up on my shore to rearrange the sand of my unconsciousness, only to be erased by the next wave.

Two men come around the corner. They seem shocked to see us. Maybe it's the blood on us that surprises them. The boy attacks the first man without hesitation. I find myself attacking the other one. No thought is involved. It seems ridiculous, children attacking grown men. We're both so small and young. But the loud crack as the boy breaks the man's arm proves otherwise. I kick mine in the groin, and then chop down on his spine at the base of his neck. He's still alive but paralyzed for the moment. There is a loud crackle like snapping trigs as the boy breaks the other man's neck, and then he does the same with my man. The boy is stronger than me, and it irritates me somehow. I pause to look at how strange they seem with their heads like that.

They are almost comical.

The boy searches for a moment and seems pleased to find a credit card – no, an electronic key for the doors. He grabs my hand, and we run again. He doesn't seem to find it strange that we just killed two men, so I don't, either. It doesn't seem wrong here and now.

The boy seems confused about what to do.

So am I.

I'm just glad I'm not alone.

We go through a door, then back out and try another, then another. The rooms seem to be operating rooms or something like that. Maybe something worse. Maybe something much worse.

I remember those rooms all too well. I'm not sure what we're trying to do. This game – no, not a game, life and death – this running is making me tired. I fall.

I am so tired. Not tired – wounded. Wounded? Some of the blood on the gown is mine. I think I must have been shot. I don't know when. My side hurts. I shouldn't have thought about it. It feels like someone is driving a hot iron poker under my ribs.

How do I know what that feels like? I don't want to think about it too closely.

The boy, young man, tears his gown and stuffs a wad of it into the hole in my side. I scream. He clamps a hand over my mouth. I shake and convulse for a moment, then get a handle on the pain. I'm okay. He whispers that we need to be quiet. I nod my head and struggle to my feet. We run some more. There are more doors ahead. He opens the one at the end of the corridor and then stumbles back with a yell.

Men come through the door, with guns. He slams the door into the first one, and we run. I'm surprised they don't shoot us, but I think they want us alive. They're going to catch us soon. They're going to put us into the machine again. This time, maybe they won't let us out. They'll hurt us till we pop and pour out of the machine like that girl last week, and they'll stand there and do nothing except take notes.

I can't go back in there.

I would rather die now and have it over with.

CHAPTER SIX

Saturday began badly for me and went downhill from there.

I consider any day that begins with a phone call to be a bad day. I usually turn off my phone on Saturdays, but the River case had me on edge. I wanted to be available if anyone needed me. There hadn't been any new developments, and I really wanted to help, but I couldn't. It was frustrating.

It took me a couple of tries to answer the phone. "Hello," I said groggily.

"Wake up, Sleeping Beauty. Did you forget about us?"

"Huh?" I 'd been startled out of a nightmare and felt like my body didn't quite fit right. I'd been expecting it to be a call from Maria, not an ex-boyfriend.

"The faire, babe. It's pirate weekend. You promised you would come and watch us perform."

"Oh, hell!" I exclaimed, sitting up. It was twenty minutes after ten in the morning. The faire would be opening soon. "I'll be there."

"We'll be looking for you," Josh said, and disconnected.

I raced to get ready.

I love to spend my weekends in the autumn at the Southern Ohio Renaissance Festival. I've been doing it for close to two years now.

Most of my time is spent wandering around with some of my friends who happen to work there as pirates. I don't work with them, but I like to play along. It can be great fun, dressing up and letting people think that you really do work at the faire.

It lets me pretend to be someone else for a while. I can sometimes get through a whole weekend without thinking about work. Everything there is an illusion. There, I get to be free.

It has some disadvantages, of course. There are often large crowds of people at the faire. Sometimes the emotions can be overwhelming. The psychic noise grinds at my shields, but I usually do okay. I have a few charms and such that I wear to help drown out the noise. No, not magic, just a focus for my own abilities.

I passed a plain white van on my street as I was leaving. Something about it bothered me, or I wouldn't have even noticed it. I ignored the feeling, though. It looked like a plumber's van or something. Probably just some guys working on one of houses along the street. My neighborhood has a lot of older houses that seem to be in a constant state of renovation.

I think it would be fair to say that I broke a few traffic laws.

I got to the faire after it opened. I was also really hungry.

Running past the food vendors to get to the back stage reminded me that I hadn't eaten anything the night before. I hadn't stopped for breakfast on the way in because I was late. I'd have to get something soon; I could hear my stomach growling even over the noise of the crowd.

The pirate show had already started when I got to the stage. There were so many people watching that I had to stand in the back. Josh was just then leaping across a wooden table, sending bottles spinning to the straw-strewn boards below. He blocked a slashing blow from a saber. I could hear the ringing blows and mock-curses from the stage. After a few minutes of feint and counter-feint, he resolved loudly to end the fight, with a vicious flurry of attacks and parries. He lunged forward and missed. As he struggled to recover, a boot was planted firmly on his butt, and he was sent crashing to the stage.

The crowd roared with laughter.

Josh was face down in the straw, slowly rising to his hands and knees. I couldn't concentrate on the comedy show; I had this nagging feeling that I was missing something, which really annoyed me. It was kind of like that feeling that someone was watching me. But I couldn't get a feel for what direction it was coming from. There were too many people around.

Josh likes to say that he jumps up and vanquishes his foes with lightning-quick strokes of his sword. Actually, he comically struggled to his feet just in time to get brained with a bottle and slump back to the stage floor, pretending to be unconscious.

The patrons like the more slapstick comedy.

The crowd was lively that day. I could feel almost-physical waves of happiness coming off them, hitting me from all sides. They roared with laughter or gasped with astonishment at all the right times. I was trying to figure out why I felt so disoriented. Something just didn't feel right; my mood kept flatlining. Normally when I'm in a crowd like this, I just soak up the ambient energy and ride the euphoria that comes from tuning in with so many people at once. Even if you aren't psychic, you've probably felt that euphoria at a concert or baseball game or something. For me, it's even better.

I scanned the crowd. Everyone seemed to be enjoying the show, except for a small group of goths sitting in the back row. I guess they were too caught up in the angst of it all. Either that, or they were miserable in the thick layers of black cloth and white face paint. I've never understood why people so determined not to have a good time go out in public at all. I was curious and looked closer at them. As I did so, my vision went out of focus for a moment. I really needed to eat.

I had noticed fake fangs on a few.

Oh no, I thought. *Fruit bats.*

Now, don't get me wrong. I have nothing against goths in general. Some of my best friends are goths. That sounds terrible, doesn't it? It's like saying some of my best friends are gay. Also true, but trite. It might also sound hypocritical, since I was standing in the hot late-September sun in black leather and cloth as part of my full pirate costume. But that's different. I was wearing appropriate clothes for my setting, and I only dress as a pirate when at the faire. Goths dress like that, and act like they're miserable doing it, all year long.

At least I *enjoy* dressing up.

But these weren't just melancholy goths; these were fruit bats. People like that seem to think they actually *are* vampires. Really. I've known quite a few of them. Now, I've seen some *very* odd things in my life, but if vampires really existed, I think I would know about it.

I also doubt that they would dress like rejects from an *Addams Family* movie audition. I concentrated on directing happy thoughts at them. After a few minutes, they seemed to get uncomfortable and left.

CHAPTER SEVEN

Speaking of batty goth friends, the short, lumpy woman trailing behind the others had looked suspiciously like Lucy Dubois. She was an acquaintance, sometimes sort-of friend, of some eleven years. I detest the term *frenemy*, but she kind of qualified. If it was her, it was odd for her to be here. Lucy never had liked renfaires. She never really liked *anything* that was actually fun.

I waved to her, but either she didn't see me, or she was in a bad mood.

Renfaires were too normal for her, I guess, or maybe too out of touch with the current era. She was much more into modern industrial settings, nightclubs and such. I'd have thought that she would have called me if she was coming to the faire. She knows that I go regularly. I'd have at least met her for coffee or something.

Lucy *had* called me on the phone a couple of weeks ago about meeting some new friends of hers. Maybe it had been last month. I couldn't remember. It had been several years since I had really *talked* to her. We'd never been extremely close. When she called, she had been overly enthusiastic about her new friends. I hadn't paid much attention to what she said; I'd been too tired. Besides, Lucy was always wildly enthusiastic about something-or-other. The only thing that seemed odd at the time was why she was bothering to tell me about it. I guess she'd just needed someone to talk to.

A badly placed boot brought my attention painfully back to the pirate show at that point. Someone in the crowd had stepped on my foot. The pirates were wrapping things up with a flurry of ringing sword blows. Thank god, I'd be able to get out of the hot sun. I guess I could have gotten out of the sun sooner, but it would have been rude. Those were my friends up on the stage. The least I could do was stay and watch till the end of their show.

After the pirate act was over, I followed my jolly pirate band down to the tavern for a quick pint, in my case a pint of ice-cold soda and something to eat. From the way I felt, I needed it. The others had pints of beer. There were eight of us in our pirate group that day. Only six members of the group actually worked the show.

If you're wondering what the hell pirates are doing at a Renaissance faire, you're not the only one. Every since that movie with Johnny Depp – before, even – pirates have been a staple at the faires. The patrons want to see pirates, so they give them pirates. The faire is a business, after all. For my part, I try to dress like an *Elizabethan* pirate. There have been pirates as long as there have been ships, so why not try for a little authenticity?

The tavern at the faire is a large, one-story wooden structure that I think looks more like a flat barn than a tavern. It has three open walls and lots of sturdy picnic-style tables and benches. The occasional wooden pillar keeps the roof where it belongs. Any time of day, you can find all kinds of people there: merchants, performers, and other people associated with the faire, taking a break.

There were also a good number of regular patrons, mundane people enjoying the faire and just wanting a chance to get out of the sun and have a bit to drink. There are a few playtrons mixed in as well, just to confuse the issue. Playtrons are people who don't work at the faire, but come there dressed up and playing along anyway, like me. I waved to the people I knew, got my drink and food, and found a seat.

"Mind if I sit with you?"

I looked up at the well-built man across the table, and groaned. Josh. Most of the time I like to pretend that I don't know him. Don't ask. "Yes, I mind. Go away." I really didn't want to play our usual games right then. My head had started to pound again, like the day before. I was afraid of what that might mean.

He sat down anyway, brushing his long, sandy-brown hair out of his face. Jeez, you make one mistake, get a little tipsy one night and sleep with a guy, and he stalks you for the rest of your natural existence. The fact that he was movie-star handsome had nothing to do with it.

Yes, I know that doesn't make sense, since I rushed to the faire after he called me.

Don't judge.

CHAPTER EIGHT

Josh tried to look hurt, but he wasn't *that* good an actor. "I just wanted to apologize. I know I was a bit of a jerk to you, Rhiannon, but you could have returned my calls."

Okay, so maybe *stalk* isn't the right word, but he'd been around me a lot more than usual, and not just because we were at the faire together every weekend, either. Maybe I was just feeling a bit more sensitive right then. Josh was a bit of a ladies' man. I wasn't sure how I felt about him. I knew that it wouldn't work out with us being together, but I'm human. I do get lonely. I just didn't like being thought of as a conquest.

"Rhiannon?" He looked like a lost puppy.

"Don't call me that," I snapped.

My name *is* Rhiannon, and no, my parents weren't gypsies. I have a more than a bit of the second sight, but I suspect it's of Welsh or Irish origin. I wasn't named after that damned Fleetwood Mac song, either; it came out a few years after I was born. I have used it to lie about my age a few times, though. I have no idea what my parents were thinking when they named me. I've gone by Michelle, my middle name, since I was a little girl. Why, you ask? Try teaching a four-year-old to say *Rhiannon*, much less spell it.

"Damn, what's up your ass?"

"Josh, don't be a prick. I just don't feel good."

"I'm sorry you're feeling under the weather."

"Well," I said, "how strange would it be if I felt *over* the weather?"

He paused for just a little too long, then laughed, and we continued to banter good-naturedly. He wasn't a bad guy, just a little too self-centered and not very bright. He wouldn't be willing to settle down with one woman – not with me, anyway. Once he got it through his head that he wasn't getting back into my bed, things would be okay between us. I think he mainly just didn't want to be the kind of guy who sleeps with a girl once and then dumps her.

To tell the truth, I really wouldn't have minded too much if he had wanted to... But no, it wouldn't work. It was hard enough hanging out with him now. Besides, he had a bit of a reputation around the faire. I think sometimes he really thought he was a pirate.

"So, Michelle, I saw you on the news last night. What was going on?"

Trust Josh to find the wrong thing to say. I sighed as all my problems came crashing back into my head. "I'm working with the police again."

"How did that work out?" He didn't believe in psychism. We'd had several conversations about my career and how "wrong" it was. That was ironic, since he's one of the most powerful manipulative empaths I've ever met. Sorry – psychologists call it *hyper-emotive*.

Whatever.

"It didn't work out. I wasn't able to figure out anything about who the killer was."

"Killer?" he asked.

"The Newport police found the body of a young boy, badly beaten and abused. The FBI got involved. They couldn't find any clues, so they me asked to help, but the body had been in the river too long. All the psychic clues had drained away. I wasn't able to help."

"That sucks. How old was he?" He seemed entirely too morbidly curious.

"Josh, I'm sorry, but this really isn't a good time to talk about it."

We sat in silence for a few minutes. I hated to end things on a sour note, so I decided to steer the conversation toward a safer topic: weapons. "I finally got that new sword I was telling you about."

He grinned, as happy as I was to drop the old topic. "So let's see it, *Rhi-an-non*." He enunciated my name carefully so I would know that he was ribbing me again.

Ignoring the teasing, I pulled out my sword and handed it to him. He's lucky I didn't use it on him. He made a few practice cuts with it as he whistled his appreciation. I rolled my eyes at him. If he wanted to wave a sword around off-stage and get in trouble with the faire management, that was his business. It was a really nice sword, though: a replica Dussack cutlass, with a long serrated edge and a guard shaped like a large shell, perfectly balanced.

"Don't cut yourself," I said sarcastically.

He gave me a sour look. "Sure this isn't too much sword for you, Rhi?"

I just glared and held out my hand.

As I sheathed the sword, I felt the subtle tendrils of a ranged psychic probe and made the motion to help ward them off. Then pain exploded behind my eyes. The next thing I knew, I was lying on the ground with Josh kneeling over me.

"Are you okay, Michelle?"

My head was pounding, and not just from hitting hard-packed dirt. I'd just been attacked again. A small crowd was starting to gather around.

Joshed helped me carefully to me feet. I wobbled for a minute, but then my legs grew steady under me. I needed to get out of there and safely home.

"I'm sorry," I said. "My head hurts. A little too much sun, I think. I'm going to get out of here, go home, and try to get some rest."

Josh offered to walk me to my car, but I told him no, I'd be fine. There was a chorus of *okay* and *take care*. These were my friends; they would do just about anything for me, even when I was acting strange.

Hell, they were probably used to me acting strange. I left the tavern quickly, avoiding the looks from the others.

CHAPTER NINE

I caught a glimpse of the goths to one side as I left the tavern. They were laughing about something. I thought it was strange to see them so animated. I went to the right, around the back of the building where I could make a straight run for my Jeep if I had to, but no one followed me. The feeling was gone; my head was clear, though throbbing. I hadn't had time to do anything, so whoever had attacked must have backed off again for some reason. Just like the day before.

I walked quickly out to my Jeep Cherokee to head home. I was glad that it was a sunny afternoon. You're no safer during the day than at night from this sort of thing, but the bright sunshine does have a calming effect on the mind. Maybe nighttime is scarier because your vision is so limited. It seems easier to believe in ghosts and other strange things when the sun is hidden behind the horizon.

I know the typical impression of a rennie, a Renaissance faire performer, is that of a struggling actor, more gypsy than anything else, and I admit that fits many of the people who work at the faires. Most of my friends work through the year, traveling from faire to faire. I see most of them only during these few months in the fall. They're good people. I was irritated that something had marred the day. I didn't want a repeat of my college years.

I'd gone to college intending to get a degree in forestry, but I had shifted to theatre halfway through and never looked back. I had a knack for costuming, and after college, I did okay for myself working the local shows. That led to me moving north. I spent some time in the theatres in New York City. In my opinion, the Big Apple is a great place to visit but a shitty place to work. I suppose my psychic sensitivities could have something to do with that opinion.

I moved back home after just a year. I started my own costume business. It hadn't worked out very well. I had mostly worked small science fiction and fantasy conventions, barely making a living. A few years later, an old friend from college told me the local renfaire was hiring. So I spent my weekends that year, from the end of August through October, working as a pirate.

I hated working at the faire. Therefore, I quit.

I know it's odd, but I just like to go and play, not work.

That was my first degree. I went back to school about ten years ago because I needed to actually do something with my life. I needed to be able to find a job and make enough money to live off. I originally went back to school to study psychology, because I'm fascinated by people, but I ended up quickly changing to anthropology. Psychology was a little too morally ambiguous for me. Anthropology seems to have a better handle on the human condition anyway. After what happened my second year, focusing on getting my PhD in criminal behavior seemed like a priority.

When I got home from the faire, I changed clothes and put the costumes away. My cat loves to shed on my costumes. I grabbed a sandwich and sat down to sort through the usual crap in my email inbox; I was left with five messages. Most of them were work related, so I ignored them for now. They could wait till Monday. If someone really wanted to get my attention, they'd call. Two of the emails were from Lucy. One was dated from last week, the other from two days ago.

Coincidence or synchronicity? I wondered.

As I read the first message, I was not enlightened, only confused and vaguely concerned. Lucy and I had never been close, but I had dated her brother in college. She got included into my small circle of friends at that time and was kind of a fixture. No one had really liked her, but no one had wanted to ask her leave, either. She'd held tragic place in our circle after that fateful March, my second year.

Lucy was really weird. I mean she was weird in a *don't-make-eye-contact* kind of way, like the guy on the subway who talks to himself. Sometimes I had wanted to choke the life out of her; she could be a real bitch. She had a dark side. Don't we all? But she had a good heart and usually meant well. At least I thought she did.

She was gushing in the first email about some guy she had met. That seemed rather odd behavior from a woman I knew to be gay. I know some guys think they can "convert" gay women, but trust me, it doesn't work that way. As far as I knew, she hadn't dated a guy since college, and that had ended badly. *Really, really badly.*

Her second email only had one word: *Run.*

And a smile emoji.

What the *literal* fuck?

CHAPTER TEN

Now she was starting to spook me.

I tried calling Lucy's cell phone, but it was disconnected. So I finished eating. Samson was twining about my ankles, looking for turkey scraps as I played a couple of games of computer solitaire. I decided to call Margaret, Lucy's...*something*. Lover? Roommate? I don't know what to call her; they have a strange relationship.

She picked up on the third ring. "Hello?"

"Hey, Marge, it's Michelle."

"Hey, yourself. How was the faire today?"

She knew my habits. Unlike Lucy, Marge and I talked at least once a month. "Hot, as usual. I thought I saw Lucy there," I said.

"Uh-huh." She paused. "Well, if you see her again, tell the bitch she owes me rent for this month."

"She move out on you again?"

"Shit, woman, I haven't seen her in three weeks. How the hell should I know?" She sounded exasperated with Lucy. "She won't even talk to me. She should at least have the courtesy to tell me to go to hell."

"She emailed me about some guy," I said as my cat crawled into my lap.

She sighed. "I know. She met this goth chick at a rave last month. Then she got into this three-way thing with the girl and her goth boy-toy or something. You know how she is. She's always bouncing from one girl to the next, from one cause to the next."

I laughed. "She always liked her fads. Do you remember when she joined the Rainbow Coalition people in college?"

"Oh my god, are you kidding? I had to stay with Christine for two months. Lucy stopped bathing, along with the rest of those freaks." She laughed. "Thanks. You're right. This is probably just another fad for her."

We talked for an hour or so. I didn't tell her about the second email from Lucy. It was too strange. No reason to make Margaret worry any more than she already was.

Lucy and Marge had this weird love affair that reached almost back to childhood. They'd met in junior high, two very different-looking girls with very similar ideas. They dated steady all through high school. When they went off to college, though, Lucy found she wanted to sample everything life could give her. Marge hadn't agreed, and I don't think they'd ever really gotten along since. They'd both been seeing other people for years, but they still lived together, at least most of the time. Lucy had left a few years ago and not come back for almost a year. Marge had pined away for her for months.

Love is, as they say, a funny thing.

I called and left another message for Mark. It was odd that neither he nor his wife Jen had called me back. Maybe they were out of town. I went to bed and tried not to think about anything. It was a little difficult, though. Two psychic attacks in two days is something of a record for me.

I usually don't get more than one a month.

CHAPTER ELEVEN

I woke up early on Sunday.

I was shaking, and I hurt all over: more bad dreams.

After a long, hot shower, I felt more like myself again. I couldn't help but think about Lucy's cryptic message and the strange events of the last two days. Had someone been trying to kill me, or just to scare me? It could go either way. The attack last week seemed nastier, but... That kind of thing took a lot out of a person.

Mark knew more about such things, hence my attempts to get in touch with him. I was starting to get worried. As far as psychic attacks go, he always said it was something that you only did if you really, *truly* didn't like someone. It was *much* easier just to shoot a person. So maybe whoever it was who'd attacked me actually wanted me dead but didn't have the balls to try to do it by their own hand.

That was not a comforting thought.

Not that I wanted anyone to try to kill me, in person or otherwise. It's just that some things are easier to deal with than others. I have a nice Smith & Wesson 9mm loaded with hollow-point bullets for anyone who wants to make my acquaintance in a manner that's unbecoming. You know what I mean?

I've never used it outside the gunnery range, but I could if I had to. On one of the recent cases I worked on, a few months ago, the killer had heard about me – I still don't know how. The police don't exactly advertise my involvement, for obvious reasons. Anyway, I started carrying the gun then. I've had it for years, though, ever since what happened to me when I went back to college.

I'd had to use a gun then, but it wasn't mine.

I'd done what I had to do.

My chance to figure out who'd attacked me was fading fast. I should have looked around the day before, but I'd been a little distracted. I called Mark again and left another message. I needed to sneak down to the river later tonight. The emotions used to attack someone should leave a trace. Maybe it had been the woman who'd asked about me. I'd start looking where the crowd had been.

I also needed to hurry up and get dressed before I was late for the renfaire opening. I'd look around there and see if I could figure who'd attacked me. The goths seemed a little too obvious. Maybe I'd find Lucy. I really needed to talk to her and see if she knew anything about what was going on. I'd get an answer out of her about that damn email, too.

I dressed in my black and green costume. It's a black silk shirt with green-and-black-striped sleeves, plus a black leather doublet with green piping. I wore it with black pants and knee-high boots. I'd read a description of an outfit like it in one of my favorite books. I then dug out all my special rings, charms, and amulets. At least as a pirate, I can get away with wearing a lot of jewelry at a time. A leather belt and pouch added to the look. I finished it with a black tri-corn hat with a green plume, which I'd dyed to match the green silk on the sleeves. If you hadn't figured it out already, I make my own costumes for the faire.

I got a croissant for breakfast on my way, and arrived early. They were just opening up the gates, and my friends weren't here yet. I didn't want to wait alone out in the parking lot, so I went on in. I tried not to think about what had happened here the day before.

It may seem strange, but shopping helps me relax. I like to go around to my favorite renfaire shops, check out what's new, and say hello to people I haven't seen in a while. You get to know a lot of people at a big renfaire. Many people work multiple faires, so you get to meet people from all around the country. I try to take small vacations and visit some of the other faires during the year.

I like the ones in Florida the best.

Florida is a beautiful state. I like to bake myself on the hot sand. The ocean has always called to me. The ocean might be why I like the renfaires down there so much. I like the Gulf side best; the water is warmer. Not that I need it to be any warmer at the faire. Historical costume is all about layers.

I stopped by the large building to the left of the faire entrance. The shop there sold different kinds of hand-made bath salts. They have huge containers of salt crystals in different colors all around the store. Each one has different herbs and oils mixed with them. I love the place. They sell the salts in glass tubes with corks. You fill them yourself. I bought six different kinds.

Moving on around the circle, I came to one of the leather shops. There are several artisans who do leather goods, but I like these guys. They do leather armor and other costume accessories. I'd bought a magnificent leather harlequin mask from them last year that was embellished with tiny little brass bells. So I stopped in to say hello. The guy who owned the shop was there working on something; it looked like a leather helmet. He talked me into buying a cool green-and-black braided belt that went perfectly with my outfit; it was braided in one of those intricate one-piece braids that look impossible to make.

I always end up buying something from them when I go in.

CHAPTER TWELVE

I almost walked into a guy in a nice suit as I was leaving the shop. It was odd to see someone dressed that way at the faire. He seemed familiar in some way I couldn't place, tall and ruggedly good-looking, with short and spiky dark red-brown hair. It was his eyes that caught my attention first: they were very green and reminded me of something or someone I couldn't quite remember. He smiled at me as I caught his amazing eyes with mine.

"Hello. You look like just the woman I've been looking for," he said, catching me off guard.

My mind raced. What? Looking for me? Did I know him? Had I gone to school with him? Dated him? I still couldn't place his face. "Hello," I said back. "I don't quite remember…" I trailed off.

"Sorry, you don't know me." He paused. "I saw you in the crowd at the pirate show yesterday."

"Oh?" How had I missed him? I was too busy looking at the vamps. Damn. We walked out into the sunshine. He was too good-looking and well-dressed to be a stalker, I hoped.

"Do you mind if I ask you a few questions?"

"Questions?"

"Sorry, I suppose introductions are in order. My name is Michael

Delling, United States Deputy Marshal. I presume you are Rhiannon Michelle Fredericks, but prefer to go by Michelle except here at the faire." He smiled apologetically as he showed me his badge. There was a faded print-out of my driver's license with it. "I do have the right woman, right?"

A federal marshal? Here? I swallowed convulsively. What would bring someone like that to the renfaire? I was suddenly worried that the guy from a few months ago had escaped or something. That would complicate things. "Uh, yeah. You had some questions? Is this about work?"

"Nothing for you to worry about. I'm conducting a routine investigation into some local matters. I just want to ask you about your acquaintance with Lucy Dubois. Have you seen or talked to her recently?"

Nothing to worry about: cop-speak for *you should be worried.* "I saw her yesterday, or thought I did, here at the faire. But I didn't talk to her."

He nodded. "Any other contact?"

I shook my head. "I talked to her last month, first time in almost a year. Then I got a couple of cryptic emails from her recently, but nothing interesting. Is she in trouble?"

"No, the investigation is about someone else. Her name came up in my investigation, and yours by association. I'm just checking on any leads." He flashed me a disarming grin. I knew he was lying, although I couldn't have said why.

"I'm glad she's not in any trouble, but we've never been close." I shrugged. "You know how it is."

"I do." His eyes seemed to bore into mine. I felt a little uneasy about him. I felt again that he was lying, but I couldn't figure out what or why. "Let me give you my card. If she contacts you, or approaches you again, please call me and let me know *immediately.*"

"I will," I said, taking his card.

"Good day," he said, and walked away. I watched him for a moment, trying to figure him out. Then I gave myself a little shake, put his card in my belt pouch, and moved on with my affairs of the day.

I skipped most of the rest of the merchants, only stopping by the pirate guys who sell swords. They have really nice stuff, but most of the prices were a bit more than I was willing to pay. I still ended up getting talked into buying a new dagger. They gave me a good discount on it, either because I'm a regular at the faire or because the guy thought I was cute; either one works for me. I know that I need another weapon the way I need a hole in my head, but I really like blades. Always have. They're kind of like shoes: you can never have enough of them.

CHAPTER THIRTEEN

It was a gorgeous day. A light breeze from the west kept things cool, and the sky was a deep blue. The trees sighed, and the grass rippled pleasantly. I wondered what would go wrong today. Everything seemed *too* perfect.

I shivered.

My friends were concerned about me, but I reassured them that I was fine. They pestered me the rest of the day to stay in the shade and drink lots of fluids. They forced so much water on me, I was running to the privies every half-hour. Oh, well, at least they cared. Even Josh was on his best behavior. I hated lying to them, but if I'd told them the truth, they would've been a lot more worried about me.

It's funny, really. People are surrounded by the mystical from the day they're born. They see ghosts; they see residuals, sometimes even demons and other strange things. Do they acknowledge this to others? No. They go through their lives pretending that weird things only happen to other people. If you try to call them on it, they just get angry and defensive, like they were back in junior high and being tricked or something.

It's not as if I try to rub people's faces in the occult; it's just that I get sick of hypocrites. I used to be really open about my beliefs, even when I was a kid. I tried to find "rational" explanations for things I saw or heard. But the only "rational" explanation they came up with was that *I* was being irrational! Why do people deny the evidence of their senses?

Anyway, nothing happened the whole time I was at the faire. I'd been hoping the goths would show up again so I could talk to Lucy. No such luck. I admit I approached the tavern with some trepidation, but shadows stayed shadows, and nothing tried to bite me, not even Josh.

I left the faire a little early.

Traffic was heavy on the expressway, and so were my thoughts. I couldn't help but think about the past, and I *hate* to think about the past. Not the recent past, but my childhood. I'm not sure what triggered the memories. Maybe the music I was listening to.

I grew up in a rural area with my grandparents. We raised chickens, which are dirty, vile, and foul creatures. No pun intended. I milked cows – which is very disgusting, by the way. We raised food for the family in a large garden. I had a couple of aunts and uncles who lived at the house, too. Fortunately, it was a big house.

I spent my summers running through the acres of forest my grandparents owned. Good times and bad, I don't think I would trade my childhood for anyone else's. Who knows what I would get? My grandparents' house was haunted. There had been some nasty murders there in the 1930s. The ghosts mostly kept to themselves, though, as long as you stayed out of the basement. Everyone in the house knew the ghosts were there, but it wasn't talked about. It was as if they thought it would give the ghosts more power if anyone mentioned them.

I think it was growing up surrounded by the dark psychic atmosphere of the house that made me into what I am now. I had to be careful what I touched as a child. There are some things kids shouldn't know about when they're that young. I never slept in an adult's bed.

I have strange blank places in my memories. I'm not talking about having forgotten things; everyone does that. I mean that I have dark, gray, formless blanks in my mind when I try to think about some things I sort of remember happening during that time. My head always begins throbbing horribly, too, in a band from temple to temple across the top. The blanks come later in my memories, after I moved in with my mother when I was twelve.

These were my thoughts as I made my way home from the renfaire. It takes a lot of effort to pull myself out of these memories and get on with my life. I have a bad tendency to brood over past events. They play over and over in my mind, and I get really depressed. I guess everyone does that.

When I checked my phone messages, there was one from Mark, inviting me to stop by and talk about the psychic attacks. So I called him immediately and told him I would be over after getting cleaned up and changing clothes. I'd raid his refrigerator when I got to his place; his wife, Jennifer, always had lots of goodies packed away.

I'd met Mark in college, like so many of my other friends. We all went through some tough times together at one point, and have stayed close ever since. Mark had been dating my friend Jennifer. I'd known Jen since grade school. They got married the year after I got my bachelor's degree, the year so many things went wrong. I don't how we made it through that semester. I stayed in school to get my PhD in anthropology; they moved out west to Phoenix. After a few years, they moved back. I think Mark's job out there hadn't panned out or something. I never was clear on the details.

Jennifer is a schoolteacher. She teaches mathematics at a local high school and probably drives all the young guys and a few of the girl absolutely mad. She's five-foot-six, blond, perfectly built, and graceful. The kind of woman who makes me feel large and clumsy, although I'm actually neither. She's a great friend.

Mark works for General Electric. He's an aerospace engineer. If you think it odd that an engineer knows a lot about the occult, then you've obviously never studied physics or mathematics. He's a Cabbalist, and a damned good one. Not one of those nutty California ones, either, but you probably guessed that. I would never have the discipline to be a good Cabbalist. But then, I wouldn't make a very good engineer, either.

CHAPTER FOURTEEN

I showered and changed into jeans, vintage combat boots, a t-shirt, and a light leather jacket. My 9mm went into the jacket, and I spent a few minutes picking what jewelry to wear. I grabbed a bottle of good wine out of the kitchen, because I knew Jen would be cooking dinner, and there are certain rules for polite visits with friends, even if it was to ask about strange psychic attacks. Maybe it was even a *better* idea to take wine when asking about that, now that I think about it.

They live out in Burlington, a few miles from the expressway. They have nice ranch-style house with lots of acreage. Obviously, they like their privacy. I usually go to their house only a couple of times a month. They have small parties on the Fourth of July and a few other non-religious holidays. Just to get this out of the way, we are just good friends, nothing else. Their parties were regular parties, not anything weird. At least nothing weirder that the occasional séance.

Jennifer answered the door as soon as I knocked. She gave me a big hug and stood on tiptoe to kiss me on the cheek. She's always been like that. She took the wine, spoke appreciatively about the vintage, although I'm sure they normally drank better, and led me into the kitchen.

She was cooking fettuccini Alfredo, from scratch, with homemade bread. The woman is amazing. If I ever get married, I'm getting a wife just like her. Not that I plan on going gay anytime soon, but while watching her move about the kitchen, the prospect was a bit more appealing than it should have been.

I really needed to get out more; my love life had sucked recently.

Mark came in and gave me a crushing embrace. Then we sat and talked about work – theirs – and friends, until dinner was done. We always did that. Jen believed in the occult – she couldn't live with Mark and *not* believe – but she had some problems with the more dangerous parts of it. They reminded her of the problems we experienced in college, and she'd gotten the worst of it then. So we talked about other things when she was around. She knew why I had come over, and after dinner she made some excuse about going to bed early so Mark and I could talk.

I settled down in a comfortable chair in Mark's study with my wine glass close at hand. As I told the story of last week's attack, he lost his customary smile and began to frown. I sat back and took a sip of wine while he digested the information.

"Well," he said, breaking the silence. "I guess it really was a psychic attack. I was hoping that you might have been mistaken, but there seems little doubt."

"Do you know anyone in the area that could do this?

"Do I know anyone who *could*," he asked, "or *would*?" He sighed and took a long drink from his glass, which had something a bit stronger than wine in it. "I don't know, Michelle. Obviously, *I* could. I didn't, by the way. As much as I like your company, I would not stoop to these methods to obtain it."

"Yeah, all you have to do is call. Besides," I said with a grin, "if you kill me, I won't be able pay you back that twenty I owe you." I'd once bet him twenty dollars that my personal psychic shielding was good enough to block anything he could throw at it. I was wrong.

He laughed. "I'd forgotten about that, actually. I don't know anyone around here who would want to hurt you. The people I know who could do it are fairly solitary and well-to-do. They could not easily be bought."

"I hadn't thought of that angle. You think someone may have paid someone else to attack me?"

"No. I don't. I'll ask around anyway. Make a few calls, that sort of thing. Is there any possibility of getting me into the crime scene?"

"Tonight?" I asked, almost choking on my wine.

"Yes, if possible."

I shook my head. "I can't think of any way. They'll have very heavy security on that place. Murderers sometimes come back around, you know. There are sure to be police officers watching the whole area. Sneaking in would be difficult."

"But not impossible? We might be able to pull it off?"

"I'm not sure I would want to try."

"It may be the only way to find out about the attack. The traces fade fast, you know. It may already be too late."

I sighed. "Well, when you put it that way, it almost sounds sane. Okay, if there's no other way, I guess we can try." I stood up and finished my wine. I was going to need a little fortifying.

I went into the kitchen and got my coat while Mark went upstairs to tell Jen what we were going to do. I filched a bottle of Coke out of their fridge while I was waiting.

Mark came down wearing all black. His outfit was not much different from mine; he just looked a bit sillier. Mark looks like an engineer, not a spy. I'm not sure what I look like. I'm not barrel-chested, with a beard, though.

After a bit of bickering, we decided to take two cars; that way I could just go straight home afterward instead of having to backtrack. I didn't mind. Mark was the one who had to get up early the next morning.

Traffic was light that evening, so the trip took only half an hour or so. We parked at the far edge of the woods, in a church parking lot, his car behind mine. We were hoping that if any police came by, they would see the cars were empty and just move on.

I led Mark to the far end of the parking lot, through the woods and over the small chain fence. From there, we had to be extra quiet. We ran across a field to a wooded area in the middle that follows the small creek down to the river. We moved along the creek as quietly as we could, but Mark sounded like a herd of angry reindeer.

The crime scene sat dark in the moonlight in the middle of the wide-open space along the river. Police ribbon still blocked off the area. I led him around to the woods father down and looked around to make sure we were alone. We were.

Mark began muttering to himself as he walked to and fro in the area where I'd been attacked. He'd sensed the place where the attack came from as soon as he got within a few yards of it. Now he was seeking clues as to who had sent it. I followed along behind him out of curiosity. My psychic abilities are mostly defensive, or at least reactionary.

We were discussing the problem in low voices when we were blinded by a light being flashed in our eyes.

"You, there! What are you doing?" A dark shape resolved itself into a police officer, bearing down on us, fast. His hand was on his pistol. I suddenly remembered that I was armed and trespassing on a crime scene.

Damn.

CHAPTER FIFTEEN

It was too late for us to run; Mark would never be able to keep up with me. "I work here," I lied. "I mean with the police, well, the FBI, and uh…"

"They are looking for something for me, officer," a familiar voice said from the darkness to our left.

The officer quickly shone his light on the other figure. "Who the hell are you?" he demanded.

The man simply held up his badge. It was Marshal Delling. Then he said, "They're working for me."

"Oh, okay, well, sorry I didn't recognize you, sir. You really need to come to the security checkpoint and sign in first, and let us know that you're going to be on the grounds. I saw the notice that you might be in and out, but you still need to tell us," the officer said lamely, flashing his light back on us.

"Of course, officer. Sorry for the confusion." He didn't sound sorry. "I'll stop by on my way out, and sign whatever paperwork you need me to. Come along, you two, back to work so we can get out of here tonight."

I waited for the police officer to walk out of hearing range. "Thank you. Why did you help us, by the way?"

He gestured, and we walked together toward the road.

"I was curious. I saw you two sneak in, and I followed you from the parking lot. I recognized *you,* or I would've called the police immediately." He smiled and looked at Mark. "Find what you were looking for?"

Mark looked startled and hesitated, so I answered instead. "I left something here last week. I was working on the case with the police. He was just helping me look."

"*Right...,*" Marshal Delling drawled. He looked back and forth between us. "Well, do you need more time, or are you finished?"

I looked a question at Mark; he shook his head slightly. "No, we really were getting ready to leave. Thank you again. Can I ask why you were in the parking lot this late?"

"No." He smiled. "Goodnight." Then he went up the street toward the police patrol car.

Mark and I walked hurriedly out toward our cars. We waited until we reached them before talking any more. He spoke first.

"I didn't find much. For the attack to have the power it did, to have entered where it did, I would say the attacker would've had to be within line of sight. They were definitely within one hundred feet," he added with authority.

That startled me. "You mean someone psychically attacked me right in the middle of a crowd of reporters and police, and not from some dark, musty basement?"

He grinned. "I suppose they could have worked out a ritual and then set it into a talisman to be called forth later. I hope not, though. That would mean they had access to some serious mystical firepower."

"So you have no idea who did this?"

"No. I didn't recognize the traces left behind. There's some similarity to my own workings, but nothing specific. I do want to ask you something else, though."

I turned toward him in the dark. "What?"

He looked nervous. "What do you know about this guy who just interceded for us?"

I shrugged. "He's a federal marshal. We talked earlier today. He asked me some questions about Lucy."

"Interesting. I was just wondering. He was loaded with amulets and talismans, real ones. He might have been able to do it."

"Really?" I leaned against the hood of my Jeep. "That's really *very* strange. I didn't feel anything. I can usually tell if a person is a practitioner."

Mark looked thoughtful. "I think one of his amulets was designed to shield him from detection. If so, he is quite good. You're sure he *is* a marshal, though?"

"I guess." I thought about it. "Yeah. I mean, he showed me his badge earlier. It certainly looked real. I've got his card. It could be easily verified."

"Hmm. Did he say what he wanted with Lucy?"

"Not really," I said, thinking about it. "He just asked if I had seen or talked to her recently. I told him no. He said something about investigating someone she knew."

Mark frowned. "Well, his power may be a bit different from mine – more like yours, I would say. I couldn't tell, but he didn't attack you. Wrong signature." He rubbed his eyes and yawned.

"You mean he could have?"

He just shrugged and yawned again.

"I'm sorry, Mark. Get home and get to bed. Thank you for your help. I'll figure something out." I pushed him towards his car.

"No, *I'm* sorry. I wish I could tell you more. I'll make those calls tomorrow. I'll call in the evening and let you know what I find out."

"Thanks. Get some sleep. Thank Jen for letting me steal you away for a while."

We got in our cars and headed toward our homes. I thought again about what had happened to me these past two days. I was no closer to an answer now than I had been before. In fact, I had a lot more questions. Why had the marshal helped me? There was something strange about him. He made me uncomfortable.

I desperately needed to get some sleep.

I didn't go right to sleep when I got home, though. First, I had to go back out and buy cat food. When I got back, I couldn't stop replaying the attacks in my head. Not exactly sleep inducing. So I sat up and read for a while, my cat purring at my ankles.

CHAPTER SIXTEEN

I slept late into the morning.

My sleep the night before had been mercifully untroubled. I wished I could have that same sense of peace while awake. It had been a difficult weekend. After a quick breakfast of granola cereal doused in honey, I decided to clean house, so I popped in a jazz album. Jazz is great for cleaning. It makes it less of a chore, anyway, if you can dance your way to the trash can.

Cleaning house is a symbolic act for me. I find that putting things in their proper places helps clean out my mind, as well. It's calming.

I was finished and bored by noon.

I should have been doing research on the River case, but I couldn't seem to get into the right frame of mind for the work. None of my thoughts was content to stay put away. They kept jumping out and making a mess of my consciousness.

I was too fidgety to sew or do any of the other things I usually do to pass the time when not working. Therefore, I decided to walk down to the local used record store and try to find a new album or something. I'd grab lunch along the way and spare myself the chore of cooking, too.

I've always liked to take walks. I'm not an exercise nut, but I do try to keep in shape. Luckily for me, I have one of those metabolisms that lets me stay fit without much effort, because I'd get bored as a gym-rat.

I left the house after changing into a t-shirt, jean shorts, and tennis shoes. It was after noon and already hot and muggy. The sky was filling with big, fluffy cumulus clouds. I thought it might rain later. A light breeze came down the hill from the expressway, carrying the smell of oil and exhaust. I cut across Decoursey Pike and started down 43rd Street to Madison Avenue. I liked the old Victorian houses in that part of town. Yes, the foundations were crumbling, and most needed new paint jobs, but they were cozy houses with long histories. Most of the psychic residue there was positive.

All the kids were in school, but their toys were still strewn along hedges and across yards. It was quiet back through there. Older working-class families and young couples living side-by-side made for an interesting contrast in vehicles, old battered Buicks and an occasional new and shiny Toyota pickup.

The ghosts were quieter during the day, too.

Crossing Madison Avenue on foot is a little like playing Russian roulette. A least there are a few lights for the intrepid pedestrian to make a crossing. After nearly getting clipped by a white van, I turned north. I passed a few closed shops and stopped at a fast food place for lunch. Half an hour and a greasy taco salad later, I left to walk over to the music store.

It's actually more than a music store. Andrea's sells used DVDs, CDs, and books, too. It's a great store. I'd found a copy of the *Anarchist's Cookbook* there a few months ago, but I decided it might not be a good idea to be seen buying that. The line between anarchist and terrorist, in the mind of the government, could disappear real quickly. I was mostly just curious, anyway, about the hype around the book.

The store has posters and flyers for local bands, and a little café-type area where you can get a latte, or better still, a Jones Soda. My favorite is the cream soda; it tastes and smells like cotton candy, and reminds me of county fairs I went to when I was a child. I'm not sure why I don't go to those anymore.

There are two entrances to Andrea's; I went in through the door near the used DVDs.

"Hey, Michelle."

I looked up. It was the guy at the counter, already waiting on another customer. You know you shop someplace too much when they know you by name. "Hey," I said, and went back to looking through the movies. They didn't have anything new except some weird anime movies with lots of tentacles and scantily clad women with blue and green hair. Not my thing. I moved on to the CDs.

I have rather eclectic tastes in music. I like classic rock and blues the best, with a smattering of classical, jazz, alternative, and punk. Just keep the rap and country away from me, thank you. I was just reaching for a Portishead album that I didn't own when someone walked up next to me, and all my precognitive senses went haywire.

"I told you to run."

I knew that voice well. I turned slowly to look at the person next to me. "Hello, Lucy, nice to see you, too," I said sarcastically. She wasn't someone I wanted to run into on the best of days. She smelled like stale potpourri.

"Didn't you get my email?" she asked.

I almost laughed. She was not exactly intimidating, if that was how she was trying to act. Lucy had always been mercurial; her moods could never be predicted. Lucy was a quite a bit shorter than my five-ten, and best described as *pale*. She had translucent white skin (without freckles, damn her), silvery blond hair, and ice-blue eyes. Those were the good parts. She was built like a Valkyrie gone wrong. You know the type, kind of *frumpy*. Take an unbaked clay Earth Mother figurine and roll it around on the ground a bit, pick off the twigs and leaves, and you'll get something shaped like Lucy. She was dressed today in some kind of too-tight, badly made, black stretch-panné gown that really did nothing to help her already unflattering figure.

God help you when an ex-seamstress feels bitchy.

"Look, Lucy, I don't know what you mean by that, but what's going on? Marge is worried about you. I haven't heard from you in weeks, and you want to be melodramatic?" I shook my head. "Oh, and someone was asking about you at the faire."

"What do I give a shit about if your friends were asking about me? I was trying to give you a warning, from a friend. I shouldn't have bothered. Victor was right about you." She turned away.

I caught a brief psychic flash of a dark-haired man.

"Victor? Is that what your androgynous, oh-so-gothic boy-toy calls himself? Could he have thought of anything more pompous?" I laughed.

She spun around, and for a moment she looked as if she was going to actually hit me. Luckily for her, she didn't. "Victor," she hissed, "will hear about this." Then she stomped off across the store and left.

Oh, I was trembling already. Yeah, right. Lucy wasn't terribly bright. What was her game? I stayed friends with her because I felt sorry for her after those problems in college with her last boyfriend. Damn, I'd meant to ask her about the psychic attack at the faire, and if she'd been there. I picked up the CD that I'd been reaching for and walked toward the front of the store.

I got a soda to go with my CD. The guy at the counter asked me if Lucy had been giving me trouble.

"No, I knew her in college. She's harmless. She can be a real bitch, though."

"What was her deal, anyway? She stormed out of here like she was really pissed." He scanned my CD and soda. "And what was with the turquoise makeup, anyway?"

"She's a Tammy Fay Baker goth," I said with a grin. He laughed so hard at that, I thought I was going to have call 9-1-1. I wish I could say I had made that up. Actually, I knew someone years ago, when I lived in central Kentucky, who had said that about a girl who was a regular customer where he worked. Come to think of it, I'm not sure if the guy knew who Tammy Fay Baker *was*. I think he'd just laughed because he always hit on me whenever I shopped there.

CHAPTER SEVENTEEN

I paid for my items and started walking back home.

There was no sign of Lucy outside. I had no idea what her problem was. That whole business about running was starting to get on my nerves. I can only sort of remember running without a fight once in my life, and that was years ago and so odd a memory that I tend to think it was just a bad dream brought on by the onset of puberty.

Just a little way after crossing Madison Avenue, I stopped to finish my cream soda and admire the architecture of a magnificent old stone church. I was getting one of those odd premonitions. I had this feeling that something was wrong, *again*. I tried to shake off the feeling. At least I was near my house; I'd be safe there.

I had just started walking again when I heard a sudden squeal of brakes beside me. I turned to look, but something slammed into me, knocking me into the wall next to the sidewalk. I pushed myself off the wall, and was grabbed from behind and thrown toward the road. I fell, and pain flared in my right hand and knee. A white van, possibly the one that had almost hit me earlier, had stopped in the road. The side door was open, and two men had jumped out, one taller than me, and the other shorter. I could barely see the driver through the open side window as I fell.

When the guy had grabbed me, I caught a flash of what was on his mind. He and his buddies had talked about what they were going to do me: who was going to go first, and so on. I had to fight down my nausea. Those flashes had been real. They had done those things to other women. Not to me, not yet.

I was not about to let these sons of bitches gang rape me.

The taller one stepped toward me. "Get up, bitch!"

Something I normally keep bottled up inside me uncoiled in my mind. I have this tight knot of rage... My friends always used to say that I just had a really bad temper, but this is different. This is like an animal growling in a cage, just waiting to be unleashed upon the world. In high school, some of the guys had a chip on their shoulders about the tall girl who could fight. They used to try to test me, to catch me unawares. They usually ended up in the hospital. I'm *much* stronger and faster than I look.

"I said *get up*," he said.

I waited till the last possible instant, glaring up at him. Just as he was bending down to grab me, I kicked him hard in the side of the knee and then jumped up. There was a loud popping crack, and he fell onto his side, screaming. I tried to run, but the other guy was in the way. He grabbed me and threw me against the wall again, hitting my head this time. The white-hot flash of pain released the last of my inhibitions. I turned and waited for him to make his move, blood trickling down through my hair. The tall guy was still on the ground clutching his knee and cursing.

Shorty may have hesitated a moment, wondering why I was standing my ground instead of running. As he moved in to grab me, I jabbed him in the nose, which broke, gushing blood. He stumbled back with a roar of pain. I kicked him but only grazed his chest. He then stepped forward and swung a punch at me, a wild haymaker. I dodged to the side, my left hand catching his wrist and deflecting it. He grabbed my hair, and I put my knee in his groin. He grunted and folded up. I spun, using my weight to add force, hitting him in the throat with my right forearm as he was falling. He didn't even have a chance to scream. I stepped away from him as he fell to his knees, his hands grasping his ruined throat, the pain between his legs momentarily forgotten as he choked.

The tall guy was struggling to stand. I didn't want him chasing me, so I planted the toe of my shoe under his chin. His head snapped back, and he flipped over. I kicked him again, hard, in the groin, just for good measure.

I could hear the driver cursing. I looked in the side window and saw him reaching for a large, ugly rifle, something bullpup. I took off running, limping slightly from my scraped knee. I wasn't able to see the license plate, since I ran past the front of the van. I ran around the church, through the parking lot. I paused then, gasping, but I wasn't being followed. I didn't stop to wonder why; I just ran.

CHAPTER EIGHTEEN

I ran straight home as fast as my legs could carry me. As soon as I had the door locked behind me, I grabbed my pistol out of my coat by the door, then ran to the phone and breathlessly called 9-1-1.

"I've been attacked!" I blurted out as soon as a woman answered.

Her voice was obscenely calm. "Slow down, miss. Are you currently in danger?"

"No, I was walking home and some guys in a van jumped me."

"Okay, miss, tell me when this occurred and where. Give me all the details you can."

I gave her a description of the van and the two attackers. What I could remember, anyway. It was kind of blurred. I told her that they jumped me and that I managed to get free and run home. I left out the part about hitting them; I didn't want to add assault charges to my problems.

She told me to wait inside my home with the doors locked while the dispatched officers investigated the incident, as if I would have done anything else. I spent the next thirty minutes shaking from the after-effects of adrenaline, until the police showed up to take my statement. They hadn't found anything except my CD and empty, broken bottle. It wasn't until the officer pointed it out that I remembered my head, hand, and knee were still oozing blood from where I had hit the wall and the sidewalk. They wanted to take me to the hospital, but I declined.

After the police left, I went into the bathroom, cleaned my injuries with some peroxide, and put a little ointment on them. They would heal well enough, exposed to air. I hoped I didn't scar. At least I had new CD to listen to while I waited for Mark to call that evening.

I was sipping a soothing peppermint tea when the phone rang. I was tempted to not answer it, but I did anyway. Maybe I needed to talk to someone about what had happened, after all.

"Hello?" I answered raggedly.

"Hello, Michelle. It's Mark. I made those phone calls… Are you okay?"

"No. Yes. I don't know," I almost sobbed. It was good to hear a friendly voice. No matter how much of a loner I think I am, I still need friends.

"What's wrong?"

I told him about my day, the encounter with Lucy, the guys from the van. He was quiet the whole time as I told my story. I think I may have cried a bit at some point. Nerves. That's my excuse, anyway. Okay, so I was a lot more freaked out about the whole thing than I had admitted even to myself.

I don't know any other women (and a few honest men) who aren't afraid of being raped. The police had also thought that was the most likely explanation for the attack. I hadn't told them about what I'd felt from the attackers. I didn't want them to think I was crazy or hysterical. Mark was quiet for a bit after I finished, letting me get my emotions back under control.

"Do think this had anything to do with Lucy's warning?" he asked.

"No." I shook my head, despite being on the phone. "I don't. I saw that van earlier in the afternoon. I think meeting Lucy was a coincidence; she often shops there. Anyway, I'd like to think Lucy wouldn't take part in something like that." I hadn't even thought that it could be related.

"It could have been what she was talking about, though. Are you sure they weren't goths?"

"They were in a *white* van, Mark. Besides, no eyeliner." I shook my head again. I hate phones; half the conversation is missed. "Really, these guys had crew cuts and worked too well together, maybe ex-military. They had no visible tattoos, no body jewelry, nothing to suggest anything about them, actually. They were kind of nondescript, apart from height."

He sighed. "What about the driver?"

"What about him? I only caught a few glimpses of him. He looked about like the others. I have no idea how tall he was. The only odd thing about him was that he made no move to help the other two, other than reach for the rifle at the end."

"That is quite odd. I'm not convinced that the explanation the police gave is the most likely. The whole thing seems strange. I admit that it doesn't fit with the goth thing, but I don't know what it does fit. Are you sure you're okay? Jen and I could swing by for a bit. Keep you company."

"Trust me, those guys were only interested in one thing. I'm fine, really, just a skinned knee and palm, a few bruises, a bump on my head. I'll be fine in a day or so. You know how I am. I'll make some more tea and curl up with Samson, and he and I will watch a movie or something."

"So, I guess Lucy is caught up in this goth thing, huh?

"Yeah, the way she's been acting, I'm not giving her any of my homemade candy this Christmas." I laughed. "Of course, she'll probably be over it and back living with Marge by then, so she'll just eat hers."

He laughed. "You're so right. I used to call her Loony Lucy, but Jen made me stop."

"To her face, right?" I grinned. "She probably didn't even notice, did she?"

"Not even once."

I stretched and relaxed a little. "Okay, tell me the results of your phone calls today. Suddenly that psychic attack doesn't seem as bad." I grinned. "I guess one horror drives out the next, you know?"

"I'm sorry to say that I didn't have much luck. No one I called wanted to talk about the details of their particular rituals. It's silly. Behind closed doors they will talk freely about phantasms, thought-forms, etc., but try to get them to chat with you on the phone, and they act like they have no idea what you're talking about."

"What did you do? Tell them you were conducting a phone survey of local sorcerers and needed just a few minutes of their time? 'Hello. When summoning demons, do you find a pentagram works best, or a thaumaturgic triangle?' Jeez, Mark!"

"Phantasms aren't demons, Michelle. They are symbolic representations – constructs, if you will – of various mental processes. Namely, they represent anger, aggression, and hatred. The will to create…"

"Mark, I was kidding. I don't really need a lesson in mystical mechanics right now. Thank you, though." He gets like this sometimes. I think it's the engineer portion of him. He still thinks he's teaching physics or something.

"Sorry. Anyway, the point is that I didn't get any real answers for you. I suppose it could have been an isolated incident. Maybe it was just some young and foolish psychic testing the water."

"That's what I've been thinking."

"I don't like that explanation, though. It takes too much effort to psychically attack someone. I cannot see someone doing it on the spur of the moment. It's not uncommon for someone to detect a new practitioner in the area and send a little something to test them, but I can't see them doing it in public. It doesn't make sense." He sighed. "Maybe I'm getting old and don't like mysteries."

"Hah! Fishing for compliments again, I see. Unless something else happens, I'm going to treat this as an isolated incident. I'm more worried about the guys in the van, to tell you the truth." I shivered a bit.

"Well, it would seem that you made them pay quite a price for their attack. They got the worse end of the deal, wouldn't you say?"

I chuckled. "Okay, go ahead. Make me feel better, just when I was getting used to wallowing in self-pity."

"Right. Now who's fishing for compliments? Are you sure you don't need us to stop by?"

"I'm sure. Thank you. Give Jen a hug for me. I think I'm going to go to bed a little early tonight. Get some rest and recuperate."

"Okay. Good night, then. If you need anything, don't hesitate to call."

"Good night."

"'Night."

I hung up the phone. I didn't even think about calling the marshal; I didn't quite trust him anyway.

It was going to be a long night.

CHAPTER NINETEEN

I woke up that next morning feeling like the damn van had actually run over me the day before. I had tossed and turned all night long. I had some nasty dreams, but I couldn't – or wouldn't – remember any of the details. I felt like shit. I probably should have taken the time to get undressed instead of falling asleep in my clothes.

My side hurt where my clothes had wrinkled up and pressed into that damn scar under my ribs. I wish could remember exactly how I got that. Something to do with a fall at school – it's all a blank. Strange how things that happen to you while you're asleep will translate into your dreams. It's like when your arm goes numb, and in your dreams, your arm gets hurt to explain it.

Well, I don't know about *you*, but that happens to me, anyway.

I got up and undressed to assess the damage from the day before. I had bruises and scrapes on just about all of my body. The side of my head hurt a lot, too. Looking in the bathroom mirror, I saw myself as a perfect model for a battered woman poster. I hadn't thought I'd been hurt so badly. I probably *should* have gone to the emergency room, just in case. But I hate hospitals. They're painful for me, and I was feeling vulnerable.

I took a long, hot shower.

The hot water and soap made my scrapes throb and burn, but I didn't care. I felt dirty and sweaty. I needed to get rid of the feeling of their hands on me. The psychic abuse I had taken made it almost seem as if I *had* been raped. I found myself sobbing in the gentle spray. That had the closest I'd ever come to having something like that happening to me.

I'm not ashamed to say it terrified me.

I couldn't remember what I'd eaten before going to bed, but if I did remember, I would never eat it before going to bed again. My stomach was trying to do sit-ups without the rest of me. I forced myself to think of other things. As I stood dripping from the shower, I began to feel better, less shaky. I dried off carefully and dressed in my blue silk pajamas. I felt like being a bum. You'll have to excuse me if I didn't feel like going outside the house.

Once my stomach calmed down, I decided to fix myself a good breakfast. I mixed up a batch of pancakes, and cooked two eggs scrambled with cheese, and four pieces of bacon. I still had some real maple syrup in the fridge and so I had myself a feast. I try to watch my weight, but sometimes you have to treat yourself to a good meal anyway. My family is prone to being a bit heavy. I exercise daily. I think getting fat scares me more than a little bit. I had this aunt who was so heavy that she couldn't move without help. I used to scream and run whenever I saw her.

After washing the dishes, I sat in my living room, soaking up the sun and doing some thinking. My life has never been what I would call dull. I've had my share of adventures, high points and low. I've even had a sordid love affair or two that ended badly for everyone. Good soap opera material, that.

My childhood was okay, barring the grief over my father and my mother's neglect. At least my grandparents were nice enough. They mostly just left me to my own devices, which suited me fine. I was sick a lot in the winters, but the summers were my time. I spent all the time I could out running in those magnificent woods. There weren't any neighbor kids my age, so I ran with kids four to six years older than me. That makes a person grow up faster than normal.

My early teen years were the worst, I think. I had moved back in with my mother, which was not really the bad part. I was actually happy to get out of the other house. My grandparents had died in a car wreck, and I was getting tired of my aunts and uncles terrorizing me. I had made the mistake of mentioning that the house was haunted, and they took unholy delight in trying to scare me from that point forward, as if having some idiot yelling *BOO!* was scarier than seeing the residual death images of people being murdered.

They used to lock me in the basement.

With the ghosts.

I was *ecstatic* about leaving.

My real problems began with the onset of puberty. Don't they for everyone? That's when my odd nightmares began, and I started having strange blank spots in my memory, missing time, that sort of thing. One weekend, I came home from school and went to take a nap in bed. I didn't wake up until Monday morning. I didn't even remember falling asleep. The whole weekend was missing. I tried to ask my mother about it, but she didn't even realize I had come home on Friday, or care. Her alcohol was the most important thing in her life.

I had a bad time in school. I was tall for my age, and skinny as a rail. Boys made fun of me and hated me for being so tall, and the girls hated me for the attention I got. I never understood that, as if I had any choice about being the height I was. I used to get beat up a lot. I tried to get myself to fight back, but it was as if I was raging inside while my body just stood there and let things happen. It wasn't until my freshman year in high school that anything really changed. I'd had a bad summer. The missing time was worse, and sometimes I found weird marks, bruises and cuts, all over my body.

That was when I decided I wasn't going to take it anymore.

CHAPTER TWENTY

The first day in high school started off bad and got worse. I missed the bus and had to walk to school. Got there late, got detention, and got branded a troublemaker because I was late. At least I'd made an attempt to get there. I would have been better off skipping school, but I didn't find that out till later. Fourth period was the worst. It was remedial math. They wouldn't let me take algebra because of my grades in junior high. I was bored and made no attempt to hide it. The teacher hated me.

I got into my first fight in high school at lunch that day. I went to the open area outside the lunchroom after I'd skipped lunch. I didn't have any money. My mother would never have given me any or signed a form for me to get free lunches. I hadn't gotten a job yet, because I was only fourteen. The school used to let kids stand around and talk in the halls around the lunchroom, or go outside and smoke.

I know: I'm showing my age.

I didn't smoke, but I went outside just to be outside. There were these girls out there who thought they were tough. Leather jackets, pieced noses (not common then), boots, spiked hair, the works. They saw me in my hand-me-down clothes and thought I would be easy prey.

To be honest, I thought so, too.

They came over and started talking shit to me. I don't remember what was said, but it was the usual crap. Then one of them pushed me against the wall while the other grabbed for my purse. Hell, I didn't have anything worth fighting for in there, but a girl's purse is sacred ground.

Something kind of went wild inside me.

I broke the first girl's nose, snapped a few fingers of the girl messing with my purse, and caught the fist of the other as she swung at me. I think it surprised me more than it did her. I broke her wrist before letting go. Luckily, the girls skipped school right after that, so I didn't get into any more trouble. None of the other students who saw the fight said anything, either. It may even have made me a few friends.

I started thinking a lot about what had happened, though. A lot of those dreams of mine had fighting in them. Is it possible for a person to learn how to fight through dreams? I didn't know. I went to the library and read everything they had on dreams and the occult. I learned about my abilities, and I started to gain some much-needed self-confidence.

By my senior year, I had a reputation as a crazy witch girl, or Satan's love slave. It really depended on whom you asked. I was never into Satanism or anything like it. I *had* read everything I could get my hands on about the occult. I followed the works of Crowley, Blavatsky, Carlos Castaneda, Buckland, and others. I was never satisfied with any of them, although they each had something to teach me. I learned more than I thought I did.

It was during this time that I starting hanging out with the local Wiccans. I'd found them through a computer BBS, bulletin board service, called The Star in the Circle. I had to use a computer at school, since I didn't have one at home. Yes, this was before the internet. I know I'm showing my age again. Fuck off.

Not all of us had a Nintendo growing up, okay?

I started college the next year. I was poor enough to get Pell

Grants, at least enough for me to go to an in-state school. While I was in college, I went to the library every day. I read all the works that came out of the Rhine Institute. I started researching psychism. It seemed to me like a better bet than magic. I know now that they are linked solidly together, but at the time, I avoided anything mystical like the plague. Some of those pagans I had known were real oatmeal-heads.

My mother drank herself to death that year. I wasn't sure how I felt about her being gone. I had never really known her. I inherited the house. I was surprised and grateful that she'd had a will. My first thought when I found her dead was that I was going to have to find a new place to live.

CHAPTER TWENTY-ONE

I had my first tragic love affair in college.

He was not my first love, by any means. I'd dated before him, complete with all the puppy love and crushes. But I never really fell for anyone until I met this guy in history class. He was big and tough looking. We talked about all kinds of things, including psychism. Robert swore he'd been part of some government experiment with psychics when he was in the military, remote viewing or something like that. Told me he would teach me.

I was an idiot.

The relationship lasted for about two years and crashed down around me, hard, in my junior year. We had narrowly missed getting married. I almost swore off men after that, but I never had much luck in my relationships with women, either, so a wild lesbian love affair seemed out of the question, much to some of my female friends' disappointment. Besides, my ego was at an all-time low. Robert had turned out to be gay.

After that, I was more open to the mystical side of psychism, I think mainly because Robert had been so opposed to it, but I also needed something to believe in. Mainstream religion offered me nothing. It couldn't even explain normal things I had experienced, much less the mystical ones. I dug out all those old books and set to work learning all I could. That led to my experiments in channeling, which of course led to my first encounter with something truly bizarre and malicious.

When a phantasm came through my bedroom wall, I was stunned. I think the first thing to go through my mind was that someone must have slipped me some acid or something earlier at lunch. I just stared at the thing as it leapt across the room at me. It wasn't until its teeth began to sink into my neck that I reacted. I grabbed a necklace that a Wiccan friend had given me years ago and screamed, *"No!"* The phantasm vanished.

I was considerably shaken by the attack. I ran to the bathroom and washed the blood from my neck. I had little holes all around my neck on the left side. I had to wear turtlenecks for the next two weeks. I still have to use makeup to cover up the scars. I know now that it was all psychosomatic, but then? Then, I believed.

After college, and my BS theatre degree, I moved to New York. I began by working the smaller venues. Then I got a lucky break and assisted with the costume design for a big show on Broadway itself. That show not only earned me some much needed cash but also got my name out there. Getting your name out is probably the most important thing when it comes to working in show business.

I got a better apartment. I continued to move up through the theatre food chain until I was lead costume designer for a new play that made it big. At least it was big for a few weeks. I started working on the side around this time, too. I made clothes for some of the hot young stars who needed a high-fashion look but couldn't afford it.

Then I met Antonio.

Antonio was young, rich, and good looking. I met him while working one of my plays. He was the hot new lead. We had a fast and furious love affair. I fell for him, hard, but I was just another conquest for him. When it all fell apart, we just barely managed to avoid the local tabloid headlines. We were upstaged at the last moment by someone more important, acting worse in public than we had.

After our spectacular breakup, I dropped out of show business and moved back home to Cincinnati. There were plenty of television and theater jobs available in the area, especially for someone who had experience in New York. That's where I met Jennifer. She'd tried to be an actress, before deciding to go back to school and get a degree in teaching.

CHAPTER TWENTY-TWO

When I went back to college, I started hanging out again with other people who were into the occult and psychism. Jennifer introduced me to most of them. Two years later, she met Mark. He had started dating Jen, and Mark and I hit it off from the start. Sometimes we would double date out to comedy clubs and concerts. I dated guys off and on, but never anything serious. I was too into my studies for that. Anthropology is fucking hard. Seriously. I had easier physics classes.

Mark, as I mentioned before, is a Cabbalist. He's Jewish, so he gets it naturally. He did break with tradition, however, in that he is only Jewish by blood. He also never lived with his parents past high school. He's more of a spiritualist, but I think it's part of some unspoken Jewish code that they have to get angry at god and stop talking to him or something. Mark told me something about that once, but I wasn't sure whether or not he was joking.

Mark and I had been even more close since the March madness in college that had struck down three of our closest friends. He almost lost Jen, too. The things Lucy's boyfriend had done... I shuddered, just thinking about that. The worse part was that we didn't know it was him until it was almost too late. Not even Lucy. The bodies of our friends just kept showing up, horribly disfigured, and we'd all sit together, scared, and talk about it.

It was scary to think that the killer was sitting with us, just lapping up our fear and pretending to be our friend. I never could figure out later why my abilities hadn't warned me about him. I think he didn't have any emotion when he killed, so I didn't get anything weird from him. After Mark was shot, and Jen kidnapped, I'd been in a panic. Things got out of hand quickly after that...

My reverie was broken by the phone ringing. I actually fell out of my chair. I ran to the phone. It was the police. They wanted to make sure I was doing all right. I would like to think the officer was just being nice, but he'd been flirting with me the day before, as if I was in the mood for that after almost getting raped. I'm not *that* good looking, for god's sake.

Men are dogs.

I got off the phone as soon I politely could, which I wasn't, really. I think he got the hint. Fortunately, I never heard from him again.

I had no sooner gotten to my chair than the phone rang again. No, I don't keep my phone with me at all times so I can check Facebook constantly. I got up again and answered it, ready to cuss out the cop.

It was Mark. I wondered briefly if he had known I was thinking about him.

"Hey, Mark."

"Hey, you hanging in there? I'm on my lunch break and thought I'd call and check on you."

"Thank you. I'm fine. Kind of stiff. I didn't sleep well last night."

"Hmm." He paused. "Having those nightmares again?"

I sighed. I'd told him about those long ago. "When do I ever stop having them? No, you know what I mean. All the stress recently has set me off. I think it's normal to have a few bad dreams."

"I didn't say it wasn't normal, Michelle. I'm just concerned. Jen has this really great therapist that she sees…"

"*No!* No, I don't want a therapist. I'll be fine."

"Okay, well, don't be a stranger."

"I won't," I said.

"Okay, I'll talk to you later."

"'Bye. Hey, Mark."

"Yeah?"

"Thanks for calling. I'd needed to hear a friendly voice right then."

"I know. 'Bye, Michelle."

I hung up the phone and went into the kitchen to get something to drink. I got a Coke out of the fridge and went back into the living room. Then I grabbed my cat and stretched out on the couch to think some more. There had to be something I was missing about all this. Some connection to what was happening now that I couldn't see. I thought back some more to the sound of Samson's loud purr.

Did I leave a trail of enemies because of my career? Of course I did. No one works in the police consulting business without pissing someone off. Did any of them want me dead? Well, probably a few, if they thought about me at all. I have helped catch killers. In court, I'm just Dr. Fredericks, a specialist in occult crimes. Once or twice, some lawyer has tried to get cute and talk about me being a psychic, but I just smile and point out how interesting their question is.

I think that if any one of them still remembered me, they would have chosen something less esoteric than a psychic attack. Since I wasn't suddenly enlightened as to who my enemies were, I decided to take care of my waiting emails. Maria had emailed to tell me there weren't any new leads in the River case, exactly what I didn't need to think about right then. I emailed her back and told her what had happened Monday and that I was taking some time off.

Then I decided to try to get some of my sewing projects done. I worked on my embroidery for a new under-dress I was making. I've always liked German blackwork embroidery, but I'd never done any before. I stitched steadily until the fading light reminded me that I needed to eat.

I got up and stretched; I felt achy and cramped from sitting all day. I ordered a pizza and did some Tai chi while I waited for it to arrive. Nothing will clear out the muscles like a good workout. I felt refreshed and energized by the time my food arrived. I took it and picked out a movie to watch while I ate.

When I had finished the movie, I remembered my plan to be a bum, so I put in another movie. I spent the whole evening watching movies, eating popcorn, just getting some much needed rest and relaxation. I took a long bubble bath before going to bed and felt good for the first time in days.

INTERLUDE TWO

I'm barricaded in a cold, white room.

The boy is with me again, but he's the one who is hurt this time. There are other children in cages along the walls, but I can't help them now. I'm not sure I want to help them. Some of them have gone psychotic. Some of the others work with the people who hurt us. They get extra food and less pain for it. They get used less.

I'll never trust them.

We tried to escape again today, the boy and I. But they were waiting for us; someone told them about our whispers. I'll kill the one who told on us if I find out who it was. I think they want us to try to escape. To see what we can do, how well we fight.

I find that I'm covered in blood again. I wonder who I killed this time. They had almost tortured me to death the last time I tried to escape. I don't think they'll let me live now, not after what I'd done.

I hope not.

We had almost made it back to the door into the other part of the building, the non-secure part, when they caught up with us again. The old doctor, I don't know his real name. They call him Dr. Green, but his accent says it's a false name. He grabbed me, and I clawed him. I think I hurt his eye. Hearing him scream was almost worth what he will do to me when he gets through the barricade.

The boy had pulled me away, and we'd run back to the room with the cages. But there's nowhere to go from here. No doors or windows. No vents large enough to crawl through, like they always seem to have in the movies.

No escape.

The doctor is outside the room with the guards. He's screaming as if he has lost his mind. That scares me more than what he's saying. He is always so calm, even when he's killing us. To hear him screaming and shouting is a shock.

He directs his comments at the boy who keeps helping me try to escape. He never addresses us females when he speaks. He has one of the other doctors talk to us instead. I heard a nurse call him a misogynist. I'm not sure what that means, but he really doesn't like us girls. He always picks a girl for his "demonstrations." That's why most of the girls are dead already, or insane like those two they took out of here yesterday.

I've thought about pretending to be insane, too, but I'm afraid of what they would do to me. They hurt me badly enough when they know I understand what they're doing. What would they do to me if they thought I was little more than an animal?

They're starting to get through the door.

I'm scared.

I can hear the doctor better now. I'm thinking about asking the boy to kill me. It would break his heart, but it would be a cleaner death than what the doctor keeps screaming about. But then he would have to face death alone. I can't do that to him. We'll face it together. I reach out and hold his hand.

Green keeps saying that he's going to kill me slowly and make the boy watch.

I know what he has in mind.

I've seen it all before.

CHAPTER TWENTY-THREE

Okay, enough with the nightmare bullshit.

Another night had been spent drenching my sheets in sweat. I needed to get out of the house and do something – to hell with would-be attackers. I'd take my gun and let anyone who dared try their worst.

I was in a foul and somewhat reckless mood.

I took a quick shower and decided to get breakfast on the road. Perhaps I would take a shopping trip to get my mind off my problems. Some of the stores in Clifton, up by the University of Cincinnati, had great clothes. I was too old to be wearing most of the crap you find in regular shopping malls.

I dressed for a fight. I put on black cargo pants, tucked into black speed-lacer combat boots. Those boots are really more comfortable than you would think, and they have great ankle support and traction. I put on a sports-bra so my breasts wouldn't bounce if I had to run. I wore a black button-up shirt over it. I had a shoulder holster for my pistol, so it wouldn't be seen. I pulled my hair back and put on sunglasses. I felt tougher already.

The layers of clothing would be hot, but they would cover up my bruises. I didn't want people looking at me funny for having bruises, as if there's something wrong with me. I felt like shouting that I am not a battered woman, damn it! I was tired of being a victim. I put two spare ammunition magazines in the pockets of my pants.

I wore a black watch and some silver jewelry that had protective wards on it. It never hurts to be careful. I took my cash, I.D., and cards out of my purse and stuffed them into my pocket. I didn't feel like being feminine today. I took one last look around the house, fed the cat, and left.

When I stopped to get gas, I put my gun and ammunition in the console. The woman at the next pump was looking at me funny as I filled my tank. I guess she didn't like my attire. I thought about growling at her, but I just finished pumping my gas. She'd probably call the cops on her designer cell phone if I made any sudden moves. She looked like a typical suburban soccer mom in her Lane Bryant clothes, flighty as a deer. There was a baby seat in the back of her minivan. I shuddered at the thought of what that woman's children would grow up to be.

I don't hate kids. I *don't*, really. I just think people who act like children shouldn't have children themselves. I was kind of indifferent to the idea of having children myself. Maybe it comes from being an only child. I read somewhere once that kids without siblings are less likely to grow up to have children of their own. One of the problems I had with Robert was that he'd really wanted kids. He wanted me to drop out of college and raise a family. As if. It turned out I wasn't able to have children anyway. I had a problem with internal scaring or something. My doctor thought it was from some childhood infection. I think that my refusal to drop out of college is what finally drove a wedge between Robert and me.

Back in my Jeep, I headed up the hill toward I-275. I got a hamburger and fries at a drive-thru and decided to eat on the road. I merged on to the expressway going west. As I took the entrance ramp to I-75 toward Cincinnati, I noticed a white van following me. Well, white vans are common enough. I decided I was just being paranoid. I do that, you know.

I put in a Tori Amos CD and sang my way through seven miles of heavy traffic. Where do all the people come from? I mean, I make my own hours during the week, so I can get out on the road at any time of day, but what do *they* do? I guess they just happen to be off work during the week. There doesn't seem to be enough people working on the weekends for that, though.

A little after crossing over the expressway bridge into Cincinnati, I noticed that the van was still behind me. I took the next exit. It followed me; it was two cars behind while I sat at the light. I couldn't see the driver. When the light changed, I went straight across and back onto the expressway. So did the van.

Okay, so they *were* following me. I had my gun, so I was fairly safe, but they could still run me off the road or something. I tried to remember what you were supposed to do in a case like this. I had no idea where any local police stations were. I could have called 9-1-1, but the police wouldn't do anything if I hadn't actually been threatened yet. The van moved over two lanes and accelerated. Maybe it was a coincidence, after all. I decided to try to ignore them.

About then, I started getting a really bad feeling. I needed to get off the road as soon as possible. Maybe I would see a cop by the side of the road and could pull over. I saw movement in the van's passenger side window as it passed me. I saw a flash of light.

I never heard the shot.

My Jeep bucked as if I'd hit a deep pothole, and then the steering wheel jerked out of my hands. The left front of the Jeep dipped down and ploughed into the road, and my seat belt jerked tight. I tried to grab the steering wheel again and almost had the vehicle back under control when a semi hit my back end at sixty-five miles an hour. I remember flashes of light, glimpses of road and sky, as I was spun around and was rolled under the trailer of the truck. Shattered glass flew everywhere. Pain flared through my whole body.

I blacked out.

When I awoke, I was hanging from my seatbelt. My shoulders rested on the caved-in roof, so I was in no real danger of falling. I tried to move, and the pain was so intense that I blacked out for a few minutes. At least I think it was only a few minutes.

Hard to say.

I could move my head just a little bit. My eyes hurt and seemed to be stuck together with blood. I managed to work them open. It looked like the truck trailer had rolled over on top of the Jeep in the end. There was a lot of wreckage above me. I could hear sirens in the distance, lots of sirens. I wondered how many other cars had been involved in the accident.

Accident. Yeah, right, I thought.

I laid my head against the roof and rested.

I think I may have slept.

CHAPTER TWENTY-FOUR

Someone was screaming and then sobbing, alternately.

It wasn't me, though.

I was sure it wasn't me.

It was getting dark outside, but the whole area was lit up with large portable lamps. I could see them through the wreckage over my head. I heard a saw grinding away somewhere. I faintly heard people talking about which cars to work on first. I wanted to yell for them to come get me, but I knew it wouldn't do any good. I think I drifted out and in of full consciousness. That was probably a blessing. I couldn't move, and I hurt very badly, but I didn't seem to be bleeding much. I think the intense emotions in the area had overwhelmed my psychic sense; I felt numb.

Finally, they were starting to work their way through the wreckage over me. It seemed to get brighter around me. I heard excited voices and looked up to see a fireman peering through the torn metal of the tractor trailer. They were going to have to cut me out. He said something about staying calm, help was on the way. I wanted to tell him that I was fine. It's not as if I was going anywhere on my own.

I woke up on a gurney. There was smoke in the air. I was strapped to a backboard; there was tape across my head, holding it steady. A thick, hard foam pad was around my neck. They were taking me to a helicopter. I had a mask over my face and nose, but I was still having trouble breathing. I tried to work myself loose but was too weak. There were several people wearing gray jumpsuits with some hospital logo. Two of them were working on me while the other two raised me into the copter. They were saying something to me, but I didn't really care. I think they had already given me something for the pain, but maybe I was just in shock. I don't know.

It was a short trip, by air, to the hospital. We spent more time taking off and landing than straight flight. It was still much faster than trying to get an ambulance through crowded city streets. The air-paramedics spent most of that time talking about the wreck. About how many cars were involved, how many lives were lost. I really didn't need to hear that. I concentrated on the beep and whir of the machines. I think they'd started an IV at some point, but I don't remember them doing it.

They took me to the University of Cincinnati Emergency Room. It was close and had room for another patient. The medical center is a huge sprawling thing. I normally tended to stay away from it. I hate hospitals; there's too much pain, fear, and sorrow in them. Too many souls trapped between worlds. It's not the dead ones that bother me.

They wheeled the gurney across the pad and into an elevator. I was then taken into a busy emergency room. Some nurses and techs took over from the paramedics. I think the medical center provides their scrubs or something, because they were a uniform drab grayish-blue. I had been hoping for a little color after the monochrome of the last few hours. No red, though. I didn't want to see any more red. Someone asked me a lot of questions that I mumbled through. They must have thought the answers I gave were satisfactory, because they left me alone after that.

Since I was physically stable and not spurting blood or anything, the unseen doctor decided to send me to Radiology before anything else. I understand that there were probably lots of people who needed the staff's attention more than I did, but I wasn't in the mood to be charitable. I was starting to hurt again.

In Radiology, they took lots of pictures of my bones, from lots of painful angles. Hospitals are strange: they strap you down and tell you not to move, and then they take you to x-ray and twist you into a pretzel to get the best angle for a picture. The tech actually twisted my head for a picture of my jaw; she had to take the neck brace off to do it. I would have smacked her if I didn't hurt so much.

After the x-rays, they took me back to the emergency room and left me alone. I lay there and listened to people screaming, sobbing, or yelling. I swear that at one point I heard a fist-fight. The sound of flesh striking flesh is distinctive. But no one disturbed me in my little curtained-off area.

Finally, two nurses came in and began to painfully clean me up. I was in that wreck for hours and not completely in control of body for most of that time, so you'll excuse me if I skip the details of what they had to clean up besides blood. It was a long and painful ordeal; leave it at that.

A doctor came in, followed by two interns, as the nurses were finishing up with my cleansing. He checked my eyes and made notes on a clipboard. A tech came in and handed him a report and pictures from the radiology department. I had slight fractures of three ribs, plus multiple hairline fractures in both arms and my right leg. Most of my cuts were minor, including some small lacerations on my eyes. I also had a concussion, which explained some of my confusion. The concussion was slight, so I should begin to feel better after a good night's sleep.

They used air-casts and pressure bandages for my fractures. Those were minor, just little cracks, really. I got numbing ointment for my eyes, followed by thick pads taped into place. They told me they were going to keep me at the hospital for twenty-three hours, for observation. I assumed they meant I could go home after that.

After the doctors left, I convinced the nurse to call Jennifer and Mark to let them know what had happened. I had to claim that Jennifer was my sister before the nurse relented. Then the nurses left me alone for about an hour before someone came in and moved me. I hated not being able to see. I could only feel the sensations: moving and then stopping, turning around corners, taking an elevator up, moving some more. I guessed they were taking me to a room. I heard whomever it was talking to someone I assumed was a nurse, and then they pushed me some place and left me alone.

I'm not sure why they call it *observation* when no one pays any attention to you.

CHAPTER TWENTY-SIX

Some time later – how the hell would I know how long? – I heard Mark and Jen talking quietly to someone. Then they came into my room. I must have looked a mess, because Jen kind of sobbed, and even Mark gasped. The nurse told them they could stay for a little while, as long as they didn't disturb me. Then I heard her walking away.

"*Hwck.*" *Shit.* I wet my lips and tried again. "Hey," I managed weakly.

"Hey, yourself. You know, I saw the wreck on the news, but I didn't know you were the instigator," Mark said teasingly.

"I was, sort of…," I choked.

"Hey, now, you know it wasn't your fault. Don't even think that! Mark, don't tease her right now," Jen said quietly.

"No, I… Shit, is there any water?" I asked.

"Sure, baby, hold on." Jen held a straw to my lips, and I drank greedily. IV fluids are fine for the body, but the mouth needs moisture sometimes. I almost cried when she took the straw away. I couldn't help but think back to those hectic days after Mark had been shot and I spent so much time sitting in a hospital room, helping him.

I told them what the doctor had said, and they seemed relieved. Then I told them about what had happened to me. We talked quietly for about an hour before the nurse noticed they were still there and made them leave. They promised to come back right after they each got off work the next day and stay with me until the hospital let me go. Jen gave me some more water before they left.

Someone kept coming in and out of the room.

I could hear people walking down the hall outside. Sometimes they stopped for a few minutes just outside my room. It was driving me crazy. I was so scared that someone was going to do something to me while I was here. Mark and Jen had told me not to worry about it, but how could I *not* worry? Someone had tried to kill me today, and they'd killed a lot of other people to do it.

Couldn't Mark and Jen see that?

What made them think whoever had done it wouldn't try again?

I squirmed in my bed each time I heard people. At least I was able to move a bit now. All my muscles were weak and sore, but I could move. I just couldn't see to do anything about it. I was afraid to remove the bandages from my eyes, though. I was worried that maybe they hadn't told the whole truth. Maybe I was worse off than I thought.

My eyes hurt a lot; maybe that was the problem. The thought of going blind terrified me. I broke out into a cold sweat. I kept trying to tell myself that everything would be okay, that I had minor injuries. The roll cage on the Jeep had saved me. But every time someone stopped outside that door, I started to feel panic again.

A little later, a new nurse came in and told me she would be taking care of me through the night. I felt by then that I must have lain there for days, but it was only a little after two in the morning. The nurse arranged the bed, fluffed my pillow, and got me an extra blanket. It was cold in that room. She also gave me water and a pill. I didn't want to take the pill, but the nurse insisted.

I was worried about whoever had tried to kill me.

Maybe they didn't know I'd survived.

I dozed off as the pill took away my pain, or at least made me not care about it.

Sometime later in the night, I awoke suddenly. I'd been dreaming about my grandparents. *Their* car hadn't had a roll cage. They'd been crushed under a semi on the expressway. That was back before the government had finally fixed the steep I-75 hill that had cost so many people their lives. Everyone used to call it Death Hill.

I hadn't understood why until I lost my grandparents.

I wasn't sure what had awakened me, but I knew it was important that I be awake. I lay there, swathed in the artificial darkness of my bandages, and listened closely. I couldn't hear anything unusual. I tried to make my mind clear enough to think. That damn pill had made me too groggy.

After a time, I became sure that I had another visitor. This one was uninvited and decidedly *not* welcome. As my senses sharpened, I could feel the malevolency of the being in the room with me. I concentrated on sensing where it was. I was scared, more scared than I had been in a long time. Whatever the thing was, it wanted me to be afraid. This was no phantasm or psychic attack. This was something much, much worse.

I took comfort in the fact that I could only sense it, not hear it. This suggested that it wasn't an actual physical threat, at least not yet, although that was a line that could be crossed rapidly and with devastating effect. I tried to clear my mind more. I could feel the thing in the room pulling at my already-low energy reserves, feeding on my fear.

I focused my mind on the area around my bed in an effort to establish a defensive perimeter of sorts. It took a lot of effort not to track that thing as it moved around the room. I was hoping it was more mystical than physical, but without being able to see it, I had no proof either way.

Some part of me began to doubt it was even there. I had been through a lot recently; maybe I was just imagining that something was there because I was afraid another attempt would be made on my life.

I was on some pretty strong medication. Maybe I was hallucinating.

Everyone has their limitations.

I had reached mine some time ago.

I started to feel *angry*. I didn't deserve this. I hadn't done anything to anyone. I had to believe in myself, or I'd never be able to do anything. If I felt something was in the room with me, I couldn't afford not to try to do something about it. Unfortunately, I tend to rely on sight for this sort of thing. Psychic barriers work really well against non-physical things such as phantasms and ghosts. They'll stop such things from getting close.

However, a guy with a knife could walk right through and stab you. I've never heard of anyone who could make barriers to stop physical attacks. I suppose it's possible, but I have no idea how you would go about it. I think you'd have to have telekinesis, and I have yet to meet anyone who has that for real.

That's why I was hoping the entity in the room with me was there only in spirit, so to speak, like a phantasm. I could feel it get angry as the barrier came into being. The entity lunged at me. I tried desperately to ignore it and hold the barrier. It stopped at the edge of the bed, and I actually heard it growling. At least, I heard that in my head. Then it slowly and carefully pushed against the barrier. I could the feel the barrier yielding to it. God, it was strong! I could feel it getting closer to me, closer, until it was just inches from my face. I could almost see a spectral image of it in my head, like an afterimage in the darkness.

My rage was starting to loosen in my mind. I was determined not to die like this. I drew upon the rage, and it fed me the energy to strengthen the barrier. The entity backed off and resumed its pacing of my room. It was quasi-solid at this point. I could hear its claws clicking on the linoleum of the floor. But it was still just a manifestation. Not real in a physical kind of way. It couldn't get to me. I was safe, at least as long as I could hold the barrier. The sounds it made might not even be real. It could just be making me hear it to try to scare me more.

If so, it was working.

I had faced an entity like this once before, when working for the Institute. I could see then, of course, but that hadn't helped much. I don't really know what it was. I'm not a demonologist. I'm not religious enough to believe in demons. I *do* believe in a something that may be the same thing, though. I grew up around ghosts; I know what they feel like. You can feel the human emotions holding them the way they are. But sometimes you encounter something else. Like a ghost in a way, except they can become almost solid. They can interact with regular matter: kill with claws or teeth, that sort of thing. Some of them are intelligent. I just call them *entities*. Whatever they are, they're malevolent.

I don't know how long I lay there with that thing in the room. I could hear the clock ticking, but I couldn't spare enough concentration to count seconds. It tested me three more times. I could almost smell its rank, non-existent breath. Each time, I could feel myself weakening.

It departed as the sun came up. I could feel its anger at me, and I knew it would be back someday. It would hunt me down and... I shook off the thought. I would deal with that when and if it happened; I was too tired and weak to think about it now. I set up the barrier at a low level and fell into a deep and much-needed sleep.

CHAPTER TWENTY-SEVEN

I faded in and out of full wakefulness through most of the day.

When I finally returned to complete consciousness, Jen was sitting by my bed, holding my hand and weeping silently. I wasn't sure how long she'd been there.

My eyes hurt, but otherwise I felt okay. That was probably the lingering effects of pain medications. I felt stiff from being in bed for so long. I vaguely remembered hearing nurses or someone coming in and giving me a pill every so often throughout the day. But now my mind was clearing, and I was waking up. I tried to sit up and quickly realized that was a mistake.

"Don't try to move too much, Michelle." Jen gave my hand a tight squeeze.

"Water," I managed.

She held a straw to my lips, and I drank. While I did that, Jen explained that she'd taken off early from work to stay with me. She had been able to get another teacher to cover her last few classes.

"Thank you," I said. "I'm glad you're here. What time is it?"

"Around five o'clock in the afternoon. Mark had to work a little late, but he just called and is on his way."

"Has the doctor been in?"

"Not since I've been here. Are you in pain? Do you need me to find a nurse for you?"

"No, I'm okay. Or at least I will be. I was just wondering if anyone had said anything about when I can go home."

"Well, they said yesterday that your fractures weren't that bad, and that they just wanted to keep you a day for observation. I don't think they can keep you longer without your insurance company complaining."

"True," I replied. "I'm just worried about my eyes."

"You'll be okay."

I tried a smile but decided against it. "How bad are the cuts on my face? I'd hate to have too many scars."

Jen snorted. "You're bruised up and have a few scrapes, but nothing that needed stitches. I doubt you'll scar. You've always healed well."

"Yes," I said softly. "I always have."

I tried not to think about the accident, but I couldn't help it. Being trapped in the wreckage had been terrifying, the pain and the crushing, overwhelming... I tried to stop myself, but my mind went blank for a moment, and then every muscle in my body spasmed. That set all my wounds to hurting. I didn't want to ask for more pills.

"Michelle, are you okay? What's wrong?"

"I'm okay," I lied. "I was just remembering the accident."

"You shouldn't do that," she scolded.

I was about to reply when I heard someone come into the room. I realized I was suddenly afraid again. I think it was just paranoia. I kept expecting whoever had put me into the hospital to come and finish the job.

It was only someone with a tray of food, though. A least they claimed it was food. It smelled so bad that, even as hungry as I was, I couldn't think about eating it. I didn't ask Jen what it was; I just asked her to get it away from me. She took it and put it someplace far enough away for me not to smell it. I felt suddenly queasy.

Jen called Mark and told him to bring me something good to eat.

I did drink the nasty, weak tea the hospital had provided. I was getting tired of water. I missed my regular sodas, my one vice. Jen and I talked while we waited for Mark. I didn't tell her about what had happened the night before. That wasn't the kind of thing she was good at dealing with.

We kept the conversation normal and talked about her work and the sorry state of the education programs in our state: Kentucky is a beautiful state, but the government doesn't want the population to be very educated. I couldn't focus on the conversation. I felt like screaming. I had so much rage and anguish bottled up inside. I was sick of not being able to see, and worried about how my eyes were doing. They had begun itching terribly.

I finally said something to Jen about that. She found the nurse call-button and explained the problem to the woman who answered. At first, the woman sounded bored and slightly unreasonable, but Jen has this voice she uses on her students when they misbehave; she used it on the nurse.

A few minutes later, a nurse came in and checked my eyes. She almost ordered me to eat the stuff I'd been given, but Jen talked her out of it by telling her that I had *real* food on the way, and since I was being discharged today, what could it hurt? I liked how she put that.

The nurse busied herself with looking at my eyes after that. She took the bandages off, irrigated my eyes with some solution that stung, and wiped my face. She said my eyes were doing quite well, that they must have erred on the side of safety in the emergency room. The damage I had was not as bad as what was written down. The nurse would have the doctor take a look when he came in later, but I could go without the bandages for now. I didn't enlighten her to the fact that I have always healed rapidly. Why start a conversation I couldn't win?

Mark came in the door as she was leaving.

Mark, bless him, had brought me an order of fettuccine Alfredo with garlic bread sticks. I don't know where he stopped to get the food, but it was good. I almost asked him to marry me when he handed me a piece of cheesecake, but I didn't think he would leave Jen for me. Hell, maybe I should ask *her* to marry me; she makes the stuff from scratch.

I had a bit of trouble holding the fork. My arms were in those odd transparent casts. I felt as if I was the kid at the pool whose parents made her wear pool-floats long after she needed them. After the meal, I sat back and sipped my Coke. I wasn't in a lot of pain now. By that, I mean that I hurt, but I could deal with it.

CHAPTER TWENTY-EIGHT

Mark knew I was holding something back in my conversation. I think he could feel the lingering traces of that thing about the room from last night. I knew *I* still could. It was like that feeling you get after you've bitten into a piece of rotten fruit, a lingering queasiness that can't entirely be explained as physical. It felt like something rotten had been in the room, besides the meal the hospital had brought me.

We sat and talked for a few hours until the doctor came in. He was short and had a thick accent, maybe Middle Eastern. He looked over my chart for a few minutes before saying more than hello.

His first remarks were addressed to Mark and Jen. "Are you family?" he asked.

"No," Mark replied.

"Then I must ask you to wait outside. It will only be a few minutes."

"They can stay," I said quickly. I didn't want to alone.

The doctor sighed; he knew I had the right to let Jen and Mark hear what he had to say. He went down the list of my injuries matter-of-factly, as if it was a shopping list. Part of me was shocked at how many there were; part of me was shocked that there weren't more.

"You'll need to spend the next couple of weeks in bed. If you have any problems, you can follow up with your primary physician or come back here to the emergency room. I'd like to see you in my office for a follow-up in two weeks. You will need to get plenty of rest."

Yeah, right. I wouldn't spend any more time in bed than I absolutely had to. Some doctors have really great bedside manners. This one did not. He had all the charm of an auto-mechanic who wants to fix something with your car that you know doesn't need to be fixed. He just wants to tinker and charge you more.

"I'll follow up with my regular doctor. Thanks anyway."

He frowned and reluctantly left after clearing me. I could go home!

A little while later, a nurse came in and unhooked me from the machines. Mark left for part of that. I didn't blame him; *I* didn't want to be there during the part with the catheter, either. Another nurse came in and gave me my discharge papers while they were doing all that. I think they hit you with the paperwork at times like that because they know you're vulnerable and confused.

Okay, I'm more cynical than I like to admit.

The nurse told me I would be able to leave just as soon as the hospital could got an orderly up there with a wheelchair. Mark came back in with a Coke for me and a Lipton Iced Tea for Jen. I wanted to walk out right then, but I was vetoed. I was in no shape to walk anywhere anyway. When the wheelchair arrived over an hour later, Mark went down to bring his blue Ford Explorer around. Jen had a little light-blue Mercedes sports car that guzzled gas like a computer geek guzzles Mountain Dew. It wasn't meant for tall people and had very small seats, so I was going to ride with Mark. Jen waited with me at the hospital entrance. The orderly had a small bag of my personal effects that had been salvaged from my destroyed clothes: some money, my IDs and credit cards, and the two spare magazines for my pistol. The orderly gave me a look as he handed the bag to Jen, but I ignored him. Someone had unloaded the magazines and disposed of the bullets. I assumed my pistol was either still in the wreck or with the police.

I was happy to be leaving the hospital; I'd felt far too vulnerable in there. As we drove away, Mark told me he hadn't actually had to work late. He'd gotten in touch with my insurance agent. Then he'd gone to the lot where they had towed what was left of my Jeep. There, he'd gotten my keys, my gun, and a few CDs that had somehow survived. I was really going to owe him after this. I was glad to have my gun back, even if I didn't have any ammo with me.

I told him about my visitor in the night. We talked about that all the way back to my house. Jen was waiting when we got there; she speeds everywhere she goes. Mark gave her the keys, and she went in, fed my cat, and got some clothes and toiletries for me. They were taking me back to their house for a few days, at least until I could get around on my own. I hadn't been asked, but I didn't argue. It would be good to feel safe again.

It should be noted that I *did* argue to be allowed to go get my own things, and I lost. I hope Jen didn't look around too much. I did ask her to grab my notebook computer. I could check my email and play games while lying around their house and eating their food.

We got to their house around nine in the evening. Jen went ahead and unlocked doors while Mark helped me inside. Damn, I hated being an invalid. *Invalid*. I've never liked that word. Just because a person can't take care of themself doesn't make them any less of a person. They are just as *valid* as anyone else. Oh, well. On the other hand, I didn't mind being pampered, either, and Jen is a great cook.

Mark sat and talked with me while Jen drove to the pharmacy and picked up my medications. I didn't really want those, but Mark and Jen both insisted. I had prescriptions for pain meds and antibiotics, just in case.

I needed to make some plans. I was tired of reacting to problems. I wanted to start taking some action. I wanted to do something about these bastards who had tried to kill me.

Damn, I had really liked that Jeep.

CHAPTER TWENTY-NINE

At least Mark and Jen's house had good mystical shielding on it. I wouldn't have to worry about any unwelcome entities while I was there. I was worried about other visitors, though. The guys in the van had been real enough. What was to stop them from just shooting me through a window? I glanced uncomfortably out the large bay window in the living room, but Mark and Jen had a long driveway.

Jen came back and fixed me bowl of spumoni to take my pills with. I was going to have to watch my figure while I was there; she seemed intent in making me blimp up. I don't know how Jen could eat that way and stay so lithe. I asked her, and she told me she went to the gym three times a week. She must do a lot there, because I didn't think three days would be enough for me to stay thin eating what she did.

I tried to use my notebook, but I couldn't type with my arms in casts. I was going to have to cut those damn things off. They had told me at the hospital that I had only minor fractures. I heal very quickly; I'd be able to get out of the casts tomorrow, maybe while Jen and Mark were both at work. They wouldn't let me do it now. The cracked ribs were honestly giving me the most problems. I'd taken an Ultram when Jen got back from the pharmacy, and that helped some, but not a lot.

I sighed and quietly resolved to kill the bastards who had done this to me. In the meantime, I had to figure out who was after me and why. I was no closer now than I had been several days ago. We sat and talked until Jen went to bed. Then I brought the subject back up with Mark.

"I've been thinking about this mess I'm in," I said by way of starting the topic off.

"No," he said sarcastically, "really?"

"Ha, ha. Really. I'm wondering who I could have pissed off enough for them to want me dead. Other than a few ex-boyfriends, I can't think of anyone, and those don't really count."

"I can't think of anyone, either. It's not as if you go around getting into vendettas with everyone you meet. Not to try to boost your ego beyond its already rarified heights, but you're a nice person. Not the type people want to kill. At least, I don't think I've ever wanted to kill you."

"Thanks, I think. Seriously, though, someone has gone to a lot of trouble to get me dead, and more than once now." I shook my head. "I guess it could be some nut-job. But they don't usually work in gangs."

Mark looked confused. "Gangs?"

"The guys who jumped me. You know, the ones from the first white van."

"Oh, I 'd set that aside as different issue, but I see what you mean."

"A separate issue! How can it be?"

"I don't know. It just doesn't seem the same style, is all. How can it be related?"

"Hmm." I paused. "Not the same style as whoever psychically attacked me, or the entity at the hospital, or the attack at the faire. I'm more worried about the attempted rape and the 'accident' on the expressway. Maybe they *are* two different people or groups."

Mark looked skeptical. "So now we have two different groups who want you dead? That doesn't make sense, either. If it is a group, then maybe different members have their own idea of how to deal with the problem."

I liked that. *Deal with the problem.* "Great, so half of them want to kill me, or rape me and *then* kill me, and the other half just wants me to be torn apart by a demon or something. Lovely."

"There doesn't seem to be any pattern to the attacks. If you lay low, you may be okay for a while." Mark took a drink of his scotch.

"Or I may be putting you and Jen in considerable danger. Maybe you should take me back to..." I trailed off at the look on his face.

"Michelle, we would both do anything for you. Even if we weren't such good friends, there is that small matter you took care of for us in college to consider. I always repay my debts, you know. I may not look like much, but I would kill to protect you."

"I know," I sighed.

"Then consider the subject closed. Jen and I will take extra precautions."

"Okay, but do me a favor."

"You have but to ask." I tried not to grin; his New England accent comes out strong when he's been drinking.

"Set a trap for anything mystical coming around." I waved him quiet. "I know you have powerful wards on the house. I mean set something up to track whoever sends the next attack. Maybe I can start going after *them*, for a change."

He grinned. "Excellent thought. I'll go do that now, if you don't mind. Then I think I'm off to bed. Do you need anything before I retire?"

I didn't, so he left me to perform my mundane bedtime rituals – difficult in casts – and go to bed. I was safe, at least for tonight. I fell asleep as soon as my head hit the pillow, maybe on the way down.

CHAPTER THIRTY

There is not much a person can do with both arms in casts. I listened to a lot of music while Mark and Jen were at work. The days passed in a haze. I recovered quickly, just as I always do. I couldn't remember actually breaking any bones like this before, but somewhere in the back of my head, I knew that I had.

I had time for a lot of reflection.

I tried to fit all the disparate pieces together in my head. First, I had Lucy telling me in an email to run, even if I didn't *see* the email until after the first two attacks. The first two attacks were psychic in nature. Rather straightforward, for someone in my business, though still disconcerting. Then I saw Lucy at the record store; she delivered more cryptic messages and seemed angry with me. After our encounter, I was attacked on the way home by some guys in a van who wanted to have their way with me.

Coincidence?

A few days later, I barely survived the attack on the expressway, and then something may have happened at the hospital. I wasn't sure about the hospital. Something didn't add up.

I mulled these through my brain. Finally, some of the glaring oddities began to sink in. One, none of the psychic attacks had succeeded. That one wasn't as odd as it seemed at first thought. Psychic attacks are extremely difficult to commit, and I'm good at defense.

That brought me to the second thing.

Why bother with the psychic attacks at all? Why shoot my tire out on the expressway, a daring but mundane type of attack, and then go to the trouble of summoning some kind of demon or other entity to attack me in the hospital? UC is a big hospital. It would be fairly easy to actually sneak into a room and kill someone. Hell, you probably wouldn't even have to sneak.

I shuddered.

I was glad to be away from there and someplace safe.

Could the psychic attack have been made without knowing where I was? No. Mark had said the attacker had been close at the river, so they probably had been close at the faire, as well. I don't think the thing at the hospital was sent after me. I *do* think it was real, but hospitals are places of suffering. Things that feed on the misery of others tend to lurk in places like that. It's one reason why I avoid hospitals when I can.

So whoever was after me had followed me to the river and to the faire, and then psychically attacked me. It wasn't the work of the same people. It couldn't be. The only answer that worked was that the people who shot out my tire thought I was dead. They may have watched for a few hours, and when I didn't make any noise, they assumed they had taken care of me to their satisfaction. It wasn't announced on the news until much later that night that I'd survived, and even then, the news would have just said that I was taken to an area hospital.

Why the tire? Why not shoot *me*? The shooters didn't know I was in the hospital, or they would have just come in and killed me there. They needn't even have shot me. Plenty of ways to kill someone hooked to an IV. Whoever had psychically attacked me didn't know I was there at all, and therefore they weren't connected to the shooter in the van.

I was wondering, too, about the guys in the van who'd jumped me. They could have just walked up to me with guns. I would most likely not have fought. I'm brave, but not stupid. There was a good chance I had seriously hurt or even killed those two men. Why would they take that chance? The driver of the van had been armed; I'd seen him drawing a large gun as I was running away. Why didn't he help his two buddies? Unless, maybe, they were meant to fail at the abduction. Maybe the driver was only concerned about defending himself. That didn't make sense, but it felt more correct somehow.

Someone just wanted to send me a message.

Whoever kept attacking me psychically wasn't much of a threat. These kinds of things have a big price – think of it as karmic payback. I've survived worse attacks. If they really wanted me dead, they would have to find some other way. They just wanted to prove something to me. I immediately thought of Lucy again. I remember Marge telling me that Lucy felt left out of our circle of friends because she wasn't good at anything. Lucy was always like that: she'd try something but not put any effort into it. Then when she failed, she'd blame everyone else.

Mark had once taken her under his tutelage in the Art. He'd kept at it much longer than I would've had patience to. Finally, he had to stop teaching her, when her sloppy technique and lack of aptitude led her to being more of a danger to everyone around her than was healthy. Could Lucy have been the one to attack me? I didn't think she'd proceeded that far along, to able to do that, but I'd ask Mark. It seemed plausible.

The physical attacks seemed to have started either as an attempt at abduction or as a test of some kind. I must have passed, because the attack on me later had been deadly. Eleven people died in that accident on the expressway. I'd read about it on the internet. I survived only by luck and the roll-cage in my Jeep. As it was, if the truck that hit me had been carrying a full load, I would have died anyway. The trailer had been empty; that saved my life.

It was two different groups, with different motivations, who were attacking me. It had to be. Was there a connection between them? They both started at the same time. There had to be a connection. Had there been some way for me to avoid this situation? Was there a way *now*? I didn't think so.

I wasn't able to avoid it, but I could do more than sit on my ass and wait for someone to come and hurt me. I could go after them and make them pay for what they had done to me. Make them pay for trying to hurt me, for killing those people on the expressway who had nothing to do with it. I would find them and make them tell me what was going on, even if I had to torture them to do it.

That thought shocked me.

I'm not normally a violent person, no matter what you may think of me. Did I mean it? Hell, yes, I meant it. I would defend myself, whatever I had to do. I didn't have any concrete evidence, or I would have gone to the police. I wasn't even sure the police weren't in on it. Probably not, but I think they could have tried harder after the guys in the van jumped me. I had to make a plan of action. I needed to find my enemies before they found me again. I might not survive another attack.

There was still a lot I had to do. I managed to get the air-casts off my arms; I left the one on my leg. I didn't really want to bend any more than I had to, with my ribs in the shape they were. I tended to get dizzy if I moved too fast, a lingering effect of the concussion or the medication. My arms felt odd without the casts, itchy. As long as I took things easy, though, they'd be fine.

I called my insurance agent and took care of what I could over the phone. The insurance company had already sent someone to look at the wreckage. There wasn't any doubt about the Jeep being a total loss. They were working with the trucking company, too. I felt bad about that. It wasn't really the trucker's fault, but he shouldn't have been that close to me.

I called my lawyer and apprised her of what was going on. I gave her the name of my insurance agent. That should take care of my hospital bills. I should also get a decent settlement in the end.

I called Josh and let him know about the accident, and told him that I wouldn't be able to attend the rest of the faire season. My bones may heal faster than normal, but I didn't want to take the chance, and it made a good excuse. I also had too much going on. The faire was too public. I told him I was staying with friends, but I'd keep him updated on how I was doing. He said he would tell the others. He'd seen the accident on the news but hadn't realized I was in it. That let me hope that maybe my enemies wouldn't know I'd survived.

I looked online at local car dealerships. I was going to need a new car as soon as possible. I'd have Jen take me out over the weekend. She's good-looking enough to get good deals on cars with a smile. I'm too tall; I intimidate most men, which is also useful sometimes. I had enough in the bank to cover a down payment, and my credit was decent enough. I wanted another Jeep, maybe a black one this time.

I played a few games of online poker while I ate lunch. Afterward, I replied to my waiting emails; there were quite a few. Although I was up to a little bit of games on the computer and such, intense activity was out of the question for a few weeks.

Jen got home early that afternoon. We talked about cars and going shopping. She didn't think much of my choice of vehicle, but I had no use for a sports car, so we agreed to disagree, at least on that. She started making dinner: pot roast with potatoes and carrots. I helped by peeling the carrots. After the roast was in the pot, Jen went to take a shower.

I moved back into the living room and decided to try some Tai chi, carefully. It would be good for my body if I could. I spent an hour stretching and moving, letting my body's energy move through me and cleanse me. Afterward, I felt energized and not as stiff and sore as I had been. As I was finishing up, Mark came in and sat in his easy chair to read.

"You look like you feel better," he said, looking up from his book as I sat down on the sofa.

I nodded. "Yes, I do."

"I see you removed your air-casts. How are your arms doing?"

I grinned. "I have a few aches and twinges now and then. Mostly they're doing well. They itch a bit."

He laughed. "I suppose you can deal with the itching, all things considered."

"Yup. That, I can." I laughed, too. "I'm just glad to be alive."

He nodded without saying anything. He didn't have to.

CHAPTER THIRTY-ONE

Jen and I left early that day to go shopping. I had taken the air-cast off my leg so I could walk a bit easier. It gave me a few sharp twinges if I stepped down a little too hard but otherwise was mostly fine. Okay, my leg hurt like hell, but I could deal with that. It had been over a week since the accident. I'd lived through worse. I must have looked a mess, with my fresh scars on my face and fading bruises.

I didn't care; I wasn't trying to impress anyone.

We took Mark's Ford Explorer so I wouldn't be too cramped. I didn't want to bend that leg any more than I had to. We went to the mall, and I bought a new purse and some clothes. Jen had picked fancy clothes for me when she picked up clothes at my house. I wanted something more comfortable, and something to replace what I'd lost in the accident. I nursed a brooding anger toward those responsible.

Later in the day, we went around to various car dealerships in the area to look at the Jeeps I had selected online. I'd thought about getting a Wrangler or a Liberty. They're kind of cool, but I am a creature of comfort. I stuck to my original choice and bought a black Grand Cherokee with all the bells and whistles.

It would do.

We spent most of the day at the car dealership. It was tiring. They can manage to make even simple things take forever. I came in expecting to put half down on a new car, to keep my payments low. I ended up putting only a quarter down and got the same payments, plus larger tires. I'm not sure why car dealers do things like that, but I'm not complaining. Not that I have any use for larger tires, but the young salesman was so eager that I decided to act impressed.

I followed Jen back to their house, but first I stopped and got myself a new cell phone. My iPhone had been smashed in the wreck. When I got back to Jen and Mark's place, we had dinner together. I wanted to get out on the road and look for that van, but I didn't. An extra day of rest would do me a lot of good. I needed it.

I spent the evening in the guest bedroom I'd taken over, working on my computer, making notes about what had been happening to me lately, trying to find a pattern. I needed a plan, preferably a plan that didn't get me killed. I wasn't having much luck coming up with one.

The best I could come up with was that I would go out the next day and look for the van. It had some rather distinctive scrapes along the right front quarter-panel, so I was sure I'd know it if I saw it. I was hoping that even if they knew I was alive, they wouldn't be expecting me to be out and mobile so quickly after the accident. My plan was to find them and follow them back to wherever they were working from. I would figure out what to do after that when I got there.

I tried not to think about everything that could go wrong with this plan. It was hard not to, though, with my bones aching. I may heal faster than most people do, but I get hurt just as easily. Well, *almost* as easily. I admit that I may be reasonably tough. When I'm not being chased by white vans and monsters, I keep a regular schedule, with plenty of exercise. I'm in fairly good shape.

I exercised for about an hour just to remind myself of that. Tai chi tends to fade from muscle memory quickly if you don't keep up with it, at least for me. It felt good to be working my muscles again. Tai chi is a really low impact workout, so I wasn't in danger of hurting myself. The workout also cleared my mind. I was ready to get this problem solved so I could get on with my life.

Mark knocked on my door later in the evening and asked me to join him in the living room.

I got a drink from the kitchen before joining him. He was sitting alone, reading, when I came in. He looked up.

"Michelle, I want to talk to you about these attacks."

"Okay, which ones?"

"Well, let's start with the ones I can help with." He paused. "There have been three mystical attacks upon this house since you came here. They were all were produced by the same person or persons."

"Go on."

He took a drink. "The first attack, last week, was from a car at the end of the driveway. The other two were from a house in Walton; I discretely traced the attack back to a house last night." He looked embarrassed. "I really hadn't intended to make the trip, but I'm afraid your impetuousness has influenced me."

"What did you find at the house? Did you see who it was?"

"I did. Are you sure you want to hear this?"

"Come on, Mark, do you really need to ask me that?" I shook my head. "I think I may know anyway."

"Really? How?"

"Deduction, but go on. Let's see if I'm right."

"I saw eleven people in the house. I only recognized one of them." He paused again.

"Lucy," I said.

He sighed. "Yes. I'm afraid she has gotten mixed up in a very rough crowd. I saw part of the second ritual through a window; they are quite crude and vicious."

"Vicious?"

He shuddered. "They used ritualistic bloodletting to gain power for the summoning: drinking of blood and all that."

"Ah, well, I suspected them of being fruit bats. Some people who want to be vampires go through the motions, you know. I've seen it in clubs." I shrugged.

"You must visit some interesting clubs, Michelle."

I just grinned.

He cleared his throat. "Well, I didn't see a white van on the property, but that doesn't mean anything. They could have dumped it by now. I'm…" He hesitated, looking at me. "What?"

"I know you don't like to think it, Mark, but I'm convinced that there are two different groups involved." I explained to him my reasoning from the day before. I included examples of how they dressed, moved, acted. I'm not sure he was convinced, but he let it ride for now. He knew I had a knack for putting together small, seemingly unrelated bits of information correctly. Jen was a constant reminder of that.

"I understand what you are saying, but it seems odd to me," he said.

"I'm quite confused, myself. I don't like the idea of groups of people trying to kill me, you know."

"I know. Let me give you the information I have."

He gave me the address of the house where Lucy was staying. I still considered them to be second in priority to the guys with the van. The vamps could wait until I had dealt with the others. I went back to my room and lay down. I had some more thinking to do. I needed to find out all I could about the second group.

I don't like people trying to kill me.

It makes me more than a little angry.

CHAPTER THIRTY-TWO

Later that evening, I called Josh. It was probably a mistake. He might get the wrong idea, but I wanted to make sure nothing had happened to any of my friends at the faire. I also wanted to hear a friendly voice that had nothing to do with this. Maybe I wanted a little sympathy, too.

"Hey, Josh. Busy?"

"Hey! How's the broken girl? We missed you today. Everyone said to say 'Hey' if I talked to you again before they saw you, so...Hey."

I laughed. Josh was crazy. "Everything go okay?"

"Oh, yeah, went perfect. You weren't there to screw things up."

"Go to hell." I laughed. "Nothing weird happened or anything?"

"No one had any bizarre accidents. Rachael punched John for real, knocked him off the stage, but didn't do any lasting damage. The crowd loved it. I told her she needed to try harder next time."

"I bet you did. Still causing trouble, I see."

"When am I not?"

I laughed again. It felt good. "So, you have any luck getting her to go out with you?"

"Now, Michelle, you know I'm not the kind of guy who goes after every pretty girl."

I snorted. "Since when?"

"Damn, I'm talking to you for five minutes, and you're already ragging on me. It's not like you haven't been doing some flirting on the side, too, you know."

"What do you mean by that?" I asked indignantly. "If you're suggesting that I've been lusting after you just because…"

"Down, kitten, I'm not talking about me. I'm talking about that Michael guy."

I was confused. "What Michael guy? Has someone been asking about me?" My heart raced. I was suddenly worried about my friends again.

"The guy you met in that shop where you buy all your leather stuff from. You know, the MIB." He said.

MIB. Man-In-Black. Government type, to Josh. "Him?" He *was* somewhat hot, in a scary big guy way. "He's a federal marshal, not a MIB. At least, not to my knowledge. How the hell did you know I ran into him there?"

"You need to ask me that, with the gossips we have around the faire?"

"People talk about me?"

"No, but someone thought *he* was cute."

"Go to hell," I said.

He laughed for almost two minutes, until I had to tell him to shut up. "Seriously, though, Michelle, he came by and asked about you, twice. He didn't say anything about being a federal marshal. I told him you'd been in an accident and wouldn't be at the rest of the faire. He seemed upset until I told him you were basically okay. You *are* okay, right?"

"I'm okay. Just a few cracked bones and a lot of bruises. A few minor cuts, as well. I'm just not up to walking around the faire for hours. I may come back before the last weekend."

"Only *you* would say you had broken bones but were okay. It would be cool if you could come by. You need to come and see everyone anyway. Let them know you really are okay. You know they don't trust me."

"Yeah, I don't trust you, either. Remember that."

"Uh-huh, I will."

"I think I'm going to get some sleep. Thanks, Josh."

"No problem, babe. You take care of yourself."

"You, too. Say hello to everyone."

We said our goodnights and hung up. So the marshal was asking about me. Interesting. I wondered if there was any connection, but I was too tired to think clearly. I'd worry about it some other time.

CHAPTER THIRTY-THREE

I told Jen and Mark I was going home over breakfast.

"Are you sure you'll be okay?" asked Jen.

"I'm sure," I replied. "I appreciate what you've both done for me, but I need to get home and get back to my life. There's quite a bit of unfinished business left. Besides, I miss my cat."

Mark made an odd noise. "Michelle, I think I know some of what you're thinking of doing, and I have to advise against any rash action at this time. We don't mind feeding your cat; you could even bring him here, if you kept him in the guest bedroom."

"I need to know what's going on. I know you're both worried for me, but there are some things that just have to be done. This is one of those things."

Mark sighed. "I understand that. I'm advising caution. You can be far too reckless when you get like this."

"It's paid off for me in the past."

There was nothing else to say. Mark carried my few clothes out to my new Jeep while I carefully got in on the driver's side. We said our goodbyes, and I headed toward my house. I didn't go directly there, though. I drove around through the connecting streets, looking for that white van. I didn't see it, so I went home and spent an hour or so with my cat, happy to be home for the first time in over a week. I changed into more rugged clothes while I was there.

I went out and drove around some more. I'd seen the van several times in this area. It made sense that they might be based near here. This part of town area had a lot of old rental homes and abandoned warehouses they could be using. I hoped I'd see them before they saw me. Just in case, my pistol was loaded and in the seat next to me.

I stopped at a gun store and picked up a new shoulder holster. I might need to carry my gun discreetly. I'd gotten my concealed carry permit several years ago, when they first became available to private citizens. At the time, I'd figured being allowed to carry a gun concealed would come in handy when going clubbing; some of the clubs I used to go to were in bad parts of town, and a 9mm pistol is a great deterrent.

I'd never thought I would need it for something like this.

I went through the drive-thru at McDonalds and got a drink. Espionage is thirsty work. I was leaving the parking lot when I saw a white van turning toward the hardware store across the street. I turned and drove down the parking lot for a better look, one hand on my pistol. It wasn't the same van. This one had bumper stickers and stuff. The two guys who got out looked like they'd rolled in white paint. Just a couple of painters. Damn.

I turned back onto the road and saw another white van two lights ahead. I hurried to catch up. It looked like the right van, yes; there was the scrape I'd noticed before on the front right fender. My heart started pounding. I followed the van up the hill towards the expressway. It went past the ramp. I wanted to know what was going on.

I was trying to stay behind enough not to be noticed, so I didn't see them pull by the side of the road until it was too late. I drove right past them. It was the same driver as the day they jumped me. My heart started beating harder. The van pulled out after me. I sped up. There was a police station up ahead.

I was starting to form a new plan. It was dangerous, but what the hell. I passed the police station. I like to think that maybe I confused the guys in the van. I hope so. They followed; a car was between us, so I didn't think they would try anything funny. Not yet, anyway. I headed out toward Taylor Mill.

My plan was to lure them onto some of the back roads of Kenton County, roads I knew really well from growing up around here but they might not. Lots of twists and turns and roads cut back and forth through the forested hills. I was sure I could lose them in a chase. I was betting my life on it.

I made a sharp turn onto Wolf Road. I went down the steep, curvy hill. I saw flashes of the van in my rearview mirror. I turned left at the bottom, back toward Latonia. After a mile or so, I made a sudden right turn onto Licking Pike; it's a long and twisty road that follows the Licking River south. I crossed the railroad tracks and shot down the road, going as fast as safely possible. In the mirror, I could see the van far behind.

I turned right and gunned it up Steep Creek Road toward Ryland Heights. They must have seen me turn, though, because I caught sight of the van again as I was going around a sharp curve. Damn. I turned left at the top of the hill; I had to go farther out into the country. There were lots of straight stretches in the road, and I was able to get quite a lead. I had the advantage n ow. Not only did I have the more stable and maneuverable vehicle, but I knew those roads. I knew when to hit the brakes in the curves and when to accelerate. I averaged fifty-five miles per hour down the long, winding hill to Visalia.

They caught up with me near the bottom, though, because I had to slow down and swerve to avoid hitting a farm tractor. I gunned the engine and shot through the lowlands out past Kenton Lakes. I was aiming for a little road up near Morning View. It cut back through the hills in a treacherous path and got very little traffic. I was thinking that if I could get far enough ahead, I could ambush them and return the favor from the expressway.

I turned at the small, red brick post office building and accelerated as fast as I could. They were right behind me. As I neared the end of the stretch of road, I slammed on the brakes and slid through the sharp right-hand curve. The van slide into the wooden fence but quickly got back onto the road, following me.

I made a hard turn onto Hempfling Road. It was narrow and curvy; I'd be able to gain some distance on them. After a mile or so of sharp turns, I saw the van take one too quickly and go off the road. They flew over the embankment and clipped a tree, rolling across a fallow field. I slowed down and stopped. I could see them from the road. It looked like one of them had been thrown from the wreck.

I couldn't just drive away.

Believe me, I wanted to.

I also wanted to know who these bastards were.

CHAPTER THIRTY-FOUR

I turned around and drove to where the van had gone off the road. I pulled off to the side and got out, my cell phone in my hand and my gun in my shoulder holster. I wanted to look over things before I called for help. It may seem callous, but these people had left me for dead in a wreck for hours, so I wasn't feeling kind and generous.

As I got close to the man who'd been thrown free of the van, I could see he wouldn't need any help, not with his head at that angle. A bulky gun lay on the ground near his hand. I'd seen ones like it in movies all my life. A little whisper of memory said it was a Heckler and Koch MP53 machine pistol, 9mm. I wasn't sure where in the hell I would've learned that.

I felt strange, disconnected from myself.

I picked up the gun. The feeling coming off it almost made me drop it. It had been used to kill a lot of people, or at least the owner had *thought* of killing lots of people while holding it. It was hard to tell the difference without checking it out, and I really didn't want to do that. The gun was heavier than I expected, loaded and chambered. I was examining it as a man stumbled from around the side of the van. We each froze for an instant, and then he went for a gun in a shoulder holster.

I yelled, "Don't!" and raised the gun I was holding, but he drew and fired at me anyway. I felt frozen in place.

I don't know how he missed me; I guess it was the blood in his eyes from a nasty-looking cut on his forehead. My hand came up, and my finger squeezed the trigger reflexively. The bullet hit the man just above the bridge of his nose; blood, brains, and bits of bone splashed out across the van.

I stared at him in horror as he slumped to the ground. His legs and arms made little jerking motions. I heard the sound of the two shots echoing off the hills. That's when I realized I had just killed a man. I fell to my knees and vomited.

After I finished bringing up everything there was to bring up, I stood and wiped my mouth, looking away from the body in front of the van. I still felt queasy, but I felt surprisingly little remorse. I was sure it would haunt my dreams for a while, but the guy had fired first. It was clearly self-defense. I wouldn't have shot him if he hadn't fired at me. Some part of me was not so sure, though. My shot was just lucky, or unlucky for him; it depends on how you look at it, I guess.

I still had the gun in my hand, and as much as I hated what I had just done, I was loath to give it up. I walked around to the other side of the van. The passenger door was open; the front windshield had a large hole it. I assumed the first guy I'd found was the driver, although his face was so bloody I hadn't recognized him. He must not have been wearing a seatbelt. I approached the van with a feeling of great trepidation. I was not looking forward to the feelings I would get once inside it. I summoned up my nerve and looked in the van.

There was a guy in the back. From the way he was half-sitting with his legs straight out, I'd say his legs were both broken, or maybe his back. He was pale and sweating, his fists clenched at his sides. He looked up as I looked in.

"Don't try it!" I said, raising the gun.

He didn't even flinch. He just glared at me with an expression of utter hatred. I looked around the van; it held racks with electronic equipment and weapons: several kinds of guns, and even what looked like a rocket launcher.

Who are these guys? I thought wildly.

"Are you alone?" He didn't answer me. "The driver died in the crash. Your other buddy didn't answer my questions fast enough. *Are you alone?*" I aimed the gun at his groin and tightened my finger on the trigger. *That ought to get his attention.* It did. His eyes widened, and a look of fear flickered across his face.

He swallowed convulsively. "There were just the three of us. We always work in three-man teams. Just like the last team," he added weakly.

"Last team?"

He took a deep breath. "The last team we sent. You took out the two retrieval specialists that time. I'm just a surveillance specialist."

"*Took out?* You mean *killed?*" I felt sick again.

He frowned and blinked at me. "Yes, I mean *killed*. You don't think you can hit people that hard in those places and *not* kill them, do you? What's your angle?"

I pointed the gun at his head. "I ask the questions. You answer them. Is that too hard for you?"

He shook his head, then winced.

I was nervous; someone could come down the road at any time. I was trying not to pay attention to the psychic emanations from the van, but it wasn't easy. There'd been a lot of pain and suffering in there. I didn't want to think about what they would've done to me if I hadn't been able to fight back.

"Tell me why you people are trying to kill me," I said.

The man just set his jaw and didn't answer.

I waved the gun at him. "Tell me what I want to know, and I'll call an ambulance for you. If you don't, I'll leave you here for the wild dogs." I had no intention of leaving him like this, but I had to make him think I did. There probably weren't any wild dogs around there, either, but you never know.

"I'm dead anyway. We failed our mission. Go to hell."

His hand flashed over to the right and grabbed a pistol I hadn't seen. The shot was incredibly loud inside the van. He had a neat hole in chest, over his heart. He stared for a moment, his mouth working, and then fell back against the side of the van.

I got sick again. I didn't even realize at first that I'd shot him. What was wrong with me?

I recovered quicker this time. Maybe it was because there wasn't as much mess. I took stock of what was in the van. I found some papers and maps. I set those just outside. I took a selection of the weapons that were in nice black hard-cases as well. If these killers were going to have that kind of firepower, I should, too.

I also found two notebook computers, along with some other hardware that looked expensive, maybe military surplus. I took everything I could carry back to my Jeep, including the registration for the van and all three wallets. I then wiped down with my sleeve anything in the van I might have touched. I went back to the guy with the broken neck and carefully wiped down the entire gun to remove any fingerprints I might have left on it. Then I gritted my teeth and put the gun in his hand, making sure to get his fingerprints in other places as well. Finally, I ran back to the car before I could get sick again and drove as fast I dared up the road.

I cut up Island Creek to Moffett Road and from there over to State Route 17. I drove carefully and within the speed limit. I didn't want to get pulled over right then. Not only did I have a carload of stolen guns and electronics, but I was afraid I might confess about shooting those two guys. They hadn't given me any choice, but that didn't make me feel much better.

CHAPTER THIRTY-FIVE

When I got back to my house, I pulled into my garage. It wouldn't do to have the neighbors see me carrying guns into the house. After I shut the garage door, I took everything into the living room. Then I mixed myself a strong vodka screwdriver. I thought I needed it for my nerves. It hit my empty stomach like a bomb, and I almost got sick again.

I decided that maybe I needed to eat something. I washed up, and then found some bread that was still good and made myself a cheese sandwich. That would do for now. I'd have to go to the store later. I threw out the rest of the vodka. It was too tempting.

I made an inventory of everything I'd taken from the van. There was quite a bit. I started with the computers, but they were password protected. I'd think about what to do with them later; for now, I turned them off and set them aside. Next were two sets of night-vision goggles. They were kind of cool; I'd always wanted a set. These had built-in battery rechargers and cords. Then I looked through a lot of papers and stuff, maps of the area around Cincinnati. Nothing jumped off the pages as I skimmed them. No circles and arrows on the map with *secret base here* written in, or anything like that.

I opened the black cases and took a look at the guns: a HK 91 rifle, a HK MP53 like the one I used earlier, and two Glock 9mm pistols. The rifle was a large, heavy thing with a bipod; I think it was meant for sniping. It took a 7.62mm by 51mm round; it said so right on the side of the gun. There were four twenty-round magazines for the rifle, two thirty-round mags for the MP53, and four mags for the pistols. There was no extra ammunition at all. I must not have found where they were keeping that.

I'd need to buy more bullets later. In a smaller case was a large scope for the rifle. Most of the equipment was new and held only faint traces of the feelings that had been on the pistol I used earlier.

I looked at the other equipment. There were two radios with headsets, a metal baton-thing that was retractable, and an electric lock-pick. I'm sure I could find a use for all that. The lock-pick had me worried. I wondered if they'd used it to come into my house and bug the place. I wasn't sure how I'd be able to tell.

I loaded the pistol mags with extra rounds I had in my dresser and put them in the console of my Jeep. I put one of the radios and the lock-pick in there, too. The baton looked as if it could come in handy in a fight, so it went in my pants pocket. The rest of the stuff got hidden in a closet. I had better make that run to the store before it got dark.

I backed carefully out of the garage. There was no one around. I shut the door and left to go to Wal-Mart. It's a big store, and always busy. I should be reasonably safe there, I reasoned.

I loaded up a small cart-load of groceries and a few other things without incident.

While I was there, I passed the sporting goods counter and noticed the rifles. I don't think I'd ever noticed before that this store sold guns. There was lots of ammunition behind the counter. I needed to stock up, maybe get some hollow-points for a little extra punch.

A large woman in a blue vest, her hair dyed dark blue, stood behind the counter, chewing gum. She smiled as I walked up.

"Can I help you, honey?" I flinched at her voice. It was high, and she had an atrocious accent. She sounded as if she was from deep in the hills of West Virginia.

"Hello. I was wondering if you have any hollow-points," I said.

"Sure do, honey. What caliber you need?"

"9mm and 7.62 NATO," I said. "The highest grain count you've got in each." I was going to hurt her if she kept calling me *honey*.

"Okay, sugar, we got lots of those. We got Remington and Winchester and…"

I growled under my breath. "Winchester is fine. What type do you have?"

She put several different boxes on the counter. One of each caliber was marker *silver-tip*. I picked up a box, opened it, and looked at the bullets. They were nice silver hollow-points. The box said they had good energy deposit for stopping power, exactly what I needed. The silver would help, as well, if I decided to add a little mystical punch to them.

"How many boxes of the silver-tip do you have in each?"

"We got six boxes of 9mm. No hollow-points in .308. You huntin' vampires, honey?"

I stared at her, too stunned to say anything. She couldn't possibly…

"Oh, that's right, it's silver for *werewolves*, ain't it? I always get them confused." She giggled, so help me god.

"Actually, I just wanted them because they make a really big hole when you shoot someone…I mean *something* with them, you know. For ah, hunting and ah…" I was thinking about shooting *her*. I wanted her to stop asking questions and sell me my bullets so I could out of there.

"Don't worry about it, honey." She winked. "I got me a gun for home defense, too. Can't go wrong with .357, honey."

I decided to forgive her when she asked to see my ID to make sure I was over twenty-one. It had been awhile.

I got back home without any problems and parked in my garage again. I don't normally do that, but it seemed like a good idea now. I wished I had a home security system. Maybe I should get one installed. Probably wouldn't do any good. Those guys had looked as if they knew what they were doing.

While I was putting the groceries away, it hit me: I had killed two men today and had been the cause of another one's death. I got sick in the sink. Damn it. I was shaking like a leaf.

I badly needed to talk to someone. I finished putting away the food, grabbed the boxes of ammo and a Coke, and went into the living room to call Mark. I got the stuff out of the closet and arranged it around me before I called him.

I was worried about what his reaction would be.

Hell, I was worried about what *my* reaction would be.

Part of me still wanted to call the police and confess.

CHAPTER THIRTY-SIX

I made the call on my cell phone.

Jen answered on the second ring. "Michelle! How are you doing? Are you okay?"

"Hi. I'm fine, a little tired but okay. I'm at home. Just got back from the grocery store." I tried to sound happy and cheerful.

"Where did you go?"

"Walmart. I like the prices there."

"I like to shop at Bigg's, myself, but then, they are closer to us here. You've got that new big Walmart over on that side of town. How's your leg doing?"

It was ten years old, but Jen would have never shopped at Walmart anyway. "It's fine. Listen, could I talk to Mark? I want to ask him about something he said yesterday," I lied.

"Sure, hold on." She put the phone down and hollered for Mark to pick up the phone. He was probably in the living room.

"Hello, Michelle," he said.

"Talk to you later." Jen hung up her end of the line.

"Hi, Mark."

"You doing okay? You sound worried."

"Yes and no. I've had a rough day." I told him about the chase and what happened afterward, leaving almost nothing out. Mark knew I could defend myself if I had to. I had killed someone once before, in college. Many of my friends couldn't handle that. They'd admitted it was in self-defense and such, but they couldn't get around the idea of me having taken someone's life. Mark had just acknowledge that it was the right thing to do, and gone on treating me the same as always. Of course, I had saved Jen by doing it, so...

He sighed. "That is a lot to assimilate. Give me a moment."

I heard him clear his throat and the ice clinking as he drained his omnipresent glass of scotch.

"Okay, I trust you. I always have. If you say it was self-defense, I believe you, though I must say I'm saddened that you went looking for trouble. Did you leave any clues that you had been there? Fingerprints, footprints, anything at all that could be used to trace you? What did you do with the gun?"

"I didn't leave any clues. The ground was firm; I'm sure I didn't leave tracks. I wiped down anything I touched in the van. I cleaned the gun and put it the hand of the driver. I put some of his prints on other places on the gun, too, so it wouldn't look like it'd been cleaned. I was hoping maybe they'd think he'd shot the others. I don't know." I wasn't so sure, now, that I'd done the right thing. Maybe I should have dumped the gun in the river.

"It sounds as if everything is taken care of. If those men really were part of something secret, there may not be much of an investigation. Even if they were not, I doubt the police will try very hard, considering the guns and such. They will probably figure it was a drug hit. That would be reasonable." He laughed. "You are one lucky lady, you know?"

"I don't feel so lucky." I sighed. "I mostly just feel sick."

"I understand, better than you may think. You need to get some rest."

"I will. I wanted to ask your opinion, and then I may need your help with something."

"Okay."

I told him about my plan for dealing with Lucy and friends; it had occurred to me as we were talking. Mark liked it, especially since it wasn't at all dangerous for us. I then asked him the other question.

"Do you still talk to Lawrence?"

"Sometimes. I hope you aren't thinking of bringing him in on this."

I shook my head — not that he could see. I should start using Facetime. "Anyway, I was thinking he could help me with these two computers. Seems like the kind of thing he would enjoy."

"He would. I've got his contact information around here somewhere. You'll have to go to him. He doesn't give out his number, you know."

I heard him ruffling papers. "I know. I don't mind going to see him. I really need his help."

"Ah, here it is." He gave me the address. It was an industrial nightclub in Cincinnati. Lawrence lived there. Really. I thanked Mark and hung up the phone. I made my plans to go out to the club the next night. But first, I needed to set my plan for Lucy in motion.

I dressed in dark clothes, hid my pistol under a light jacket, and snuck out of the house. I have pale skin, but at least I have dark hair. I didn't my pale skin to stand out in the dark. I walked down to the corner and used the pay phone — not many of those left around — to call the police. I told them a bogus story about having been taken to a house by a friend after a party, where dark Satanic rituals were taking place. I gave them the address for the house where Lucy, Victor, and her vampire-wannabe friends were hanging out and practicing their rituals. That should get them off my case for a while. I told the police I would rather remain anonymous, and they didn't press the issue. The only people they hate worse than terrorists are cultists.

After I got off the phone, I jogged back to my house, making sure no one was around. The streets were empty, as usual. I went in and decided to go straight to bed. I'd look at the other stuff from the van tomorrow.

CHAPTER THIRTY-SEVEN

I spent most of the morning trying to figure out how to track down Department of Motor Vehicles records online. I had no luck whatsoever. I had hundreds of sites trying to sell me criminal records and copies of birth certificates, but I couldn't track down the ownership of a white van with Ohio tags. I wished I'd been friendlier to that cop a few weeks ago, but then, I didn't want to be connected to the incident out there in the country, either.

There was no mention of it on the news.

I paid too much money to do background checks on the names of the guys from the van. I had to cover their pictures while I was working with them, to keep from being sick. I found nothing at all on any of them. Their identities were aliases, as I'd feared. Even the social security numbers were bogus.

I ordered a pepperoni double-topper pizza from LaRosa's for lunch. I was too busy to get out of the house and didn't want to be bothered with cooking. I tipped the delivery guy extra because he got it to me in twenty minutes; they know me up there. I gave Samson a piece of pepperoni while I was looking at the maps. I think after that, he decided to forgive me for being gone so long.

The maps from the van seemed fairly mundane. Whoever these guys where, they had good maps of the whole area; even the little country back roads were marked. That explained some of their ability to follow me. I pored over the maps for two hours, but there was still no big red X marking the location of their base of operations. I guess I was out of luck on that front.

I still got the shakes from time to time during the day, but my stomach had finally settled down. I'm not sorry about killing those guys; they had it coming. I just get a little queasy over how easy it was. I used to get the shakes badly back in high school after fights, too.

Maybe I just don't like violence.

Some part of me I don't like to look at laughed at that.

As the day drew on, my patience grew thin. I kept running into dead ends in all my researches. The other papers from the van had lots of information, but none of it made any sense. I hoped the two computers had better stuff on them. I didn't like having to involve anyone else in this, especially if it turned out there had been no reason.

Oh well. Lawrence was an old friend. It was not as if he was going to run to the police. Besides, I thought maybe he could hack into the DMV or something. Whatever they call it these days. He's a cybersecurity consultant, and he makes good money. I hoped he wouldn't charge me. I don't think I could afford him.

After a quick sandwich for dinner, I took a shower and spent some time trying to figure out what to wear. Black has always been a good color for me, so that helped in my decision. I wore my old tanker combat boots with tight black jeans. I added my black suede strapless renfaire bodice. My 9mm went under my arm in a shoulder holster. I topped off the outfit with a leather biker jacket. I picked out my usual assortment of silver jewelry. Just because Lucy's crowd was indisposed at the moment, or so I assumed, was no reason not to be vigilant. I dropped an extra mag in the jacket pocket and stuffed the extendable baton in my boot.

It was still a bit early, so I played with my cat for an hour. Then I had to find some tape to remove all the cat hair off my clothes. That took even more time. It was just past eight when I set out on the road. I had the directions Mark had given me on the seat next to me. I hoped I wouldn't get lost; that wasn't the best part of town.

I watched the mirrors as I drove, but no one followed me. I wasn't so naive as to think I was over my troubles, but I might have bought some time for myself. I was really nervous as I drove through the place on the expressway where the accident had happened. I kept my hands clenched on the wheel and just drove as fast as I legally could. I tried to ignore the twinkle of broken glass and burnt places on the road.

The flashes of pain and terror were harder to ignore.

The club I was heading toward is near the University of Cincinnati main campus. There are a lot of clubs in that area, but this one isn't marked in the tourist directories. I found parking near the club and walked across the street to the door. An iron sign above the door said *Machinations*. It looked burnt. I think they must have a gas fire burning through the sign on the weekends.

The guy at the door looked bored. Mondays are not the busiest nights for clubbing, but they do see a good crowd in the late evening in most clubs. He looked me over as I as walked up. He didn't look all that impressed. I guess he was used to babes with boob-jobs or something. He just moved in front of the door.

This could get ugly. I wasn't in the mood to deal with his type.

"You looking for someplace, miss? Maybe I can direct you."

He had this soft, slightly high voice. Maybe he had been kneed in the balls too many times as child or something. No wonder he worked out so much. "I'm sure I'm in the right place. What's the cover?"

He didn't even blink. "This here club is invitation only, miss. I never seen you around before, and since there ain't no cover, I figure you got the wrong place."

Damn. "Ah, well, it so happens that I do have an invitation. I'm a good friend of Lawrence."

That made him blink... a lot. "Hold on," he said finally. He then rapped on the door behind him with his thick knuckles, never taking his eyes off me. Someone inside said something I couldn't hear, and then he said, "What's your name?"

"Rhiannon." That should get Lawrence's attention. He might know other Michelles, but how many Rhiannons could he know?

The door opened a few minutes later. A big guy quickly looked me over, then asked me, "You got a scar on your side?"

Damn, these guys were paranoid, and I'd thought *I* was bad about that. "On my right side, just under my ribcage. It's shaped like a star." Actually it looks more like small, pale asshole, but I wasn't going to say that.

He nodded. "Okay, come in, but I'm taking you right to him. If you aren't who you say you are, you're going right back out the door. Understood?"

I nodded curtly and then stepped inside the door. At least he didn't try to frisk me; I would've fought that. What was this place, Fort Knox? We walked down a short hall, then through another door.

I had to stop and stare.

CHAPTER THIRTY-EIGHT

I don't know what I expected, but this place wasn't it. The patrons were a mix of people from their mid-twenties though some who had to be in their sixties. Techno-industrial music poured from speakers all over the place, nothing I recognized.

The room was huge and dark. Like most nightclubs in that part of town, it looked like a converted warehouse. Tables and comfortable-looking chairs and couches were scattered chaotically. There was an open upper level, too. Half-naked dancers gyrated in cages in the corners and suspended on chains from the ceiling. Damn, I hadn't even known there was a place like this *in* Cincinnati. I hadn't been to a club like this since I lived in New York. No wonder they had tight security here.

The Midwest is far too uptight for a place like this.

The bouncer led me through the room to a table near the back, one with a wrap-around couches like you see in some restaurants. Lawrence saw me as we approached and stood up with his arms wide. We embraced. The bouncer quickly left with a mumbled *sir* directed at Lawrence. Several other people sat at the table: some dressed more like me, others like Lawrence, in suits.

"Michelle! You are looking quite well. How is my Amazon

Voodoo girl? It has been so long. Come, sit with me." He took my arm and steered me to the seat.

"Could we talk privately?" I asked, ignoring the *Voodoo* remark. He knew I didn't practice Vodun. The *Amazon* part, I'd give him; I do tend to tower over most people.

He nodded, and the others got up and left without being asked. Lawrence seemed to be doing all right for himself these days. He's only a little taller than me and twenty years younger, and built much slighter. His naturally light brown hair was bleached white and cut short and spiky. He was wearing a very stylish silvery-gray silk suit and tie with a white silk shirt.

It all looked great on him. He'd lost his pudgy baby-fat that he had when we were in college together, and looked like he was quite fit. The last six years had been kind to him. He poured me a glass of wine, a good merlot. The deep purple of the wine matched his eyes. He probably picked it for that.

"I assume I have dear Mark to thank for your fine company," said Lawrence.

I almost choked on my wine; he was even more full of himself than he'd been in college. "I asked Mark about how to get in touch with you, but I needed to see you for my own reasons."

"Hmm," he said, pausing to sip his wine. "Mysterious, as always. Why would you need to contact me?" He raised a bleached eyebrow.

"So I assume I have your attention?"

He eyes roamed over my chest. "Always, darling."

I rolled my eyes. He was queer as a three-dollar bill. "I need your help with something. I assume you're still into computers?"

He choked with laughter. "Oh, Michelle... Am I still into computers?" He lapsed into laughter again.

"Whatever. Look, I need your help. I have two computers with encrypted files that I need unlocked. Just tell me how much it will cost for your cooperation and discretion."

"I am always discreet. As for the cost, keep your money. You know you couldn't afford me. I could always use a favor from you, however."

I narrowed my suspiciously. "What favor?"

He waved his wine glass airily. "Any favor, something I might ask of you in the future. Not," he added with a smirk, "anything that you would find overly distasteful."

"Right. A favor, then, but I can refuse any specific favor asked of me. I pick and choose what I do with my life." *And my body*, I thought.

"Agreed," he said too quickly. I wondered what trouble I was getting myself into. I could almost hear the gears grinding in his mischievous head. "So tell me about these computers."

"Not here," I said. "You want to know about them, you have to come with me back to my house. We can talk there privately."

"Whatever would make you the most comfortable, of course. You have piqued my curiosity. I shall see this through to the end."

We stood up to leave.

"Oh," I said, just then thinking of it, "do you have any way to tell if a house has been bugged?"

He raised that damn eyebrow again. "I do. Hmm. This gets more interesting by the moment. We will have to stop off at my flat upstairs and get some equipment. I'd need my own computers anyway."

His *flat*? He was definitely trying to shed his past. *Hard.*

I followed him through the club to a private elevator that required a key. I was beginning to wonder if he owned the place, but I wasn't going to ask him. It would only inflate his ego more if I asked that. His apartment was decorated in a tasteful 1920s Art Deco style, with several pieces of art by well-known painters on the wall. Lawrence had been doing very well for himself, indeed.

I followed him into an office that looked like Mission Control at NASA. He had computer equipment on every available surface, lots of notebooks and desktops, and two server towers off to the side. The open framework at the end of the room looked suspiciously like a super-cluster. He walked around to a corner and picked up two hard-sided briefcases. He then gestured for me to go back out the way I had come.

He paused in the living room. "I assume you wish for me to work on this problem of yours at your house. I may take a day or two. You *do* have a guest bedroom?"

"Of course," I snapped. "You can stay there for a long as you like." I was irritated by the opulence of his décor. I've done okay for myself since college; I'm comfortable, but not rich. I was maybe a *bit* jealous. He'd been a punk in college. He hadn't improved.

Lawrence left the room and came back a few minutes later with a small overnight bag. "Ready when you are, Michelle," he said.

I turned and went back to the elevator. He followed with his bag and the two steel cases. He stopped to give directions to one of the bouncers, and then we left the building. I led him to my new black Jeep.

"Very nice, Michelle, and it is so *you*, elegant and yet hard."

"Fuck you, Lawrence," I said under my breath, but he heard me and laughed.

I unlocked the doors as we walked up. He put his gear in the back seat and climbed in; he took one of his cases up front with him. I got in and started the Jeep. He opened the case and did something with some device inside, and then declared that the vehicle was clean. I'm guessing he meant free of electronic bugs. He didn't elaborate, and I didn't ask.

"So, tell me about these computers, Michelle, before I die of curiosity," he said as I pulled out of my parking space and head back toward the expressway.

"I'll need to fill you in on current events first. Do you remember that stuff that happened back in college?"

CHAPTER THIRTY-NINE

Lawrence paled. "Of course. How could I forget? The bastard killed Cindy, and a lot of our other friends too." He shuddered as he said it. A little bit of his native Eastern Kentucky accent crept in, too.

"I hadn't forgotten, either. I just wanted to set the importance of this in your mind."

"Okay, so this has something to do with what happened back then? How could it? Richard is dead. Isn't he?" He looked around as if he expected Richard to be in the back seat or something.

"He's dead, and this has nothing to do with that."

"Then what are you saying?"

"I'm saying that what I'm into now may be worse."

"Oh, so like this is a big conspiracy with lots of murder, chaos, and destruction?"

"Something like that," I said dryly.

"Cool. Count me in."

I glanced at him as I drove. "It could be dangerous for you."

"No problem. I got you to protect me. Who do we kill first?"

I sighed. "This isn't a game, Lawrence."

"I'm not a child, Michelle," he said, turning suddenly serious. "I was serious about what I said back in the club. I was a smart-ass, pimply hacker when we were in college, but I make my living now doing consulting work in cyber security for banks and other businesses. If you think that isn't dangerous, you don't know anything."

"I'm sorry. I just… Okay, let me tell you everything." I gave him the full story of what had happened with the guys in the van. I told him about being jumped, about the car wreck, the chase and accident and shootings of the day before. Lawrence took it all in without comment. Afterward, he sat for a long time before saying anything. We were almost back to my house.

"That is a lot of bad shit to happen in just a few weeks, you know. Damn, I heard about the twenty-car pile-up on the expressway, but I had no idea you were in it." He said this in a low, slightly awed voice. "I guess that explains why you are armed today."

I looked a question at him.

He smiled. "I felt the gun under your arm when we embraced."

I just shook my head. He never changes.

I opened the garage and backed in. Lawrence got out his gizmo and started walking through the house, muttering to himself. He could get quite single-minded at times. I followed him around, opening doors and trying to stay out of his way. I don't think he noticed me. When he got back to the kitchen, he announced the house clear of surveillance equipment. He sounded almost disappointed.

"This is a nice place, Michelle."

"Thanks." I wasn't sure if he meant it or not. "I like it."

"You do have fiber, right?"

I smirked. "Of course."

"Good. I simply *have* to have some science fiction to function. I still need my Classic Trek every day, you know."

"Lawrence, you are not going to watch *Star Trek* every day in this house. I like the show, but I have my limits."

"If I miss one of my favorite shows," he said, "I'm going to work twice as slowly as normal."

I glared at him. "This is life-and-death. Hell, I've got the damn things on DVD."

He looked surprised. "They are out on DVD?"

I shook my head in disgust. "For a techno-geek, you can be really dumb."

"Are you sure they are out? I thought the studio wasn't going to put them out for some reason."

I grinned. "I bought them years ago."

"Oh, you have the originals, not the new ones with updated special effects."

"Lawrence, just watch the damn things on Netflix or Amazon or something, okay? Can we talk about these computers?"

I led him into the living room where all my contraband was. He glanced around the room, taking in the guns, ammunition, and miscellaneous electronics. He just grunted and left the room to go get his other stuff out of the Jeep. I grabbed a couple of cold Cokes and sat them on the coffee table. I then grabbed a load of my stuff, carried it into my bedroom, and dumped it on the floor.

By the time I had changed clothes, Lawrence was on the couch. His cases were open on the floor, and there were wires and cables strewn all across the coffee table. He had two of his own notebook computers set up on the table, and one of the black military ones from the van. He was making little sounds of appreciation as he tinkered with them.

I pushed a drink over to him, and he opened it, took a sip, and recapped it without even looking up. I took my drink over to my desk and played solitaire while he tinkered. After an hour or so, he sat back and sighed, loosening his tie. I didn't know if that was good or bad. So I asked him.

"Huh? Oh, good and bad, both, I guess." He gestured at the computer. "This is some serious shit you have here. It is definitely military grade. I can bypass the password protection on the operating system easily enough, but the encryption is going to take some time." He took a long drink from his bottle of soda.

"How long of a time?" I asked.

"I'm not sure. If I can break the encryption, I'll have all the files for you fairly quickly, but until then," he said with a shrug, "it *could* take a long time." He got up and stretched. Then he went around and looked at everything else. The guns didn't hold much interest for him, but the electronics did. He took a stack of papers back to the couch and sat looking through them.

I decided this was a good time to show Lawrence the guest bedroom. He took his bag and followed me. He tossed the bag on the bed and took off his jacket. I told him I was going to bed; he just nodded and muttered goodnight. I took the guns and locked the door to my bedroom before going to sleep.

It's not that I didn't trust him; it's just that it paid to be extra careful.

CHAPTER FORTY

When I got up the next morning, Lawrence was sitting on the couch, already working. Or maybe he was *still* working. Two empty bags of Doritos and half a dozen empty pop bottles lay around him on the floor.

He looked blearily at me as I walked through.

"Have you been to sleep yet?" I asked.

He shrugged and continued typing.

I decided that I would need to make a run to the store later for soda; I had a feeling I was going to run out before the end of the day. I went into the kitchen to fix breakfast. It's strange, but it seems easier for me to cook breakfast for more than one person. Maybe I'm just lazy when it comes to taking care of myself, but hospitality to a guest is important. I don't know. Lawrence grunted thanks and started eating when I placed a plate in front of him. I could see that he was going to be terrific company.

I made a trip down to the local grocery after I cleaned up the kitchen and changed clothes. The weather was getting cooler outside, clouding up and looking as if it might rain. The checkout clerk asked me if I was having a party. I guess the ten bags of chips and dozen two-liters of pop had caught her eye. I mumbled something to her, paid, and took my cart outside. I hate small talk.

A fine drizzle was coming down. Just my luck. It did nothing to improve my mood. I had a vague sense of foreboding. Being away from home was making me uncomfortable.

I got home and pulled into the garage. Everything seemed fine when I went in. Lawrence was sitting in the kitchen, drinking coffee. I guess he had needed something with more caffeine than Coke. His eyes lit up when he saw me carrying the bottles of Mountain Dew. I put one in the fridge after I carried the rest into the kitchen. Lawrence had disappeared into the living room with one of the two-liters. Yuck: warm, fizzy syrup. I guess he was used to it, though.

I went into the living room. Lawrence looked a little fresher than when I'd left. His hair was slightly damp; he must have taken a shower. He was wearing black sweat pants and a gray henley-style shirt. He had his feet propped up on the coffee table and was stretched out, his laptop in his lap. His other computer was to his right on the couch, and the one from the van on the left. The pop was nestled in the crook of his arm. He looked comfortable.

I remembered many times in college when we'd all be together at one apartment or another, sitting around watching movies, drinking, and laughing. We sat up all night, talking about the occult, magic, psychism, computers, history class, or whatever. Those were good times. It's strange to think that they came to an end so quickly. After all the murders were over and things settled down, most of our circle of friends drifted away, drawn into other pursuits. I always though it strange that Lawrence stayed around with us. He didn't have any inclination toward the occult at all, and didn't really have much interest in it. But we were friends, and I guess that was enough.

He must have had a rough time in college, being just sixteen when he started. He'd been a child genius. Too bad his family had been too poor to send him to any of the really good schools. He struggled through grade school out of boredom. Finally, he dropped out and got his GED. He then scored some ludicrous score on the SAT and ACT. That got him into the local college, and he did great in an environment where learning was more important than fitting in. He'd still had some trouble from people who thought he was too young to be there, but we were very protective friends.

I was sitting at my desk updating my notes when I heard a knock on the front door. A moment later, the doorbell rang. *Who the hell?* Lawrence and I looked at each other across the room. The doorbell rang again. Whoever it was, they had to know I was home. It was dark and stormy outside, and I had half the lights in the house on. I picked up my pistol off the desk and went to find out who it was. Maybe it was just a salesman or something.

It wasn't a salesman; in fact, it wasn't anyone I wanted to see right then. It was the federal marshal, Michael Delling. *Oh, shit,* I thought to myself. I had to answer the door. I opened it slowly; I kept my hand with the gun out of sight. I didn't need more trouble right then.

He smiled as I open the door, the bastard. "Ms. Fredericks, how are you?"

I hesitated. "Fine. Um...How did you get my address?"

He didn't say anything, just raised an eyebrow.

"Right, federal marshal, law enforcement resources, got it. What can I do for you?"

"Actually, I looked you up in the phone book. May I come in? I'd like to talk to you."

He wanted to come in. Of course he did. "Ah, now is not really a good time. Maybe you could come back later?"

He narrowed his eyes slightly and nodded slowly. "Of course, but then I'd have to come in an official capacity. I'd have to have a writ for search and seizure. I'd have regular police officers with me. It would be a real mess, not to mention a lot of paperwork for me. Maybe I could come in now, and we could talk, unofficially, just a friendly chat." He smiled again.

I gritted my teeth. This was not going to end well at all. "Come on in. Um, I have a gun in my other hand, by the way."

"Are you planning on shooting me, Michelle?" he asked, stepping inside.

"Huh? No! I just had it in my hand as I answered the door. I didn't want you to be alarmed, that's all."

"Consider me not alarmed. You don't mind if I call you Michelle, do you?"

I tried my best to smile. He was taller than I remembered, standing there in my hall so close to me. He looked to be about six-six. He was better-looking than I remembered. Smelled good, too. I swallowed convulsively and said, "Not at all. I assume I can call you Michael? Come on into the kitchen. I'll fix some coffee."

I led the marshal to the kitchen. He sat down, and I placed the gun on the table and started a pot of coffee. While I was doing that, he picked up my pistol and began looking at it. That made me a bit nervous. I tried not to spill the water as I filled the coffee machine, but my hands we shaking; at least my back was turned to him.

I heard a *click-slip* noise and turned to see him removing the magazine and looking at it. I gritted my teeth. He looked up at me and smiled disarmingly. It didn't work.

"Silver bullets. That's not a normal round for home defense," he said, smirking.

"I bought them at Walmart. Want to see the receipt?"

He laughed softly. "I don't think that will be necessary." He then said, "Look, I'm here in town for an important investigation. I don't normally do investigations. I normally take care of witness relocation, fugitives, et cetera. The problem is, I have a case that involves all of the above."

I sat down across the table. "So what does this have to do with me?"

He smiled again. Why did he have to smile so much? Did he know the effect that smile had? Probably. The bastard. "Ms. Dubois – Lucy, if you will – was in witness protection until a year ago; at least we thought she was. Turns out, she had contact with a number of people she wasn't supposed to. That is neither here nor there, though. The important part is that I feel a bit responsible for her. I helped her out originally."

I frowned; I had no idea what he was talking about. "Okay, what in the hell could Lucy have gotten into that she needed protection?"

He nodded. "That is exactly the right question. She got involved with a vampire cult up in Detroit. The guy she was with murdered a lot of people. She testified and went into witness protection. So you see –"

I cut him off. "Wait a minute. Are you sure about this?" My mind was racing. I had a sick feeling in the pit of my stomach.

He frowned for a moment. "I'm quite sure. Why? What's wrong?"

I swallowed hard before speaking. "Do you know anything about when Lucy was in college?"

"I know you met there. You had some occult club or something," he said.

Just then, Lawrence walked in. "Do I smell coffee? I've almost got the code cracked on the file headers and..." He trailed-off in confusion when he saw the guy sitting at the table. "Did I interrupt something?"

CHAPTER FORTY-ONE

It's amazing how quickly things can go from bad to worse.

"Lawrence, this is *Federal Marshal* Michael Delling. He's here about Lucy," I said stiffly.

Lawrence is such an idiot. "Oh, cool, nice to meet you." He grabbed a cup of the now-ready coffee and walked back into the living room. I prepared cups for the marshal and myself to cover my new round of shakes. Michael didn't say anything until I had set the coffee down in front of him.

"I see we'll have other things to discuss later. But first, why ask about college?"

I cleared my throat. "When we were in college, our group had a lot of people in it. One of them... God, I can't believe you don't know this. One of them killed several members of the group."

"Let me guess," he said. "He was Lucy's boyfriend."

"Yes. It never went to court because he died."

"What, did he just happen to step in front of a car?" he asked sarcastically.

"No, I shot him in the head. Twice." My voice was shaking.

"Very professional. Were the police involved?"

I stiffened. "As a matter of fact, yes, they were. They decided it was self-defense. He'd kidnapped my friend Jen and shot her boyfriend Mark. I tracked the bastard down and tried to rescue Jen. He caught me, and I killed him."

"Hmm. I admit I didn't pull a complete report on you. I now see I should have. I just looked for an arrest record. So there *is* a pattern here. Interesting."

"You said you were also looking for a fugitive. What's that about?"

"A woman escaped from federal prison during a transport to a more secure facility. Unarmed, she managed to overpower and kill four officers. She also killed the other two prisoners who were being transported. We're not sure why."

"What does this have to with Lucy?"

"Absolutely nothing directly, as far I can tell. But she was tracked to this part of the country. A person she listed as her brother lives here, and that is a different story."

Oh, no, now I knew what the sinking feeling was for. I knew what he was going to say.

He nodded; he must have seen the comprehension in my eyes. "Yes, Victor Owens is her brother, or she claims he is, anyway. He also happens to be Lucy's new boyfriend or something. The relationship seems to be more platonic. Lucy has a talent for finding the sick ones, doesn't she?"

"Or she pushes them into it," I said.

"No, she may help instigate the crimes, but you have to be really sick to do what they do. Mr. Owens has a long record of criminal behavior. I'm sure that guy in college did, too."

I just nodded my head. I didn't trust my voice right then.

"All of which leads me back to you, Michelle."

"Me?"

"Yes, you. I want to know why you called the police on Lucy and her gang this last Sunday. I asked you to call me! Damn it, Michelle, you blew my one solid lead back to Julia."

"I didn't...," I started.

"Don't insult my intelligence. You called from the payphone at the end of your street. It wasn't that hard to figure out."

I looked away. "Listen, I told you Lucy had been bothering me. I found out where she was and took care of it in a manner that seemed safe and reliable."

"Ah, so you *weren't* going for revenge for your accident."

My breath caught for a moment. "That had nothing to do with Lucy."

"Are you sure, Michelle? You should have called me Monday after you were attacked. I might have been able to help. I would've looked into it far more thoroughly than the local police did."

"I didn't even think about it. It didn't seem connected to Lucy." I didn't tell him about seeing her right beforehand. I had a feeling about what he would say. "Also, I don't have any particular reason to trust you."

"No, I suppose you don't. So, what's the connection with the guys in the van and your accident?"

"What makes you think there's a connection?" I asked.

"Humor me."

I clenched my fists; he was going to make me tell him everything. Then I'd be lucky to get out of this with just life as someone's bitch in prison. I took a deep breath. "The van from the assault the other day... It followed me on the expressway. I took an exit or two to make sure they really were following me. They got close to me and –" I had to bite back a sob, damn him. "– and they shot out my tire as they drove past." I was breathing hard. I took a long drink of my coffee; it needed more cream.

Delling was silent for a few minutes. Then he looked deep into my eyes and held them. "How do you know it was shot out? It could have been just a freak blowout."

"No, I saw the muzzle flash out their passenger window." I sobbed and hated myself for breaking down in front of him, even a little. "You don't believe me, do you?"

"Actually, I do," he said, surprising me.

I looked up and met his eyes. He nodded. "Why?"

"Because I can tell you're not lying to me this time." He grinned without humor. "Call it a gift." He pushed his spoon around on the table for a minute or two. "Did you have anything to do with the accident and shootings out in Independence this past Sunday?"

I met his eyes again. "If you mean the white van," I said, and then hesitated, "yes." What the hell, all he could do was arrest me. I suspected he already knew anyway.

"Thank you for being honest with me." Delling finished his coffee. "There's no open case for that crime. The local police wrote it off as a drug hit. If the case is reopened, and I'm asked about it, I'll tell them what I know. But —" he held up his hand "— I'm not going to mention it to anyone until that time. I doubt it will ever come up. I personally feel that whatever they were up to, they got what they deserved."

I nodded. There was nothing I could say, and I had a feeling that he knew a lot more about what was going on. There was some other reason for him not to call attention to the van and the fact that I'd killed several people. I couldn't figure out what it could be, but I could sense it.

"But," he said slowly, "if you interfere in this case again by not coming to me first with information, I'll nail your ass to the wall. I'll make sure they lock you in the darkest, nastiest prison in the system for murder. Do we understand one another?"

"Yes." I was shaking. "Thank you."

"Don't thank me yet," he said. "I want to know everything, all the details you can remember from the *incident* in college and everything since that has anything to do with this case. I want to know what you took from that van. I'm going to be very disappointed if it was drugs."

"It wasn't drugs. It might be easier if I show you while we talk."

"Okay. I'll want to talk to this Lawrence guy, too. Later, we can go talk to your friends Mark and Jennifer; they might remember important details from the events in college."

"Okay." What else could I say? If I'd had balls, they would have been clenched in his fist.

CHAPTER FORTY-TWO

I led him into the living room. I saw his eyebrows go up quite a few times as I showed him everything I'd gotten from the guys in the van, and introduced him to Lawrence again. He told Lawrence he really didn't want to know what he did for a living; he would just assume *computer programmer* and leave it at that. I think we were all grateful. After he spent a few minutes looking through the papers and such, he took me by the arm and led me back into the kitchen.

He took a small black notebook and pencil out of his pocket and then told me to begin. I started with the events in college. Then I told him about all the details about that had happened to me so far. I thought about leaving out the psychic stuff, but I remembered what Mark had said last week, so I bit the bullet and told it all. He never even twitched. He just took notes, saving his few questions till the end.

After asking about a few minor details, Michael closed his small notebook and sat back. I couldn't begin to guess what was going through his mind. I was right; his next question came out of left field. At least that's what it seemed like at the time.

He cleared his throat. "Okay, I have one burning question that still remains unanswered."

When he didn't elaborate, I had to ask. "What?"

He seemed strangely hesitant to continue. "I've wanted to ask you about how you managed to fight off the two guys that jumped you."

"What do you mean? I told you. It just happened."

"Taking on, in a fight, two military-trained men who out-mass you, killing them, and coming out of it with only a few bruises is *not* normal. Then facing down two other armed men who were most probably also very professional, and killing each of them. It takes a lot of training to be able to do that."

"So I got lucky."

"Luck certainly played a part, but you did everything right. That suggests good training," he insisted.

"Well, I'm sorry to disappoint you, but I wasn't in the military. I've never studied any martial art except Tai chi, and I majored in theatre and anthropology in college, not warfare. I've never had any kind of training." Even as I was saying this, I was thinking about those horrible dreams I've had for half my life.

But those were just dreams.

Right?

"You don't seem like you quite believe that, Michelle," he said." Either you've had training, or you haven't."

"Maybe. I don't know. Maybe I was a soldier or something in a past life." I laughed a little, but it sounded weak even to me, and hell, *I* believe in reincarnation.

"Right, and maybe I was a cop. What the hell does that have to do with anything? If you were a soldier in a previous life, at most you would have an inclination for similar types of work. You're a criminal anthology consultant." He sounded irritated.

If he was trying to tell me something, I wasn't getting it. "What are you saying, then?" I asked angrily.

He sighed. "I'm trying to understand. You were born in '72, right?"

"Yeah. June fifteenth. Last time I checked, lots of people were born in 1972, same as any other year." I blushed a little at admitting my age. I look younger. That counts, right?

"I'm looking for any bits of information, no matter how disparate, that might help me figure out what's going on."

"Well, you've lost me."

"It puts things in perspective. Data should never be ignored. Coincidences rarely are actually coincidences."

"Coincidences?" I asked.

"Synchronicity, my dear. Seemingly unrelated facts that *are*, in fact, related."

"I know what synchronicity is. What I don't know is what the hell you're talking about."

He smiled. "You're the same age as Julia and Victor. In fact, you share many of the same traits as Julia."

"So what? You're saying what? Julia looks like me?"

"I'm saying that there's a connection between you." He rubbed his eyes. "You have a talent for fighting, yes?"

I shrugged. "I guess. I don't know. I've never really thought about it."

"No? I think you're lying. I think you have thought about it – a lot. Tell me, do you ever find yourself wanting to kill, to hurt people? Do you ever think that you might be just a half-step away from being a serial killer, Michelle?"

"Stop it!" I was enraged. "Goddamn you! How dare you say something like that to me? I have suffered enough!"

"How many, Michelle? You've admitted to me tonight about killing at least four people. How many others have you killed? Did Lucy's boyfriend kill your friends in college, Michelle, or did you? Did you like it as they screamed?"

"Get out! Get *out*!" I was screaming. My head was pounding. How dare he say those things to me? My friends had been killed, and he dared accuse *me* of doing the killing? A black rage filled me, and I wanted to lash out. Make him stop.

"Michelle."

I was losing it. I wanted him out. I kept screaming, tears running down my face. I just wanted him to shut up and get out. I couldn't handle it. I felt guilty about not being able to do enough to help my friends that had died. Something was tearing loose in my mind. The thing in the cage was getting free, the lock broken.

"Michelle."

I finally realized that I had stopped screaming at him some time ago. He'd said nothing except my name for several minutes now.

"Michelle," he said tenderly. "It's okay. Put the gun down."

Gun? I realized suddenly then that I'd picked up the gun off the table and was now holding it pressed against his forehead. I carefully lowered the gun and placed it on the table. Then I ran to the sink and vomited for what felt like an eternity.

It wasn't until the spasms stopped that I noticed Michael was holding my hair out of my face and had turned the faucet on. He'd filled his coffee cup with water and was holding it for me to sip. I washed out my mouth, suppressed the impulse to spit on him, and wiped my face with the dish towel. I felt like a limp rag. I shrugged him off me and turned to lean against the counter.

"You are fucking bastard," I said quietly.

CHAPTER FORTY-THREE

"Hear! Hear!" Lawrence said from the kitchen doorway. "You guys sure do know how to have fun." He brushed past me and got another two-liter out of the fridge. "I'd keep him, if I were you," he whispered as he walked by to go back to the living room. "He's cute."

I couldn't help it. I laughed, and then sobbed. I had to wash my face again. I probably looked like shit right then. I said so.

Michael half-grinned. "Not really. I'm sorry, Michelle. I had to get you worked up so I could see what was really going on inside your head. I needed to know."

I cleared my throat. "So you really thought I might have done those things? You really *are* a bastard. Do you know that?"

"Yes, I do, actually."

"How did you manage to stay so calm when I had a gun to your head?" I asked, irritated.

He smiled. "I took the round out of the chamber when I was looking at it earlier."

"Shit. That's what I get for not checking it after you messed with it. You ever do something like that to me again, and you'll be the one needing a gun." I was still pissed.

"I'm carrying three right now, so I've got it covered," he said.

I just blinked. *Where the hell?* I didn't want to know. I sighed, and went and sat back down at the table.

Michael sat down across from me again. "You have the inclination and the aptitude to be a killer. So do I. So do many people. Like me, you also have a conscience. That's what sets us apart. It's also what draws us together. We have the ability to think the way they do. We make sure justice is done."

"You do, maybe," I said wearily. "I just help find a few clues."

"I do, but so do you. You *do* get involved. You took heroic action in college. No, hear me out. That took guts and brains to pull off. You've been trying to figure out what to do about this problem. You should have gone to the police. You should have gone to the professionals."

"Maybe. I guess. I didn't know how deep it went. I didn't know if I could trust anyone else. So where do we go from here? Are you going to take all this and confiscate everything I took from the van? I can understand that you might have to. You want me to do *what*? Go into hiding or something?"

He shook his head. "No. I don't want you to go into hiding, and I'm not taking anything. I want us to work together. I can make it official. Hell, I'll even backdate the paperwork, just in case anything does ever come out about the van. I need your help to solve this."

"You mean it?" I couldn't help myself from sounding eager.

"Yes. I don't know who those guys in the van were. I agree with you that they seem connected somehow to the whole issue with Lucy, but I don't know how." He sighed and looked at his watch. "I should be going. It's late. If you don't mind, I'll be back in the morning. We can talk more then. Maybe later in the day, we can talk to Mark and Jennifer, get their perspective on things." He stood up.

I wobbled a little as I stood. "I guess I'll sleep well tonight."

He smiled and turned to leave. I walked him to the door.

What a strange man.

Lawrence and I talked for a few hours before I went to bed. He couldn't believe Michael hadn't arrested both of us. He didn't think that it was a good sign.

"I'm telling you, Michelle. These federal agent types, they *use* people."

"I know. I think he had his own reasons for not wanting the van looked at too closely. That scares me. I don't know a lot about him."

"Are you sure he really *is* a federal marshal?" Lawrence asked.

"No, I'm not," I admitted. "I'm not sure about anything anymore. I guess I'd better call a few friends at the FBI and make sure."

"What was all the screaming about?"

"You don't want to know, and I don't want to talk about it," I said warily.

Lawrence nodded. "Okay. Why don't you get some sleep? You look bushed. I'll work on this stuff some more, and we'll talk more tomorrow. Okay?"

"Okay," I said.

It was going to be a long night.

INTERLUDE THREE

Pain.

I'm being crushed everywhere at once.

I've already screamed myself hoarse. Now I'm just gasping. Each breath takes all my strength. All my concentration is on staying alive. I fought hard this time, but it didn't do any good. The boy with the green eyes is here. They made him go first in the machine; now they're making him watch as they do it to me. They have his head clamped and those things on his eyes so he can't blink. I always hate that part when they make me watch, almost as much as what I'm forced to watch.

They're going to start cycling again soon. Then I'll be screaming again, whether I have the strength or not. The people in the coats are taking their notes again today. They call it the chair; we just call it the machine. The pressure builds. I'm choking. I can't breathe. I'm stuck between breaths; they're holding it steady there.

They always do.

I convulse. The pain is too much, too much. I... The pressure is beginning to ease off.

No. No! It drops, and I'm dying again. I can feel my skin stretching as my internal pressure exceeds my environment. God, that damn lecture they keep giving us is going through my head now? The machine tightens down around me, keeping my fluids where they belong. Most of them, anyway.

The pressure is rushing back toward normal. I can feel the blood running down my face from my eyes. Then the shakes hit me as they always do. I puke; I'm choking on it. The smell of vomit and blood and shit is strong around me. Maybe they're going to let me die this time. I wonder if I can choke myself to death before they can open the machine and get me out.

I try.

I start to fade.

Rough hands are slapping me. I'm slapped again and again, until I begin to scream and thrash. Then they hit me with the hose. Washing out the machine and cleaning me in the process. They do it for themselves, not me. They leave me gasping in the corner. I wish I could run. I'm so weak. I hurt so badly. I wonder how long they kept me in there this time. From the dark bruising on my skin, I would say a long time.

Time has no meaning in there.

I hear footsteps. I look up as I'm grabbed. Two men carry me over to a chair, a normal one with clamps for my head, arms, and legs. They hold my head while one of the men in a white coat puts those clips on my eyes. Then I see who is in the machine, and I start to scream.

They're just going to keep doing this to us over and over. The boy's breath is coming in short, ragged bursts now, as the cycle begins again. He starts screaming.

I can't stop screaming.

CHAPTER FORTY-FOUR

Lawrence was asleep on my couch when Michael arrived the next morning. I answered the door in my blue silk pajamas. I swore to myself as I opened the door that if he so much as smirked, I was going to slam the door in his face and go back to bed.

I'd had a rough night.

He didn't, so I didn't.

I hadn't thought he meant *this* early when he said he'd stop by in the morning. I'd decided the night before that I wasn't going to be nice to him. That lasted about thirty seconds. I needed to work on my convictions.

He was quite polite as I invited him in.

"These are for you," he said, handing me a box of Godiva chocolates.

I must have looked confused.

He smiled. "It's down payment for being a bastard last night. I know I pushed you too hard. I said some harsh things that you didn't deserve. I'm sorry."

I searched his face. He seemed sincere.

"Well," I said, "thanks." I ran a hand across my face. "Look, I'm a bit out of sorts this morning. Why don't you make yourself comfortable? I need to get dressed."

He nodded and headed for the kitchen. He had a briefcase with him.

I sighed and retreated to my bedroom to change out of my pajamas. I needed the time to get my wits back. He'd unsettled me. I'd expected him to be an ass, not kind and apologetic.

I still had echoes of my dreams running through my head.

It's hard *not* to think about something that bothers you.

The dream last night had been too vivid, too real. I didn't like to think that my mind could make up something so horrible. I knew I'd never read or seen anything like it, though. What did that say about me?

Once I was dressed, I walked back into the kitchen. Michael was sitting at the breakfast table, drinking my coffee and looking over a sheaf of notes. I fixed myself a bowl of cereal, and we sat and talked. I had a cup of hot tea with breakfast; I'm only a coffee drinker in the evening.

"So," I asked. "What now?"

He looked up from papers. "Down to business?" he asked. "I can do that."

He handed me two thick folders, full of forms and such.

"What am I looking at?"

"Those are my dossiers on Victor and Julia. Flip to the back for pictures."

I did as he suggested and almost dropped the folders. Victor and Julia both looked frighteningly familiar. I didn't get it until he pointed out that they both bore a bit of a resemblance to me. No wonder he'd thought he needed to test me. It was eerie.

"It's more than that," I said hesitantly. "*Julia* seems very familiar. I'm sure I've seen her before."

"I'm sure," he agreed cryptically.

I was about to ask him what he meant when Lawrence stumbled into the room and blearily begged for coffee. I got up and made him a cup with lots of sugar. He took his cup and wandered off to the guest bathroom. Michael and I just exchanged amused glances.

The day was bright and sunny, as it often is after a storm. The light was streaming in through the kitchen windows, picking up glints from small motes of dust in the air. It fell across Michael's face and made his green eyes seem to glow. It was strange and somehow intoxicating.

There was something about him. Something about those eyes…

"I'd like to ask Lawrence a few questions," he said suddenly.

The spell was broken. He was just the marshal now. I shook my head to clear it; I'd been having odd thoughts.

"I don't mind, if he doesn't. Go ahead. I'll meet you in there."

I got up and retreated to my bathroom to splash cold water on my face. My nightmares last night had been much worse than usual. I'm always shaken by them, but this was ridiculous. I needed to focus on the task at hand, and my thoughts were all over the place, along with my emotions.

I found myself drawn to the marshal. I was attracted to him on several levels, and that scared me. He was a very intense man. I concentrated on building some professional detachment. If we were going to be working together, I needed to keep a clear head. I did *not* need to be thinking about his eyes…

The guys were in the living room talking when I came out of my bedroom. Lawrence was in his now usual place on the couch, sprawled with his computer in his lap again. Michael was also sitting on the couch, looking at the screen of Lawrence's other computer. I came around and sat on the edge of the coffee table so I could see, too. Lawrence was looking far too smug, so I asked him why.

"I broke the file headers. I knew I was onto the right track last night. Look here." He did something on his computer, and a file opened on the one we were looking at. "This is a list of the file names on this other baby."

There were *a lot* of files on that list, thousands.

"It's going to take weeks to decode all of these files," Lawrence explained. "This is an important first step. You can pick files for me to work on first. I can concentrate on those and try to get them done first."

I groaned.

I'd hoped for some kind of miracle, I think. Michael traded seats with me and handed me the computer. I skimmed over the list, with Michael looking over my shoulder. Nothing jumped out at me.

"So, Michelle, where are you taking me out to eat?" asked Lawrence.

"*What?* What are you talking about?" I was too absorbed by the list to pay much attention. There was a section marked *Special Projects*; I'd have him start with that one.

"Dinner, Michelle. *Food.* Real food. Not this junk you have around here." He waved at the stack of empty chip bags around his feet.

"What do you want? I can order a pizza."

He made a retching noise. "Do you understand the concept of real food, Michelle?"

I looked at Michael for help, but he was pretending to be more interested in the list of files than in the conversation. "Sorry, Lawrence, but to me LaRosa's is real food."

He gritted his teeth audibly. "You owe me something a little classier than that, don't you think?"

"What do you want, Texas Roadhouse?" I said it just to bug him.

He eyes bugged out in horror until he figured out I was just having fun harassing him. Then he got a mischievous gleam in his eye. "Do you fondue?"

"Do I what? I don't eat any of that sushi crap, so this had better not be anything like it. I remember what you used to eat back in school." I shuddered.

Michael laughed and spoke up at that point. "Actually, Michelle, you're not far wrong. They do bring you platters of raw meat."

"Okay." My stomach churned. "Pick somewhere else."

CHAPTER FORTY-FIVE

Lawrence glared at Michael. Then he said to me, "They bring you out a pot of broth with a small flame under it. You get to cook the food yourself; they just prepare it. They also bring out a vegetable tray. You can start with an appetizer of different breads that you dip in a pot of melted cheese and wine. Oh," he added, and his eyes got really big, "don't forget *desert*: a pot of melted chocolate, white and dark swirled together, with a tray of fruit, cookies, and cake to dip into it. Ah. We have to go. You *must* try it."

We all laughed for a moment. "Okay, make your reservation or whatever, and we'll go later. What's the dress code?"

"Nice evening casual," he said. "Jeans would be okay, but frowned on."

"Right, so we'll feed you well later. What have you done to earn it? What *is* this crap? Tell me what I'm looking at."

"Well, most of it doesn't make any sense right now, but look –" he scrolled down the list "– here."

"That's my name. I have a whole file devoted to me?"

"Actually, Michelle, it's an encrypted folder. You have *lots* of files about you in there."

"But," I said, looking from Lawrence to Michael, "that doesn't make any sense. Why me? I'm not important enough to have a single file, much less a folder full."

Lawrence shrugged. "Nevertheless, there it is."

"So how soon can you decrypt it?" Michael interjected.

"I don't know. A week, maybe two."

I started to interrupt, but he held up his hand.

"I know what you're going to say, Michelle, so don't. It took me a couple of days just to get the headers. Even then, I would be S.O.L. if the list itself had been encrypted. As it was, only the shell for the file was. If those docs in that folder are completely encrypted, you'll need a miracle to unlock them."

"Actually, all you need is the key. I'll make some calls. Excuse me." Michael got up and went into the other room, a cell phone appearing in his hand out of a hidden pocket in his coat.

I decided this was a good time for me to go and take a bath. I prefer baths to showers, but I tend to take more showers. Don't ask me why; I couldn't tell you. After I was feeling more myself and less human – *human* being defined as a stinky and dirty animal – I dressed up. I wore a long, dark-blue skirt and a lighter blouse. I cut the jewelry down to the basics. I pulled my hair back after blow-drying it. I'd be brushing stray stands out of my face for the rest of the day, but I liked how it looked.

Michael was polite and said I looked *nice*. I suppose that's a compliment; that man can be entirely too laconic sometimes. Lawrence was not as restrained and wolf-whistled when I came in. He fawned over me so much that I blushed. I kicked him – quite accidentally, I assure you – on the way to my desk. I could see he was trying to push me toward the marshal, but I wasn't going to play his game.

"I've made us reservations for four o'clock at The Melting Pot," Lawrence told me.

"You, sir, are an idiot," I said. "That's a terrible time to be driving through Cincinnati."

He just shrugged. "I guess we should leave early, then, shouldn't we?"

I think he was planning on getting Michael and me drunk or something.

Worse things could happen.

I drove us all in my new Jeep. The meal was every bit as good as they'd both said. I avoided the weird tiger shrimp; I don't eat things that are green unless they're plants. Lawrence and I had a good time reminiscing about the exploits of various friends from college. Michael told us some truly bizarre stories about cases he'd handled. It would have been a perfect evening if things had stayed going so well.

Lawrence drank most of the wine.

We were working on our second bottle, after the meal, when a woman walked up to the table. I don't think I noticed her until I saw the expression on Michael's face and looked around to see what was wrong. Julia Owens was standing there with a big smile on her face.

Julia was about my height, maybe a bit taller. Her hair was darker than mine, more black than brown. Her eyes were blue like mine. We had very similar features. We were even both a little broader than average through the shoulders. I have a better nose than hers, though.

She was dressed in a tan pantsuit. Somehow, I had expected her to be in prison fatigues or something. Or maybe dressed as a biker. Hell, I didn't know what to expect. The corporate executive look seemed out of place on her. Meeting her eyes, I revised my expectations. She should been wearing black combat fatigues.

"Well," Julia said, "isn't this nice? Fancy seeing you here, marshal. Shouldn't you be out chasing the bad guys or something?"

"You are under arrest," Michael began. "You are a federal fugitive wanted for murder." He reached into his jacket as he started to stand.

"Now, marshal, don't go and get hasty. I'd hate for the two young girls my dear brother is entertaining out in the parking lot to come to any harm. I know *you* wouldn't want that to happen."

Something about the way she said *entertaining* made the hair on the back of my neck stand on end.

Michael sank back into his seat, his face pale, but his hand remained on his pistol. "What do you want, then, Ms. Owens?"

Julia smiled. "That's more like it, nice and friendly. Of course, I would feel a lot better if your hand was on the table."

"Forget it," he said. "Get on with it."

"Okay." She looked at me. "I want to talk to you. Alone."

CHAPTER FORTY-SIX

"Like he said," I replied angrily, "forget it."

"Oh, but you will want to hear this, believe me."

I looked at Michael; he shook his head. "No deal. You want to talk? Do it. I'll tell them what you say anyway."

"Ah, yes, but you might not want them to know what *you* say." She waited for a minute, but when I didn't answer, she frowned and said, "Look, you want to frisk me? I need to talk to you."

"Then talk," I growled.

She pulled a chair around and sat down, keeping a fair distance from any of us. She looked a long time at me before continuing. She directed her first comments at Michael, though. "Do you know why I was in federal prison?"

"The question should be, do I *care*? I don't," he snapped.

"Sounds like a personal problem. You don't care that I should never have been in that place? You don't care about what they did to me there?" She glared at him. "Justice!" She spat the word.

Michael shrugged. "If you were there falsely, you should have made an appeal. Do you deny killing the guards and the other prisoners on your transport during your escape?"

Julia took a deep breath and looked away for a minute. "I neither confirm nor deny anything. I did what I had to do."

I couldn't stay out of the conversation any more. It suddenly made sense. Two groups after me, but both of them linked. "Oh, you mean like sending three guys to rape and kidnap me? Or when you sent them to try to murder me on the expressway?"

Julia smiled humorlessly. "Yes, I sent a team to pick you up. You took care of them, didn't you? They overstepped their bounds, both times. They were just supposed to give you a warning, not try to kill you." She looked at Michael. "I assume that neutralizing them was your work? I may have misjudged you."

He raised his eyebrows. "Actually, I had nothing to do with it."

Julia looked quickly at me. "*You* took them out? Interesting. My trip here might not be wasted, after all. Looks like I'm not the only who does what she has to do to survive."

"I did what I had to," I said, blushing.

"So did I."

Michael was starting to look uncomfortable. "Listen, why don't you turn yourself in? I guarantee that you will be treated fairly. I'll even help you find someone to represent your case. You'll be safe."

Julia smiled humorlessly. "No." She looked at me again. "I came here to see you, Michelle, firsthand. I admit I thought about killing you. Now, though, maybe we could work together. What do you say?"

I didn't even hesitate. "Go to hell."

"I've been there, bitch. So have you." She stood up and leaned over the table. "I haven't forgotten what they did to us. Maybe you want to play patsy with your boy here, but I know you'll see my way in the end. You betrayed him before; you'll do it again. If I wanted you dead, you would be –" she snapped her fingers under my nose "– like that!"

Michael placed the barrel of his gun to her temple. I hadn't seen it before. It was a large, black .45-caliber automatic, maybe a Sig. "I think we need to get this over with now. You're under arrest."

She froze, and then laughed; it was almost a bark. "How sweet.

Still pining for her? Or don't you remember, either? You two make me sick," she said viciously, then stepped back slowly. Michael never wavered with the gun. "You don't want those girls hurt. I know you. It doesn't matter. Follow me out. Victor is in the lot. We can make the exchange there." She turned her back and started walking.

Michael got up so quickly that his knees hit the table, but he kept the gun on Julia. As soon as he was past the table, he tucked the gun in his pocket. "I'm sorry, Michelle, I have to –"

I cut him off. "I'm coming along. Lawrence, do you mind staying and talking care of the bill? I'll get you back for it, I promise."

Lawrence swallowed loudly. "After that crap, I don't want to be anywhere near that lady. Go. I'll be out in a minute." He stood and motioned to the waiter who had just come up. I hurried after Michael.

They were out in parking lot. Victor was nothing like I had thought he would be. He was actually handsome. He looked a lot like Julia, certainly enough for them to actually be brother and sister. He and Michael had made their exchange already. Two young girls, maybe early teens, were standing huddled together near Michael. Julia was standing next to Victor; he had a rifle in his hands, similar to the one I had taken from the van. Michael was holding his pistol openly off to the side.

Julia placed her hand on Victor's arm. "Time to go," she said.

I walked up beside Michael. I wished I hadn't allowed myself to be talked out of wearing my gun. I vowed that until this was all over, I would never be unarmed again.

Victor turned to leave.

Julia looked at me. "I'll be seeing you again." Then she followed Victor around the cars to a sedan. There were two guys in the front seat.

I looked at Michael. He was talking to the two girls. Apparently, their parents were inside. The girls had snuck out to smoke, and Victor had come up to them and starting talking. Then Julia had come up with the rifle, said they would do, handed the rifle to Victor, and went inside. All of this came out in a confused rush from the girls. Michael decided to go inside with them to explain things to their parents. He didn't need to ask me to follow; I wasn't going to stand outside alone and unarmed.

I met Lawrence inside the door, and we stood there talking, in plain sight, while Michael explained to the concerned parents and manager that he was a federal marshal and that there had been an incident. I was glad I didn't have tell people things like that. Michael looked exhausted when he joined us a few minutes later.

"Let's go." He steered us both out the door by our elbows.

Michael checked my Jeep carefully, but he couldn't find anything wrong with it. Julia must have followed us. I hadn't been paying attention as I drove here. We realized that we were going to have to be more careful. Julia obviously had a larger organization than we'd thought.

I was nervous on the way home. Michael was angry; he kept muttering to himself and clenching his fists. Lawrence sat in the back and went to sleep. We didn't have any problems on the way home. Michael went through my house first, checking it, and then he made some phone calls. I woke Lawrence up and got him to the couch in the living room. I then went and put some coffee on, because I figured we were going to up late talking.

CHAPTER FORTY-SEVEN

I was wrong.

Lawrence wanted to go home.

"Look," he said, getting up, "it's been fun, Michelle, but I never planned to stay for more than a day or two. I need to be back home, around my own stuff again. I'll take the notebook computer I've been working on with me." He turned to Michael. "If your friends find anything useful, let me know. I'll leave both of you my cell phone number. Michelle has my email; that can be just as quick for me. Which one of you wants to give me a ride home? On the other hand, I'll take a cab. You should stay here with Michelle; she shouldn't be alone." He threw a wink at me.

He packed quickly and had a cup of coffee while waiting for the cab. We didn't talk much. What was there to say? When the cab pulled into the drive, I walked Lawrence to the door and gave him a hug and a kiss on the cheek. He promised to keep me up on what was happening, and left. I went back into the living room, where Michael was looking through the papers again.

He looked up and smiled at me as I sat wearily in a comfortable chair. Samson immediately jumped up in my lap. He didn't like Lawrence and had stayed under my bed most of time. He started licking my hand and purring loudly. Michael looked interested, so I introduced him. Samson liked Michael, and plopped over on his side on the couch and started grooming.

"So how are you holding up, Michelle?"

"I'm doing okay. Julia is…intense."

"Hmm. Most psychopaths are."

I frowned. "I don't know what I think of her, actually. She seemed so strange – fragile, maybe. Like someone who's had too much happen to them. I had an uncle like that; he'd served in Vietnam, and, well, he was a bit brittle after that."

"Julia is the same age as us," said Michael.

"Did she serve in the military?"

He hesitated for a moment. "I don't know."

"What? How can you not know? Or is it that you won't tell me?" I asked.

"I said I don't know, Michelle. Her records are classified as *need to know*. I've only seen the personal history portion. That was all it was decided that I needed." He didn't sound happy about that.

"Could you get the rest of it?" I asked. "It seems that now it could be important."

"I don't know. I doubt it." He shrugged. "Ever since 9-11, the federal government has been more cautious about what information gets disseminated, for any reason."

"It's crazy."

"I agree, but what do you want me to do? I can't raid the offices of the FBI or storm the Pentagon. I use the information they deign to give me and count myself blessed."

We didn't say much for a while after that. Michael sat looking through the papers, and I read through Julia's file again. There was nothing interesting in it. The only useful things were the information on Victor, and Julia's picture. There was something odd about the picture, which didn't do her justice. I tried to figure out what was off about it.

She was dressed in black. Her face was just a pale blot between her clothes and her hat. She was wearing a beret or something like it. Her hair was pulled back. No, it was really short. I turned on more lights and got a magnifying lens out of my bedroom desk. I sat next to Michael and got his attention.

"Look at this."

He took the lens and looked at the photo, then again without the lens. He frowned and seemed as if he wanted to say something but wasn't sure what. He looked at the picture with the lens again.

"It looks like black fatigues, doesn't it?" I pointed to the beret. "There's some kind of emblem on that." I pointed lower in the picture. "That could be a rifle."

The skin between Michael's eyebrows bunched up as he frowned. "I don't know. If the picture was better, maybe I could tell." He scratched his head. "It could be."

He saw my look.

"Okay, so let's say it is," he said. "So she was in the military or CIA or something, like she said. What does that have to do with anything?"

"She may not have been in prison legally."

"It's the government, Michelle. They can legally imprison someone for lots of things. All they would have to say is that she had terrorist inclinations, and they could put her away without a trial. Or," he said with a snort, "they could say she was suspected of having had contact with aliens; they can hold you in CDC quarantine indefinitely for that one."

I laughed, and he grinned. I think he'd been trying to lighten the mood.

I *hoped* he was joking, anyway.

He took my hand. "I promise you, I will make sure there's an inquiry after I catch her. I'll make enough noise that someone will have to do something. Okay?"

I looked long into his eyes. They seemed sincere, but what did I really know about him? I nodded my head; I didn't trust my voice. I could feel the heat off his body. He was so close. I leaned forward

slightly.
     Then my cell phone rang. *Damn!*

CHAPTER FORTY-EIGHT

I sat back and caught a quick breath.

My phone was sitting on the desk.

Michael gave me a lopsided grin. *Damn* again.

I got up and answered the phone.

"Hello?"

"Michelle, are you doing okay? We haven't heard from you in a day or two." It was Mark. I really should have called him yesterday.

"I'm fine. I'm sorry, Mark. A lot happened yesterday; I forgot to call. I'm sorry." I could see Michael was paying attention to my side of the conversation. He mouthed a question to me. He wanted me to ask about him talking to Mark and Jen.

Mark was saying something. "We were worried, that's all. So what has happened in the last two days? Hopefully nothing like Sunday."

"No," I said with a grin, "nothing like Sunday happened at all. There have been other developments, though." I told him about Lawrence coming over. I then told him the condensed version of Michael coming over, and then today's excitement.

"Right," he said. "Well, you have been a busy one, haven't you? So the marshal wants to talk to us about Lucy and college. I can't say I'm happy about that, but I'll comply. Didn't take you long to get on a first name basis, did it?"

I could hear him chuckling through the phone. He knew I was blushing. I could see Michael's eyebrow going up. I'll pay Mark back for that someday.

"When can we come over to talk, then?" I asked.

Mark sighed. "It's late tonight. I'll talk to Jen later and let her know you two are coming over. How about tomorrow for dinner? Around seven p.m.?"

"Hold on." I pressed the phone against my chest and looked at Michael. "Mark wants to know if tomorrow at seven p.m. for dinner and conversation is acceptable." He nodded. I held the phone back to my ear. "That's cool, Mark. Just make sure it's Jen and not you who does the cooking. I have a delicate stomach." He agreed with a laugh, and we said our goodbyes.

"So they'll both be there?" asked Michael.

"Yes. Mark isn't happy about you asking Jen questions. She had a rough time of it in college. The guy raped her and beat her badly. All the while, she thought Mark was dead and no one was going to save her. She's been a little delicate since."

"I can understand that. You've given me enough information on that front," Michael said. "I'll wait till after dinner, and maybe Mark will talk to us alone afterward."

"That would be great. Hold on and let me call him back." I did, and Mark was quite relieved. He'd be able to keep Jen from this. After I got off the phone, I sat down across the room from Michael. Why tempt fate? "He said to say thanks. He'll be a lot more open with you without Jen in the room."

"Thanks. I didn't know about the other stuff, or I wouldn't have asked. So do you need me to stay here, or are you okay by yourself?"

I wasn't sure how to answer that one. If I said I wanted him to stay, he might think I was weak. If I said I didn't want him to, he might think I was pushing him away. I was damned either way.

I compromised. "Either way is fine. If you stay here, you'll save on hotel expenses. I have a guest bedroom empty again." I smiled. Put the ball in his court.

He narrowed his eyes at me. His damn built-in lie detector again. "I suppose it would be more convenient to stay here, since we are working together on this." He smiled. "I wouldn't have asked, but it'll be nice to get out of the hotel. I've never liked them. I'd be worried about Julia getting to you without me around."

We decided to take my Jeep again. I don't think he really liked to drive much. I didn't mind, though; I *do* like to drive. Michael was staying at the Marriott in Covington. It was a quick trip. He had only one small bag there. Checkout went smoothly. No one questions law enforcement types too much about why they're leaving; they're just happy to see them go.

We made it back to my house without being chased or followed. I was almost disappointed, but I guess Julia had an *only one harassment per day* rule or something. When we got back, I changed the sheets and pillowcases in the guest room and told Michael where everything was. He was to help himself to whatever he wanted. I meant just about anything, but he limited himself to the stuff in the kitchen cabinets.

Oh, well.

I spent an hour cleaning up pop bottles and chip bags. Lawrence can be a real slob when he gets busy working on something. I left the trash in the garage; I didn't feel like going outside after dark. Michael went to bed early, so I did, too. It had been a really long day.

I seemed to keep having those.

CHAPTER FORTY-NINE

It's a good thing I sleep in my pajamas. When I got up the next morning, I wasn't thinking too clearly. I remembered that Lawrence had gone home, but I'd forgotten Michael was still here. When I walked into the kitchen and saw him sitting at the table, reading some papers, I almost took off running for my gun. He'd scared the crap out of me.

I recovered quickly, though, and he wisely pretended not to notice, but I saw the smirk over the edge of the paper he was holding. I ignored him and made myself a cup of Earl Grey tea. I made Michael a cup, as well, just to be spiteful. Then I made us both egg sandwiches.

"I would prefer to at least spend breakfast thinking about something besides Julia and Lucy and all the related problems," I said. "Okay?"

"Sure, Michelle," he agreed, and put down his papers. "What would you like to talk about?"

I smiled and shook my head. He wasn't going to make this easy for me. "Tell me a little about yourself, Marshal Delling," I said. "Where did you grow up? What was your sister like? All that jazz."

"Hmm," he said over his mug. "Okay, what the hell."

I waited expectantly.

He sighed. "I grew up on a farm in Rabbit Hash."

I chuckled.

"What?" he asked, scowling.

"I'm sorry," I lied. "I just can't hear that name without laughing. It's like Turkeyfoot Road or Buttermilk Pike. It's too silly. Go on, please."

"My sister lives somewhere out west, said Michael. "I'm not sure where. I haven't talked to her since I was a teenager."

I sensed a lot more that he didn't want to talk about. We talked about him for quite a while. I had to keep steering the conversation *back* to being about him. He was just as curious about me. I finally relented and told him about growing up, and school and stuff. He looked thoughtful at times. Our lives had some odd similarities. We both had bits missing from our early teen years. He saw my discomfort, though, and asked some less painful questions.

"So how did you end up with a name like *Rhiannon*?" he asked.

"Now you see, you have an unfair advantage on me. I usually lie and say I was named after the Fleetwood Mac song that came out in the mid-seventies, but you already know my age."

He laughed. "Well, at least I don't think you look your age. That may be some small comfort."

I glared at him. "Don't change the subject. Your flattery will get you nowhere."

He smirked. "Really? Oh, well. I'll have to try harder."

I swallowed, suddenly very nervous. "Okay, you can change the subject."

He laughed. "So what would you like to talk about?"

"Are you married?" I blurted out. I couldn't help it; I needed to know.

Now he looked nervous, but he smiled after a moment. "Sorry, took me a second to track the non-sequitur. No, I'm not married. Never have been." He cocked his head slightly to look at me.

"Good." I didn't elaborate. Let him sweat it out. I smiled once my back was turned and got myself some more tea.

He cleared his throat as I sat back down. "Well, moving right along..." He grinned. "I supposed I put my foot in it, huh?"

I just smiled and sipped my tea. It was time for me to play coy.

He grinned wider and shook his head. "Okay, you win."

I laughed. "That was almost too easy. What made you want to be a marshal? Why not be a regular cop or something?"

"Did you ever see *The Fugitive*? The movie, I mean, not the old TV show."

"I think so. The one with Harrison Ford? His wife is killed at the beginning?"

"Right. I liked the marshal in that movie. He was cool and sarcastic and made the regular cops look like idiots. He seemed above corruption. He was an enforcer of justice." Michael shrugged. "That's it."

"So some form of law enforcement was your first choice of career?"

He hesitated; I wondered if he would ever relax around me. "Actually, military was my first choice. I joined in '90, just in time for the Gulf War. Twenty years served. Eventually, I took a bullet through the hip. Then I came home and went to college."

He hadn't mentioned that earlier. "So, were you in the army, then?"

He looked away for a moment. "Something like that."

"Special forces?" I guessed.

He frowned.

Dumb question. If he had been, he couldn't talk about it. "Okay, what did you do?"

"I really don't want to talk about that. I'm sorry. It's a little too painful a subject for me." He looked uncomfortable.

"I'm sorry, I shouldn't have pushed."

He didn't say anything, but he nodded.

Something he'd said before made me remember something... His war injury brought to mind my dream from last week. My side immediately started throbbing. I must have looked upset.

"Are you okay, Michelle?" he asked.

"I don't know, actually. I was thinking about what you said, about getting shot. It reminded me of a dream I had recently, one I've had before. I get shot in it."

"That is weird. Do you often have dreams of death?"

"It's not like that. In the dream, I'm shot in the side. When I wake up, my side hurts." I met his eyes. "Would you know a bullet scar if you saw it?" I asked.

He frowned. "Well, I guess so. They tend to be fairly distinctive. A least any direct hit does. I might. Why?"

I didn't answer; instead, I stood and carefully raised the edge of my pajama top so he could see the scar on my side. He reached out slowly and touched the scar so lightly that it tickled. I had to struggle not to jerk away. Michael's face had gone pale. He looked as if he was going to be sick. I was surprised; he didn't seem squeamish. The scar wasn't *that* bad.

"I've had it since I was —"

"Fourteen," he said, cutting me off. It was my turn to be stunned. How the hell did he know that?

"How?" I stammered.

He took a minute to compose his answer. "Michelle, do you remember anything else about those dreams? Had any others like them?"

He was starting to scare me. "Maybe. What in the hell is going on? You're scaring the shit out of me, Michael."

"I'm sorry. I don't mean to scare you. It's just that what you said seemed very familiar to me."

"Yeah, so how did you know I've had it since I was fourteen?" I demanded.

"Before I answer," he said, "would you please answer my other question? Have you had similar dreams?"

"Yes, I have. Now what the hell are you taking about?"

"I've had dreams, too, Michelle. Bad ones. About a place where I was taken and things that were done to me. That's what you're dreaming about, isn't it? About a place where bad things happened to you when you were thirteen or fourteen?"

CHAPTER FIFTY

I didn't answer him.

I was shaking and had a cold sweat, remembering all those horrible dreams. The pain, the anxiety, the suffering: it was too much to think about. Before I knew what was happening, I was sobbing. Somehow, Michael was holding me, and I was holding on to him as tight as I could. I couldn't stop crying. It was embarrassing and scary, and being held felt so damn good that I never wanted it to stop. He just held me, said soothing things, and stroked my hair and back. He let me go as soon as he felt my sobs lessen. He got up and came back with the box of tissues from the living room.

I felt like a fool. But I did feel better. I had never truly let any of that out before.

"Feel better?" Michael asked.

I nodded. "I've been holding on to those dreams for years, keeping them just under the surface. Not letting myself remember. So what's the deal with them? How is it we've both had dreams so similar? Is it some kind of Jungian archetype or something?"

He smiled without humor. "Haven't you guessed?"

I started to shake my head, but I didn't. Maybe I'd guessed that they were more than just bad dreams. The thought that they could actually be *memories* was too frightening for me to contemplate. Yet there was no way to deny them now that they were on the surface. The dreams were self-consistent and all had the same theme. I was stuck someplace I didn't want to be and trying to get away. I almost always had help from a young man with bright green eyes.

I looked and met Michael's bright green eyes. "You're the boy in those dreams of mine, aren't you?"

He nodded. "You're the girl in mine." He laughed. "You want to know something funny?"

"I think I need something to laugh about right now."

"Before I met you, I thought *Julia* was the girl from the dreams."

I started to laugh and then met his eyes again. "I think maybe she might be in some of mine. She and Victor both must have been in that place. What the hell is going on? What was that? It can't possibly be real, can it?"

"I'm not sure. I've been telling myself for years that I was crazy, that something like that couldn't possibly have happened." He stopped and shuddered. I reached over and held his hand. "When I was in the military, Michelle, I learned about some of the things the government could do. I was part of some of those things, overseas."

I had a feeling he knew more than he was sharing. "Do you think it was some kind of government project? I saw this show on the Discovery Channel about some CIA project called MK-Ultra. It was freaky. They did all these mind control studies. They used drugs like LSD and other hallucinogens to try to create sleeper agents or something. Scary stuff," I said. "I never thought it could apply to me."

"I don't know if it was government or not. I never remember seeing any soldiers. Everything took place in that hospital or whatever it was. The security was tight, but not like military installations. If the government was involved, it was only in the form of black-project money, I'd say." He looked thoughtful.

"What," I asked, "is the deal with black projects, anyway? I've always wondered, but never could find any answers."

He smiled mirthlessly. "Black projects were first initiated by Abraham Lincoln. During the Civil War, he decided that the military needed to have money to work on secret projects that they didn't have to answer to Congress for. He felt, rightly so, that Congress was incapable of keeping a secret. Nowadays, there's a special congressional oversight committee that keeps track of what money is going where. The various government agencies don't have to say what they're doing; they just report a project called such-and-such is using X amount of money and is X amount close to completion."

"That's terrifying. They don't have to answer to anyone about what they do?"

"Not really." He paused. "There was a big case that made headlines in the late eighties that involved handicapped children in New York being feed radioactive isotopes with cereal to view the long term effects of radiation sickness. There was a case here in Cincinnati about comatose patients being used in coldsleep studies. They'd take people and rapidly cool them down to just thirty degrees and leave them in these meat-locker things like that for hours, sometimes days. Then they'd try to revive them. It should be noted that all this was without consent. In the mid-nineties, some survivors of MK-Ultra who'd come forward with the assistance of their therapists actually brought their cases before Congress. They were awarded large settlements for what had been done to them."

I shook my head. It was too much. "It all seems like so much conspiracy theory crap to me." I smiled. "Maybe I'm naive."

He shrugged. "It's not easy to believe that our own government would do stuff like that, and worse, but they do. Imagine how bad it must be in nations where the people don't have the freedoms we do."

I shuddered. I could imagine that all too well.

He continued, "All the stuff I mentioned is a matter of public record. The public doesn't want to know about it, though."

"I can't say that I blame them. So where does that leave us? Have you ever found anything about what we may or may not have been involved in?" I asked. "I'm not sure if I can believe that we were both in some sort of project. It seems too much like TV or something."

"Michelle, how can you say you don't believe that something happened? You said you had the dreams. You have the scar on your side. Isn't that enough proof to believe it?"

"No," I said frankly. "It isn't enough." I was trying to figure out how to say it. "How do we even know that we've been having the same dreams? So we both have bad dreams. So what? Wait." I held up my hand to cut him off. "Hear me out. What we need to do is write down what we can remember, separately. Then, if the details match, we'll know that we share something. Maybe nothing ever happened to us, but we share some kind of psychic link and live out each other's nightmares. We have to be sure."

He was nodding. "You're right. I just got excited at the idea of finding answers. I'm sorry." He seemed embarrassed. "I've kept notes on all I can remember in my black notebook. Go write your memories down; we'll compare later."

"Sounds good," I said. I stood and gripped his shoulder. He smiled up at me. I could feel my heart beating hard against my ribs. I left the room before I did something foolish. How could I be having feelings for him? I'd only just met him. Or had I? If he was right, I'd known him when we were teens.

I went into my bedroom and shut the door. I took a quick shower and changed into jeans and a t-shirt. Then I sat at my desk and wrote all I could remember. It wasn't a lot: bits of corridors, getting shot, a room with cages, and the machine. A lot of it was painful and embarrassing, but I wrote it all down. I knew he would have.

CHAPTER FIFTY-ONE

As I walked into the bathroom to wash my face again, my phone started ringing. Why does the phone always ring when you're in the bathroom? Or for matter, why can I never remember to just carry the damn thing around all the time like everyone else seems to?

"Hello?"

"Hey, Michelle, it's Marge."

"Hey." I felt vaguely guilty. I should have called her when I first had news about Lucy. "How are you?" So much had happened.

"Fine. Look, have you seen Lucy? I bailed her ass out of jail the other day, and she's split again. She's driving me nuts, Michelle."

"You bailed her out of jail?" I had a sinking feeling in my stomach.

"Yeah, those freaks she got involved with got arrested for being a cult or something stupid. I'm worried about her. If she misses her court date, she's going to be in serious trouble."

"Yeah, if I see her, I'll let her know, but she hasn't made any contact."

"Okay. Well, thanks anyway."

"No problem." I said. She hung up. I wondered what this meant to me.

I went out to find Michael, taking my notes with me. He was

waiting in the living room. He had taken his gun apart and was cleaning it. I told him about the call. He looked worried. Hell, so was I. Lucy was something of a wild card. We didn't know what she was up to or even capable of.

"It never rains but it pours, eh?" He sighed deeply and frowned at the parts of his gun as if they were to blame.

"Well, nothing we can do about it right now, anyway. We were already on guard. We'll just have to double it," I said.

"Yeah." He looked at the papers in my hand. "Looks like you got your notes finished before she called, at least." He held out his notebook.

I was strangely hesitant to take it and read it. He had marked the parts I needed to read with a few scraps of paper for placeholders. I took it, handed him mine, and sat on the couch.

It was pretty much like mine. He'd written down more details about what each person looked like, the doctors and stuff. It was from his point of view. He had a few more locations than I remembered. It was also the most frightening thing I had ever read. He finished reading before I did, but he didn't say anything till he saw me look up.

"It looks like we have a match, doesn't it?" he said.

I took a long, deep breath before replying. "It does. You have more details than I do, but we remember enough of the same things in the same way to make me believe it's not just a coincidence. What about the shared dream thing?"

"You don't really believe that, do you?"

I shook my head. "No, I don't. I don't know. Maybe. If it really happened, then that *really* terrifies me, Michael. How can something like this have happened? Why don't we remember better?"

"Drugs and hypnosis can be used to selectively cover or erase memories. I learned all about that in the military." He looked pained. No wonder.

"Michael? What about your sister? Was she there?"

Some odd emotions flickered across his face. "I'm not sure. She may have been. It would explain a few things."

"Like what?"

He sighed. "She had a severe nervous breakdown when we were teens. She was still in an institution when I left home. I haven't talked to her much over the years. She lives out in New Mexico. Taos, I think. I guess I need to get in touch with her when all this is over."

We sat and talked until early afternoon. Then we had lunch and talked about other stuff for a while. It was agreed that we wouldn't discuss business during meals; it was too hard on the appetite.

The big problem we faced was that nothing could be proved. We knew better than to try to talk about it openly with anyone else. People would think we were nuts, even more than they usually did. We tried a few searches online, but the conspiracy websites were so filled with oatmeal junk that we couldn't find much that was useful. I even tried the Dark Web, but finding stuff there is impossible.

Mark called and said he was going to be a few minutes late from work, but that we should go on over. After the call, we got ready. I changed into nicer clothes, and so did Michael. I think he was a bit nervous.

We left for Mark and Jen's a little early so we could stop and get a good bottle of wine. Michael found an expensive bottle of Merlot tucked away on a back shelf of the store. He insisted in paying for it, since he was the one who'd wanted to talk to Mark and Jen. I thought he paid way too much.

I drove, of course.

I pulled into the drive just behind Mark. He'd had to work late, he explained again as we got out of the car. I gave him a quick hug and introduced him to Michael. They'd met before, but it hadn't been under the best circumstances. Mark led us inside, where dinner was waiting. I don't know what Mark had told Jen about why we were there, but she spared nothing on dinner that night.

She had cooked smoked salmon with mashed sweet potatoes, rice pilaf, fresh yeast rolls, and mincemeat pie for desert. It was too much. She accepted the bottle of wine with delight, and we had it with dinner, thus confirming my guesses that I knew nothing about wine. I'm sure she had never opened a bottle I brought over. The wine had a rich, smoky flavor that Mark explained came from it being aged in oak casks. I knew that, but let him have his fun.

I'm not a big seafood fan, but I will make an exception for good salmon. This was *excellent* salmon. I resolved to ask Mark later about how much the meal had cost. I never did, of course. He would have been deeply insulted. We chatted about local events and about how Michael and I met. I thought Mark must have dropped some hints to Jen about us getting along really well. She kept pushing subtly. I was tempted to just tell her that he wasn't married and no, we hadn't slept together yet. But why spoil her fun?

After dinner, we moved to the living room and had a bit more wine to go with our conversation. I got Jen and Mark talking about some silly things that we'd done together. I even got Michael to tell them some of the funnier stories he'd told Lawrence and me when we'd gone out to eat. I know it seems like I may have had a lot of wine, but two glasses over three hours with a full stomach is not too much for anyone. I was a bit flushed, and my tongue was looser than normal, but we had a good time, and I got to sit next to Michael on the couch.

Jen excused herself around ten o'clock.

CHAPTER FIFTY-TWO

All good things come to an end. It was time to talk business. I really didn't want to. After a few minutes of the three of us sitting there in silence, I couldn't stand it anymore and started laughing. We were a fine bunch of cowards.

"Okay," I said. "I guess I'll start." I told Mark about the call earlier in the day from Marge. I thought he should know right off about Lucy being out of jail. After I was through, Michael took over.

"First of all, thank you for talking to me about this. I know it's difficult for you. I'd like to start with what you can remember about Lucy and what happened in college. I'll tell you the information I have afterward so it doesn't spoil your account." He took out his little black notebook and a small pencil.

"Very well," Mark said as he sat back. "It was almost exactly ten years ago. You know about our small group of friends and their interests?" When Michael nodded, he continued. "Well, Lucy brought this guy to the group. She was always bringing someone new to the group, but they were usually female. We never could understand why she latched onto this guy. I can't remember what his name was, though. Funny, isn't it?"

"Richard," I said without thinking.

"That was it. He was quite the bastard, even from the first. I know that you like to give people the benefit of the doubt, Michelle, but I couldn't stand this guy from the beginning. I didn't know why. Maybe it was the way he looked at the women in the group. He was like a wolf that had just found a flock of sheep."

He took a long drink of wine before going on.

"I never trusted him. That is why we drifted away from the group after the first murder. I didn't think it was him. Not really. I would have called the police if I had. I just knew that a friend had died. When another one died, I knew that the killer was somehow connected to the group. But by then he had stopped coming around, hadn't he?"

I nodded.

"So," Mark said, "that led to us being attacked that night on the way home from a late-night study session. Come to think of it, Lucy was the one who asked us over."

Michael and I exchanged looks.

Mark went on in a rush, "The guy jumped me. I just wasn't paying attention. I should have sensed him near, sensed his intent, but I didn't." He paused. "I was shot in the chest. If Michelle hadn't been looking for us, I don't think I would have made it. He took Jen, of course. I was certainly in no shape to do anything about it. I managed to tell Michelle who had done it. That's about the extent of my knowledge until it was all over."

Michael looked at me. "How did you know where to find him?"

I frowned. "Lucy."

"Ah." He made a note of it.

Mark was looking at me curiously. "I never did get the story of what happened that night from you. Jen, of course, has had a lot of problems. She can't deal with anything of an occult nature anymore. Whenever she tries anything, she says she can feel him on the other side, screaming."

"You passed out from the pain, and I stayed with you until the ambulance got there. I went straight from there to Lucy's apartment.

She didn't want to let me in. I pushed her aside. I was so angry." I smirked at Michael. "You've seen my temper now. Imagine for yourself how I got the information out of her. I was unarmed, but that didn't matter. In the end, she told me where Richard had been staying. It was a house on the edge of town. Not far from where we were. I washed Mark's blood off me in her bathroom, then called the police and told them what was happening. I then took off running. I didn't have a car at the time."

"Go on," Michael said. "You've got my attention."

"I ran to the house; it was only a couple of miles. I don't know what I was expecting to do when I got there." I shrugged. "Anyway, I got to the house and walked around it looking in windows until I found Jen. She was unconscious and laying on some kind of alter-like table. She was bloody and naked. For a moment, I thought she was dead. Then I saw that she was breathing. I didn't see anyone else around. I broke the window with my elbow and unlocked it. Richard grabbed me as I was climbing in. He must have been in the corner or something."

Mark looked a little pale, but he gestured for me to continue.

"He threw me across the room and pulled out a knife from his back waistband. I was next to the table, and picked up a brass candlestick. We fought. I broke his nose with a left jab, and he cut me along the stomach. It was shallow, though. When he swung at me again, I caught his hand and gave it a quick twist. I think I fractured his wrist. He screamed, his first sound, and dropped the knife. I made a mistake and went for the knife. He kicked me in the head, sending me sprawling, but I got the knife. He darted behind the altar, and I knew he was going for his gun. I rolled to my feet and threw the knife at him as hard as I could." I paused for a drink of wine.

"Jen was still unconscious?" asked Michael.

"Yes. She didn't wake up until she was in the hospital, thank god." I sighed. "The knife hit Richard in the face. I missed my target. I'd been hoping for his throat."

"What happened then?"

"Then? It sank into his left cheek and stuck in his jaw. He dropped the gun and stumbled back, clutching at his face. I ran forward and picked up the gun. I could hear the sirens now. He had this look in his eyes, like a wounded animal. He drew the knife out of his face with his left hand and took a step toward me." I swallowed quickly. My heart was racing from remembered fear. "I shot him in the head, twice. He was dead with the first shot, but I walked up to his body and put another round into his head, just to be sure. Then I walked over to Jen and did what I could to stanch her wounds and get some clothes on her. The police burst in a few minutes later, and I had a difficult time getting them to understand what had happened. I went with them back to the station while they took Jen on to the hospital. I had made the 9-1-1 call, so it all sorted itself out fairly quickly. I was reprimanded for not letting the police do their job. Basically, I had my hand slapped and was told not to do it again. They didn't take me in front of a judge."

"That's a lot of new data. Are you doing okay?" Michael looked concerned. I started to nod, when I realized he was talking to Mark, who was looking very pale and shaking slightly. I got up and sat on the arm of his chair so I could give him a hug. He looked like he needed one right then.

Mark took a long breath and answered. "I will be. It's a little scary; you form strong visuals when you remember like that, Michelle. I almost felt as if I was there with you, watching everything that happened. It's also scary to think of how close I was to losing Jen forever." He took my hand and smiled at me. "Remind me not to doubt your actions from now on, okay?"

"I certainly will not. I need someone to give me a little humility now and then." I smiled. "Maybe we've done enough damage for one night." I looked a Michael. "What do you think?"

"I think Jen is a wonderful cook, and I hope to be invited over for dinner more often. Also, if you remember anything else, please tell me. I can use all the help I can get. It's late, however. I thank you for telling me this, both of you." Michael stood up.

I stood, too. Mark was a little slower getting up, so I teased him about getting old, even though he's two years younger than I am. That broke the aura of gloom in the room, and he laughed.

"Thanks. I think I needed that." He looked at Michael. "You sure you have enough information? I didn't help much. I also thought you wanted to discuss something about Lucy."

"It can wait," Michael said. "I think I, for one, am too worn out to continue tonight."

Mark smiled. "Then we will call it a night."

He led us to the door and bid us goodnight. I got another hug, and Michael got a handshake. I told him later that Mark must like him; Mark normally avoids physical contact with anyone but close friends. We didn't have any incidents on the way home. I went straight to bed when I got there. I'd had a long and uncomfortable day of recollections.

CHAPTER FIFTY-THREE

The day started rather badly for me.

I was awakened by the phone. I hate waking up that way. My body never seems to fit right after I'm jerked back to consciousness from the land of dreams. I started to be irate as I brought the receiver to my ear, but a glance at the clock told me it was after eleven a.m. I'd slept much later than usual.

"Hello?" I croaked.

There was no answer, just a dial tone. The caller ID said the number was blocked. It was probably some damn marketing company. I got up and took care of my morning business. I was feeling out of sorts. I didn't remember having any nightmares, which surprised me. I usually do after dragging up so many painful memories. Michael was up and watching Netflix. It was so incongruous that I just stood and stared at him for few minutes.

He noticed me and promptly said good morning. Samson was curled up in his lap, the traitor. I mumbled a reply and stumbled into the kitchen. I decided to forego eating and got myself a Coke from the fridge. I usually drink tea in the morning, but I didn't feel like bothering today. Besides, it wasn't morning any longer. I felt oddly irritated that my home had been invaded. I'm just not used to being around people so much, and I'd had a lot of company recently.

I went into the living room and played some games on the computer. I was tired of talking about something I couldn't do anything about. I needed a break. I couldn't get into my games, so I went and sat on the couch and watched some program with Michael about how the first nuclear bomb was developed. I wasn't really interested, but one advantage of cable is that it seems to sap IQ points. I just sat there and didn't have to think. It felt good.

Michael's cell phone rang. When he got up to go answer it, I grabbed the remote and started channel surfing. Nothing interesting caught my eye. I had an odd combination of being fidgety and not wanting to do anything. I could hear Michael in the other room on the phone. I couldn't quite make out what he was saying, though. He came back a few minutes later, and the grim look on his face made me forget I was bored.

"What's wrong?" I asked, suddenly concerned.

He frowned. "I have to go. There's been a development with the case."

"Can I come along? I don't want to be here alone." I stood up.

"I don't know if you want to do that. There has been a murder. It matches Julia's usual M.O. I need to get there and talk with the police."

"So can I come along or not?" I asked.

"You'll probably have to wait in the car. I haven't had time to take care of any paperwork for you yet. You might be safer here." He shrugged. "Come along. Maybe I can bullshit the local police into letting you come on the scene. You may need to know what she's capable of."

I didn't like the sound of that, but I ran and changed quickly anyway. He let me drive again, but he got two bulky, black plastic cases out of the trunk of his car first.

"Just for insurance," he said without elaborating as he placed them carefully in the back seat.

It was around noon, so the traffic was a little heavier than normal.

He directed me to a house in Fort Thomas. It was nice little brick cottage in what looked like a pleasant neighborhood. All the lawns and hedges were neatly trimmed. The houses had spotless paintjobs that couldn't be more than two years old. There were over a dozen police cars parked in the drive and along the street, plus an ambulance and several unmarked cars that looked official.

It was difficult to find a place to park, but an officer helped us find one once he stopped trying to wave us on and saw Michael's badge. We made it across the lawn and just inside the door before anyone questioned us. Michael flashed his badge again and told the detective in charge that I was a civilian attaché to the United States Marshal's service. He didn't ask any more questions after that, but called another officer over to show us around and tell us what they had found out. The officer looked a bit familiar; I may have worked with him before.

Nothing had been moved yet. A forensics team had already gone through the house, looking for clues. The team hadn't wanted the bodies moved until Michael arrived and gave his okay. He had jurisdiction over the case, as it may have been done by a fugitive he was hunting.

The inside of the house was a wreck. Furniture was smashed. Broken glass was everywhere, but it wasn't from the windows; they seemed intact.

I noticed the splashes of blood on the walls first, as we were led to the master bedroom. There were four bodies in it. Three were children of various ages up to late teens or so. It was hard to tell, considering the condition they were in. The other was an older woman, maybe middle-aged. It looked as if they'd been lined up kneeling on the floor, facing away from the doorway. Then they had each been shot in the back of the head. From the mess, I would say it was something larger than the traditional Mob .22-caliber. The officer said forensics thought it was a 9mm round. They weren't sure, though, because no empty brass cartridges had been found. It looked like someone had swept through the house and removed as much physical evidence as possible.

"Naturally," Michael mumbled to himself. "I would have, so of course Julia would."

He actually got down close to look at the bodies. I stayed back by the door. I was glad I hadn't eaten yet. My stomach was doing flip-flops, and my mouth was doing that hyper-salivation thing it does right before I vomit. It wasn't the bodies. I've seen lots of bodies. It was psychic aura of rage, tinged with madness, that clung to every surface of the house.

Michael looked around the floor a bit, too, I guess just in case the CSI team had missed anything. It wasn't likely, but checking couldn't hurt.

"Are these the only bodies?" Michael asked.

"No, sir. There is one other." The young officer looked uneasy.

I wondered what could have shaken him up so badly. The bodies were unpleasant, but surely he had seen worse. I doubted he could feel the same things I was sensing.

When Michael indicated he was ready, the officer led us back through the house to the kitchen. We stayed in the doorway, as the forensics team was still looking for evidence. Even that was too close for me. I had to walk back into the living room after a minute of looking in there.

There was a dead, middle-aged man in the kitchen. His arms, hands, feet, and head had been taped down to a tall wooden chair with several layers of duct tape. He looked as if he'd been badly beaten, but that wasn't the worst part. There was a clear plastic bag over his head; he'd been suffocated. The officer helpfully explained that the medical examiner thought the man had been tortured with suffocation for hours. The actual cause of death looked as if it might have been a heart attack. The police would have to wait for the autopsy to be sure how he'd died. I wished he hadn't told me that.

My head was reeling from the pain and grief in the house.

CHAPTER FIFTY-FOUR

Michael walked over and put his hand on my shoulder. "Are you okay? I guess I should have warned you."

"It wouldn't have done any good. I would have come anyway. I had to see."

He nodded. "Any doubt it was done by Julia?"

I just looked at him.

"What I mean," he said, "is, do you feel anything?"

"Yeah. Lots of fear. Rage. Madness." I closed my eyes and tried to filter for a minute. "Yes, she was here. She..." I took a deep breath. "She was really angry. *Enraged*, I would even say. Much angrier than when we met her. She was crazy with hate."

"Specifically at the victim?" he asked.

I swallowed hard against the waves of psychic emotion washing over me. "Yes. So who was that guy? Does she just pick someone at random to do this to, or what?"

"No, it doesn't seem to be random." He didn't say any more, because we were interrupted.

"Who the hell are you two, and what are you doing at my crime scene?"

We both turned to look at the belligerent person who'd spoken.

He was shorter than Michael, about my height. He wore a nondescript black suit. "I said —"

"I heard you." Michael said coldly. "I'm Deputy Marshal Delling. This crime may have been committed by a federal fugitive. That makes it my business."

"You can get out and wait for the report. I've seen nothing to link this to anything or anyone," the man said.

"I reported to the all local police departments about the M.O. of my fugitive. Maybe you should read your memos."

"Maybe you should keep your nose out of this."

"What is your problem? This is a federal matter. End of discussion," Michael snapped. He was starting to look angry; it was a bit frightening.

"You're right, there. It is a federal matter, but not yours. Special Agent Henderson, Office of Homeland Security. I've taken over this case," he said with an irritatingly smug smile.

"On what authority?" asked Michael. "How can this be a national security issue?"

"Sorry, but I doubt you have the necessary security clearance that would allow me to tell you. Now get the hell out of here." He turned slightly to look at me. "Who the hell are you?"

"She is a civilian attaché whom I asked to look at the crime scene. She has certain skills that may be useful. She's a specialist in occult crime."

Agent Henderson's smirk and roving eyes suggested what skills he was thinking of. "She can take her *skills* and get the hell out, too." He walked up close to me. It might have been intimidating if he'd been taller than me. He just glared and said, "If you talk about this case to anyone, it will be considered a breach of national security, and you *will* be persecuted to the full extent of the law."

"I think you mean *prosecuted.*" Michael took my arm and led me outside. I was so angry, I wanted to kill the bastard right there. We walked over and got in my Jeep before talking. "God damn it!" he said explosively.

I flinched. Michael was angry. At least it wasn't at me. I felt the same way, but I guess he was less used to such behavior than I was. The police were never overly friendly with me when I was working with them. I figured that the Office of Homeland Security would have even less use for anyone with paranormal abilities; they tend to be rather 'white bread.'

"Sorry," Michael said more calmly.

"It's all right. I feel the same way. Does Henderson really have the authority to take over the case like this?"

He shrugged. "Yes and no. I doubt he'll actually take the case. He was just blustering. He knows I can't push this one because there's no direct evidence linking it to my fugitive hunt; *that*, I have complete authority in. This Homeland Security crap is starting to get on my nerves. There's nothing like inventing an enemy to make it easier to take away a country's freedom."

"What about 9/11?"

"Oh, it was real enough, I don't mean that. I had a couple of friends who died in New York City that day. My first thought when I heard about it was that I couldn't believe we'd let them do it."

"You think the intelligence agencies looked away and let it happen?"

"I don't know. They had a lot to gain. I do think that they weren't trying all that hard to *stop* it. Always think about who gains the most from something. The CIA got a blank check after that. Don't forget that we didn't have Homeland Security before that, either."

I didn't say anything. It was weird to think about. I did appreciate Michael trying to distract me, though. I hoped this didn't trigger any bad dreams tonight; I was worried that it might. Seeing that dead man like that... I had to stop thinking about it before I started shaking.

I started my Jeep and pulled out onto the road. Michael made a few calls on his cell phone on the way. He was asking for paperwork to be made ready at the local marshal's office. He wanted to get me officially on the case so we wouldn't have any more problems. I turned into I-471 to go to downtown Cincinnati. Michael just nodded when he saw where I was headed. I figured the Marshals Service would be located in the Federal Building.

Once downtown, it took me a bit to find a parking space; it was always busy downtown. I left my gun and mags in the console. Michael led me into the building. There's a lot more security on federal buildings these days. We had to sign in, and I had to go through a metal detector. Then we took the elevator up to the floor with Marshal's offices. I was apprehensive when we arrived. After meeting Agent Henderson, I wasn't too sure about meeting a bunch of federal marshals.

I need not have worried. They were polite, professional, and a few were even friendly. They didn't act as if what I did for a living was weird; I guess they hear about that sort of thing fairly often. I was glad I'd dressed up nicer than usual. They took my picture twice for my new identification badges. Then we had to fill out more papers to make it legal for me to carry a gun everywhere. Michael didn't want me unarmed any time we were out, not even in the Federal Building.

All of this lasted until early evening. When we were done, we left and got something to eat at a drive-thru. I was exhausted. There had been *lots* of paperwork. That sort of thing always wears me out. Before we went into the house, Michael warned me about talking on the phone about anything. He didn't know how serious the agent from Homeland Security was, and he didn't want to find out.

He was worried that the phone might have been tapped.

I was irritated. It felt like an invasion of privacy, and it was, but there was nothing I could do about it. If the phones were tapped, Michael would know by the next afternoon. Until then, I would use my cell phone. They can be tapped, too, but it's a lot more difficult. He didn't think the Homeland Security would bother with it. They may not even know I had it, since it was a recent acquisition.

CHAPTER FIFTY-FIVE

I checked my phone after I got in the car. I didn't have any messages, but someone had called four times over the course of the day. The caller ID said it was a hotel. I told Michael about it, and he suggested I call the number back. I called the number. A man answered on the third ring. He sounded nervous.

"Hello. You called me four times today," I said. "Who is this?"

"Who are you?' he asked.

"Michelle. You don't get a last name. Now, tell me who you are and why you called me four times today, or I'm hanging up and calling the police. I've had a long day."

"My name is Christopher. I really need to talk to you, but I have to be sure first."

"Sure about what?"

"That you are who you say. Then I'll prove that I have something worth knowing."

"Okay, ask away," I said. I figured it couldn't hurt to play along a little.

"How did you get the scar on your right side?"

I stiffened for a moment; I hadn't expected that. "I fell at school."

"Perfect. Now for the truth. You were actually shot."

I was suddenly leery. "Why do you think that?"

He laughed. "I don't think it; I *know* it. I was the doctor who sewed you up. I suspect you know it now as well, since you've been talking to the marshal."

"So is that what you have to tell me?"

"No, I have a lot more to tell you than that. Would you be willing to meet me? Alone?"

It was my turn to laugh. "No way in hell. Marshal Delling comes along, or you can forget it." I was not about to deliver myself to some nutcase, especially one who might be connected with my half-remembered past.

"I need to talk to you. You need this information." He sounded pained.

"Why? Why give it to me? What is it to you?"

"You'll understand if you come meet me."

"I can't do that."

"Will you meet me someplace in public? How about the courtyard at the mall, maybe? The marshal can come to the mall with you, but not inside the food court. What do you say? It will be public, but we can have a private conversation."

"Florence Mall, I assume?"

"Yes."

"Okay, that sounds reasonable," I could see Michael shaking his head; I held up my hand to get him to wait a moment. "Don't even think about screwing with me, though."

He coughed lightly. "I wouldn't think of it. I know better than you do what you're capable of."

"Okay," I said. "What time, and how do I find you?"

"I'll find you. How about three p.m. tomorrow afternoon?"

"Fine, but you'll need to make sure it's me. I'll be wearing –"

He cut me off. "I know what you look like. I wouldn't mistake you for Julia."

I suddenly got goose bumps.

"Is it agreed, then?" he asked.

"Yes."

"Goodbye, then." He hung up.

Michael pounced as soon as I clicked off the phone. "What the hell are you thinking? You can't meet this guy alone."

"Relax, Michael, I'm not. You're coming along." I sat on the couch and told him the whole part of the conversation he had missed. He still looked vaguely irritated. I told him I would remain in view of the entrance by the pet store at all times. He nodded.

He finally quit pacing and sat down. "I don't like it. It feels like a trap. I guess we have to take that chance. It could be really important. We'll go over everything tomorrow in more detail before we go. We will both be armed, of course." He took out his notebook and starting writing everything down.

He obviously didn't want to talk, so I went and took a long bath. I dressed in a clean set of red silk pajamas and a thick bathrobe. I probably looked silly with my hair up in a towel-turban, but I didn't care. It took me a while to figure out where my slippers were. I never did find them and ended up in thick socks.

Michael was talking on his cell phone when I walked in, so I continued on through to the kitchen. I fixed myself a nice cup of tea. I hadn't had any for a day or so. I was rummaging through the cabinet while my tea steeped when Michael sat down at the table. I was looking for some cookies that I thought I'd stashed in there a few weeks ago. I hoped that Lawrence hadn't found them, but he must have.

I sat down and sipped my tea.

"Your phone line is clean. I had a friend do a line trace on it," Michael said suddenly.

I smiled. "Great. So what's bothering you?"

"Is it that obvious?"

I nodded solemnly, hiding my smile in my cup.

"Damn." He shook his head. "I guess I'll have to confess."

I just raised my eyebrows.

"I'm worried about you doing this tomorrow, Michelle."

"Thanks, but I should be safe enough. He's not going to shoot me or abduct me in the middle of the food court at the mall."

"I know. I just wish he'd told you whatever it is over the phone."

I shrugged. "Me, too, but he didn't. So I'll go to meet him. You'll be no more than fifty feet from me. I'll make him keep his hands in plain view the whole time. If he tries anything, I'll break his arms." I grinned.

Michael nodded. "You probably could, at that. Okay, I can't stop from feeling that something's going to go wrong, but I'll stop being overprotective. I'll try, at least."

"I was actually joking about the arm-breaking thing."

"I know, but I know you could do it if you had to," he said seriously.

"I wish I had your confidence."

He patted my hand. "You'll be fine."

"So what's really bothering you?"

He gave me a rueful grin. "I'm worried about what we saw today. Julia never used to toy with them like that. Did you recognize the victim?"

"No, should I?" I asked.

"I don't know. There has to be a reason she picks the people she does. I just don't know what it is. They're always older men or women, usually fifty or older. They tend to be professionals in the medical field. Some of them are just businessmen, though. I don't get it. Maybe she really is just acting out a single event with random victims in whom she sees her original tormentor. I don't know."

"What's that?" I asked. He had lost me for a second.

"Sorry, it's from her psychological profile. The psych people think she's just a typical killer who sees certain people as a threat because she was hurt badly by someone like them in the past," he explained.

"So you don't think it's linked to what they did to us?"

"What do you mean?"

"Michael, she straps them down to a chair and suffocates them. That doesn't seem a bit familiar to you?" I was agitated; it seemed obvious.

His brows knotted together. "You think that she's reenacting the events that you and I have dreamed about? That she, too, was put into that device and suffered in..." He took a shuddering breath. "You know what I mean," he finished quickly.

"I think it's more than that."

"What?" he demanded after I was silent for I minute as I putt all the pieces together.

"I think that the people she's killing were actually part of whatever happened to us. She's giving them a taste of what we went through. That's what you were thinking, wasn't it?"

"Yes," he admitted. "I didn't want my thoughts to interfere with yours. I thought maybe you would see some other explanation."

I just smiled and sipped my tea. I was beginning to understand how his mind worked.

"If he was a doctor who worked on the project, I want him to come into protective custody. We'll need him." He paused. "We might even be able to bait Julia with him."

I met his eyes. He was serious.

I finished my tea and went to bed. Saturday was going to be a long day.

INTERLUDE FOUR

I'm standing before a keypad.

We've gone through more doors than we ever have before. We hope freedom lies on the other side of this one. This door has a keypad lock instead of the swipe card like the rest of them. The boy is torturing a guard. He is trying to get the combination to the door. I don't think the guard knows it. He would have given the answer by now. No man can withstand having his genitals crushed slowly under your heel. They just taught us that trick last week. It was good to be able to use what they taught us against them.

There's something strange about the keys. It seems that there is some kind of memory there that I can't quite place. I don't think it's my memory. My hand drifts toward the keypad. I stop myself. If I enter the wrong code, it will set off the alarms. The boy has given up and broken the guard's neck in disgust, or maybe pity. He wouldn't want to live as a crippled eunuch, so maybe it was mercy. That was a trait they keep telling us is a weakness. I resolve to work on my sense of mercy.

Anything they don't like it, I do.

My hand wants to move. I let it. The boy is watching me with an odd look on his face. I just close my eyes and let my fingers move on their own. I type in a sequence. Nothing happens at first. I'm worried. We exchange looks, ready to run away. Then the door opens with a sigh.

I am suddenly slammed into the door, which shuts. The boy howls in pain and falls to his knees, clutching his lower back. I turn to see the girl who looks a little like me. She has a metal bar and raises it to hit the boy again. I knock it out of her hand with a kick. She tries a killing strike to my throat. I block it. I am better than her at unarmed combat, and she knows it. We're often paired up together in the classes, since we are of a similar build.

She's angry. She says that every time we try to escape, they make it worse on everyone. She says she's been here the longest, and we should do as she says. I don't care. I just want to go home. She might not have a home, but I do. She performs a roundhouse kick at me. I duck and dart back, realizing too late that I've done what she wanted me to do. She hits the keypad with her foot, pressing several keys at once. Alarms go off. She's going to get us caught. She laughs and runs away.

I grab the boy, helping him to his feet. Maybe we can make it back to the cages before they notice that we were the ones who tried to escape again. They will punish us all if no one confesses, but it will be less severe than what they did to the boy and me last time. I can't take that again. Maybe the girl will keep quiet.

She doesn't talk to them.

She hates them in a way I understand but could never match.

CHAPTER FIFTY-SIX

Other than the one brief nightmare, I slept much better than I expected. Maybe it was the promise of finally getting some answers to my problems. My other dreams were odd but not actually bad. I guess these things become relative over time. I got up and took a shower. It was only eight o'clock. The afternoon was a long way off. Michael seemed asleep, so I had the house to myself again for a while. I felt good. I played with Samson until I heard Michael stirring. Then I went into the kitchen and started breakfast.

I made scrambled eggs, bacon, and toast. I put some coffee on for Michael and made tea for myself. Michael came out of the guest room looking freshly washed and smelling of some pleasant aftershave. He grinned as he came into the kitchen and saw the food I was cooking. He told me the smell of the bacon had rousted him from bed, and it had been everything he could do to make himself take a shower before rushing out. I took that to mean that he really liked bacon, so I put some more in the microwave.

We sat and chatted while we ate. I told him about some of the strange cases I'd worked with the police on. Michael asked me questions about some of the ones he'd heard of; he had an astonishing memory for case files. I was lucky to remember that I *had* worked on a case. He could call up details of any he'd read about. I was envious.

We spent the rest of the morning talking about what we were going to do later. We tried to think of things that could go wrong, and ways to come out of it alive. Meeting someone like this doctor was always dangerous. We didn't know if we could trust him. We didn't know if he'd be alone, or have backup. We didn't know anything for certain, really.

When the time came, I dressed in business attire. I wore one of the dark pants suits that I wear when I'm working with the police on a case; it makes it easier for them to take me seriously if I look professional. I put my new federal IDs in my jacket pocket. My cell phone went in the other pocket. I wore my pistol in its new shoulder holster. If I kept wearing guns with my suits, I was going to need to have suits made that would hide it. At least my pistol wasn't too bulky.

I wore a few discreet protective charms; they tend to blend in nicely. I was as nervous as I could possibly be, jumping at little noises. I finally snapped at Michael. I needed him to stop trying to reassure me, because it was having the opposite effect. We left at two o'clock, to give us enough time to get to our meeting. I drove, and Michael watched for anyone trying to follow us.

All was clear. Traffic was light.

We got to the mall around two thirty. I parked near the pet store so we would be close to where we'd be inside. We went in, and I looked at the cute kittens while Michael did a quick sweep, looking for anyone suspicious. At ten till three, we decided it was time for me to go into the dining area and find a table. I stopped by the sandwich place just inside the courtyard and got myself a drink. I didn't want to be sitting at the table not eating or anything; that would look odd to anyone.

Right at three o'clock, I noticed a distinguished-looking older man walking by for the second time. He wasn't looking at me, but I could tell his attention was focused on me anyway. Sometimes it helps to be psychic. Finally, he quit circling and came over to the table. He looked nervous. I didn't blame him. He sat down without asking.

"You are Michelle," he said." I'm Christopher."

I'm glad he cleared that up; I was wondering who I was. "Prove it," I said.

He swallowed and looked around. He was going to end up calling attention to himself just by how upset he appeared. "The scar on your right side looks like a puckered star, a typical gunshot scar."

"What caliber round was it?" I asked. I had no idea; I was just curious what he would say.

"It was a 5.56mm bullet, the standard M-16 round," he said without hesitation.

"Really? I didn't know. So what do you have to tell me?"

"I knew your father, Michelle. He was a good man."

That caught me off guard. "My dad died when I was young."

"I know. You were three. You went to live with your grandparents after that, and lived with them until they were killed in that dreadful automobile accident. Then you lived with your mother until you moved into an apartment for college," he said. "After New York, then back here. Then off to college again. You've had quite a life."

"So far you're not telling me anything I don't know. How did you know my father?"

"We served together in Vietnam. Medical."

I hadn't even known my dad was in Vietnam, much less a doctor. I'd have to call one of my aunts and ask her when all this was over. "Go on, and stop looking around like that. You're going to call attention to yourself."

He paled. "Right. Well, I obviously don't have the same skill set as you do. I'm just an old country MD."

"And I work with the police to solve weird crimes. I'm a criminal anthropologist, not a spy. Tell me something I don't know, before I lose my temper." I was betting he was scared of me. I was right.

He jerked as if he'd been slapped. "Okay, look, I just want you to be clear on this. All I did for the project was keep the subjects as healthy as possible. Okay? I never hurt any of you kids. The things they did to you made me sick. I couldn't believe how much punishment you could take and still be functional."

"Excuse me?" I said, glaring.

"Sorry, it's nothing personal. It's just that it was easier to stay emotionally detached. I meant that you kids recovered amazingly from severe injuries."

I needed to ask something that had been bothering me. "How could we have? I mean, were we genetic super-soldiers or something?"

"No." He scowled. "Nothing silly like that. You were given booster shots all your life that were actually different types of steroids and enzymes. They were designed to keep the body's natural abilities of regeneration working into adulthood. All young children can heal quickly and even regenerate a little. The first phase of the project pushed that as far as we could with the technology available. That gunshot wound healed in less than a week."

I had a million more questions. Which ones to ask first? "So that's what the project was about? Healing and stuff?" That wouldn't be so bad, I guess.

CHAPTER FIFTY-SEVEN

Christopher shot that down quickly. "No, that was only the first phase. They needed to toughen the subjects so they could survive phase two."

So much for that idea. I noticed how he went from *we* to *they* when talking about the second phase. I needed to be careful with this guy; he was just trying to cover his ass. "So what was phase two about?" I had to know.

He started shaking slightly. "Phase two was the testing part of the operation. They weeded out the subjects that were not suitable, and pushed the rest to prepare for the third phase."

This was starting to sound wrong. He wasn't really telling me anything. "What was the overall project about, then? How many phases were there?" I was getting angry at this old man who could talk so calmly about *weeding out.* "Tell me, or I'll give you to Julia myself!" I growled. That should do it.

He almost jumped up, but my look stopped him, and he sank back down into his chair. "Dear God, no. Please," he whispered. "Do you know what she has been doing?"

"Yeah, a lesser version of what was done to us. Now talk."

He nodded sharply and then continued. "Okay. The project was initially to design an apparatus to assist in trans-location, out-of-body experience under conscious control. It was a side project to work along with the remote-viewing projects of the time. The military engineers built a machine that would recreate the near-death experience but keep the subject alive, at least theoretically. The first two dozen army 'volunteers' died in the machine."

He paused for a few quick breaths.

"Go on," I said.

"That's when they outsourced it to a private company to do a research and feasibility study. They picked up a few local orphans and began to work on them. By the time the subjects were three years old, they knew they were on the right track and opened up the first phase of the project to four dozen children with the correct backgrounds."

I broke in. "What backgrounds?"

"They decided that they would use children of direct German and Irish heritage. Germans have produced many powerful occult figures throughout history, and the Irish have always been known for their *second sight*, as they call it."

"Okay, weird, but go on."

"Anyway, the new subjects were given the boosters and such at regular times. They lived normal lives with their parents – in your case, grandparents. The orphans were kept at the facility as a control group and were subjected to much more rigorous testing and training."

I sighed. "Let me guess. Julia was one of the orphans."

He nodded. "Yes, her and her brother. I think they were the only two of the orphans still alive at puberty when phase two came online."

I just shook my head.

Hell, I'd be dealing with the pain from this conversation for a long time.

He went on, "Phase two was started at puberty, because that's when most children begin to seriously manifest psychic abilities, poltergeists and such."

I nodded. I knew that.

"Since the subjects were intended to be special espionage agents, you were all given extensive training in the martial arts. Some of the children – you were one – had a special knack for combat. The government almost started a side project."

"So what about phase three?" I asked.

"The project never went that far. The subjects that survived, sane, manifested a wide range of psychic abilities. Only a few were considered of worth militarily. The machine could force the subjects out-of-body, but there was no way to control them once it did. Once a person has felt so much pain, what else can you do to them? The project was terminated and the children sent home with memory caps in place."

"How were the memories suppressed? It doesn't seem to have worked real well," I said. "I have a few; Julia seems to have all of hers."

Christopher twitched when I said Julia's name. "The memories were suppressed in the usual manner: a combination of drugs, hypnosis, and electro-convulsive therapy. Julia never had a full cap placed on hers. She was sent to another special project – CIA, I think. Her brother didn't exhibit any useful psychic skills, so he was sent to a foster home."

I was almost afraid to ask. "What was so special about her skills?"

He started to answer and then paused with a little cough.

I didn't recognize the first shot for what it was. It wasn't until I heard the longer burst of a machine gun that I realized there was trouble. People in the food court were turning to look. The shots had come from the direction of the pet store. *Michael.* I turned quickly to tell Christopher that I had to go, but he was already gone. Damn. Several of the mall security officers, actually off-duty police, were moving quickly in the direction of the gunfire, talking on their radios. I heard several more single shots, and then silence.

Christopher had bolted in the other direction. I could see his back as he ran out of the courtyard. I wanted to follow him, but I also needed to make sure Michael was okay. When I got to the area where

I'd left Michael, he wasn't there. I was starting to turn to look for some sign of him when someone yelled.

CHAPTER FIFTY-EIGHT

"Freeze!" Three cops had their pistols out and pointed at me. I realized my gun was in my hand.

I froze.

I spoke up at that point. "I'm working with a federal marshal. My ID is in my right jacket pocket." Michael had made sure I took the ID with me. Just in case. I was feeling thankful, but also worried about him. He should have been there, and wasn't.

I changed my grip to put my finger away from the trigger. One of the cops moved up carefully while the other two kept him covered. He took my gun. Then he reached carefully into my pocket and removed the badges. I remained perfectly still. It never hurts to be extra cautious. It can hurt a lot *not* to be, though.

The cops relaxed a little as they looked at the IDs. I told them that I had been talking to a potential witness and that the federal marshal I was working with had been supposed to wait for me here. The gunshots had happened near here.

We were still talking when the service door across the way opened, and Michael walked out. He had his badge out and called to the police officers. There was blood on his arm.

The officers put away their guns and walked over to talk to him. I looked a question at the cop next to me. He smiled and handed back my ID badges and gun. I must have looked surprised.

He smiled. "We worked together on a case last year. I thought I recognized you. Wondered why you were running through the mall with a gun. You go on over. I think I'm going to call for some assistance in crowd control." There was a mob of people standing around gawking. I turned my back to them and walked quickly to Michael's side. I took his arm and checked it while he was talking to the police.

"I suggest," he said, "that we step in here to talk." He gestured toward the service door he had come out through.

One officer led the way, and the other went off to help keep the crowd back. I followed Michael. He started talking again as soon as the door was shut. We were in a long corridor; there were shapes at the end that looked like bodies. There were bullet holes along the floor and both walls. I couldn't figure out how Michael had managed not to get killed.

"I was standing out in the corridor when someone jostled my side. At least that was what I thought, until I felt the knife. He tried to slip it under my ribs, but my holster caught it. I grabbed for him, and he ran in here. I followed. There was a second perpetrator at the end the hall. He was the one with the submachine gun." Michael smiled grimly. "I had my gun out as I gave chase, so when he opened up at me, I took them both down."

The officer spoke up. "Do we need to take them into custody, sir?" He was reaching for his cuffs.

"They're both dead. I'm afraid my instincts took over. The one with the gun was wearing a bulletproof vest; he took two rounds and then returned fire. I put a round in his head. The other also took one in the head as he went for gun the first perp dropped." He shrugged. "I've already called in a clean-up team."

"Right," the officer drawled. "I'll need a copy of your report later, if you don't mind, sir. This sort of thing..." He shook his head. "Not good for publicity."

"There is a zero-news policy in effect. If asked, say there was an electrical malfunction that sounded like gunfire. You responded to it and found nothing was amiss. An electrician was called in for repairs. They'll be here soon."

The officer sighed. "Yes, sir." He went out to tell the others and to disperse the crowd.

I looked at Michael. "Are you okay?"

"I've been better. I'll be okay. It hurts, but it isn't serious." He walked down the hall toward the bodies.

I followed.

"Recognize these two?" he asked.

I shook my head. They didn't look familiar at all.

"They look like a couple of metal-heads – no pun intended. Sorry," I said at his quick look.

They were dressed in black jeans and rock band tees. The gun was a small Ingram .22 caliber, the kind that people always call an Uzi but isn't. One of the shooters had on an army surplus flak vest that appeared to have been spray-painted black. It would pass for a thick vest-like jacket to most people. Besides, with the number of piercings and tattoos on these guys, no one would get too close or ask too many questions.

"They certainly don't look like Julia's people," I said.

"No, they don't. I wonder who the new player is."

I took a deep breath, took the ring off my right hand, and then knelt and lightly touched the gun with the back of my fingers. I got several flashes of feeling, including the two guys dying. Then I got what I was looking for. I stood up, wobbled for a second, and put my ring back on.

"It was Lucy. She sent them."

"You're sure?"

I just gave him a dirty look.

"Okay, sorry. Your specialty, not mine. So Lucy is playing hardball now. Interesting." He lightly kneaded his injured arm.

"So how bad is it?" I asked, pulling at his sleeve.

"Not too bad. I just caught a couple of ricochets that had mostly spent themselves against the walls." He frowned at the wounds. "The bleeding has mostly stopped already. I'm more irritated about the jacket, to tell the truth."

I smiled and shook my head. He nearly gets himself killed, and he's worried about his suit. I wondered if he would heal as fast as I do. By tacit agreement, we didn't talk about what I'd learned from Christopher. That could wait until later.

We didn't have to wait long for the clean-up people to arrive. Michael talked to them for a few minutes, and then they got busy. He explained to me what they were going to do. Two of them took photos of everything before they started. Then they put the bodies into body bags. They would wait for the mall to close before they removed the bodies, backing the van right up to the door. They would then take the bodies to the closest hospital and bring them in as John Does. The Federal crew cleaned up the blood, pried bullets out of the walls, and patched what they could. It wouldn't look perfect when they left, but it would pass casual inspection.

We left once they got started.

CHAPTER FIFTY-NINE

I drove us back to my house. Michael got cleaned up while I ordered a pizza. I didn't feel like cooking again. I tried to call Christopher, but the desk clerk at the hotel said he'd checked out. I wasn't surprised. I helped Michael bandage his arm while we waited. I was somewhat disconcerted to see him there without his shirt on; he was well built, densely muscled, and fit.

Luckily, the pizza guy arrived early.

We sat in the living room, eating pizza and talking about what Christopher had told me. It was almost surreal. It didn't take me long to fill Michael in on everything that had been discussed. Our informant and I hadn't been able to talk for long. I asked Michael if he thought Lucy had us followed, or if she somehow knew we were going to be there.

"I think," he said, "that she must've had us followed. Christopher was vague and guarded, but I don't think he was trying to set us up. It doesn't feel like it, anyway."

I nodded. He trusted his instincts; so did I.

"I wonder where they got the gun?" he mused.

"Probably at the flea market," I said. "You can get just about anything there if you know who to ask."

He raised his eyebrows. "Automatic weapons?"

I shook my head. "I doubt they were automatic when they were bought. You know how easy it is to file down an Ingram."

"I," he said with a laugh, "must have missed that class."

I smirked at him. "I learned it from a movie."

He just laughed harder.

"So how much of a chance is there that they'll try again?" I asked.

That sobered him. "Well," he said, "I suppose they'll keep trying until we put them away. When these two show up in the morgue, it will make the others less sure of themselves. Do you know what kind of financial resources Lucy has?"

"I have no idea." I shook my head. "I don't think she has a lot. She's never worked much, just enough to get by."

He nodded.

"Do you think Julia has given up for now, or do we have her to worry about, too?"

"I'd say that we will have to stay on guard at all times from now on. At least until this is resolved," said Michael.

"You think we can find a way to get them before they get us?"

"Of course I do." He grinned at me. "My ego won't let me admit defeat. Seriously, though, we need to be careful for a while. Julia has a certain code of conduct, twisted as it may be. I believed her when she said she didn't intend her men to actually hurt you. Lucy and her goons are unpredictable. They're like rabid dogs. We'll just have to take them down if they come near us. At least they don't seem organized or well trained."

"I hope Christopher calls again. I was hoping to get more information out of him. I guess I shouldn't be greedy, but I felt as if there was something else he wanted to tell me, something important."

"I don't know, Michelle. I'm sorry about disrupting things this afternoon."

I laughed. "Yeah, how dare you get stabbed and then shot, and then make such a big deal out of it?"

He smiled. "Okay, no apologies. I'm not actually sorry about those two anyway."

"How do you do it?" I asked suddenly.

"What?" He looked confused.

"How do you manage not to get sick and have the shakes and stuff after violence?"

He shrugged. "I hold it inside till later. Trust me, it bothers me. I worry that I like doing it too much. I used to worry about becoming what Julia is."

I shuddered. "I've worried about that in myself, as well."

We didn't say anything for a while after that. There are some emotions that you don't really want to share with anyone. We talked about other stuff for a bit before turning in for the night. There were things I wanted to ask Michael, but I didn't want to ask them while all this was going on.

Why give him more to worry about?

I called Mark from my bedroom. I wasn't supposed to be talking about the case with anyone else, but I needed to talk to someone.

"Hello, Michelle," he answered.

"Hey, Mark. How's it going?"

"Fine, although our life seems a bit dull, compared to yours. How are you and Michael doing?"

"We're doing fine with each other, but we've had the usual problems with everything else. I met someone today I want to talk to you about."

"Okay, what's up?"

"I know I've told you about the odd dreams I have sometimes," I said.

"Hmm. Refresh my memory."

"I mean the ones with the violence when I was a young teen."

"Ah, yes." I heard him take a drink. "I remember some of that. Have you been having them again? I seem to remember they were especially bad after what happened in college."

I lay back on my bed. "Oh, they were bad before then, too."

"They've gotten worse? Maybe you should see someone. As I said before, Jen has a really great therapist. I'm sure you could get in for an appointment."

"I don't want to see a therapist, Mark. I don't think they could handle me."

He laughed. "Okay, you may have a point. So what *do* you want, Michelle?"

I paused. It was a good question. "Resolution, I think."

"They're just bad dreams. I should tell you some of mine." I could hear him sipping again. The man was going to become an alcoholic if he wasn't careful.

"Are you so sure? What if they *aren't* just bad dreams?" I heard my voice crack a little on that. It was hard for me to lie to him, even by omission.

Mark snorted. "What are you saying? Listen to yourself. I think you have been under a lot of stress recently. Maybe you should think about resigning from the police work. I'm sure you could make good money doing normal lectures for the CRI."

"What if I had proof?" I said quickly.

"Then I would be really scared for you, Michelle. Are you saying you *do* have proof? Have you talked to Michael about this?" He sounded concerned for my mental state.

"I'm fine. Maybe I shouldn't have called you about this. Yes, I've talked to Michael about this. Quite a bit, actually. He's had dreams like mine since the same age."

"I see. And this is your proof?" He sounded skeptical. I didn't blame him.

"No, I met today with a doctor who was part of a secret project."

"Someone who *claimed* to be part of something secret. It was probably someone wanting to scam you out of money. I hope you didn't give him a credit card number or anything."

I sighed. It was no use. "I'm sorry to bother you, Mark. I've got to go. I'll keep in touch."

"Wait. I'm sorry. You obviously believe what you are saying, but I think you're just tired and worn down. Rest for a few days, okay?"

"I will. Say hi to Jen for me. 'Bye, Mark." I hung up the phone. I'd thought that Mark, of all my friends, would understand.

CHAPTER SIXTY

I woke up early the next morning and decided that I was tired of my life being on hold. I called Josh to see how he was doing. I missed my weekends at the faire. They were the only time I really got to relax and forget about work for a while.

Josh harassed me about not at least stopping by to say hello to everyone. I promised I'd see what I could do, but I told him I doubted I could make it this weekend. We talked for about an hour about what had been happening around the faire. I got to catch up on my gossip; it felt good. Josh had finally gotten Rachael to go out with him. I tried to suppress the twinge of jealousy I felt.

He didn't owe me anything.

Hell, I didn't even want him. I just wanted my old life back.

To my surprise, Michael was not against the idea when I mentioned going to the faire over a breakfast of eggs and toast. He said the faire was where this had started for me, so it might be good to go back and take another look around. We talked about the plan for a while. He even mentioned that he was looking forward to meeting some of my friends.

I wasn't sure how to take that.

I liked Michael, and I wanted more from our relationship than just a working partnership. He was good looking and smart. We'd shared an extraordinary experience in our youth. We had a connection that went deep into our souls. I wanted to see if that connection would grow into something more. I was also afraid of seeing what that connection would do to me. I'd avoided getting seriously involved with anyone for years. I wasn't sure if I was ready for a steady lover.

I was nervous about Michael and Josh meeting each other, but I guess I'd just have to let things settle where they would. Josh was getting involved with Rachael anyway. Not only was she really good looking, but she was the co-owner of the acting company Josh worked for. Did I mention she was rich? They'd known each other for many years, and Josh had wanted her for as long as I'd known him. I really was happy for him. I was also sad that I hadn't even had a chance with him. I had known that all along, though.

Maybe it was better this way.

It was close to the middle of October, and the weather was starting to turn cool. We were able to wear our suits without dying of heat stroke. Suits are pretty much a necessity if you're going to wear a concealed gun in public. I drove us to the faire just after lunch. I played Loreena McKennitt's *The Book of Secrets* while on the way. I love that album; it really gets me in the mood for a renfaire. Michael had never heard the whole album before, just the second song. "The Mummers' Dance" had gotten a good bit of airtime when the album came out, and for good reason: the tune is irresistible.

I'd bought passes for every weekend in advance, so I didn't need to pay for us to get in. I brought the extra passes I had left over, to give to my friends – they'd find someone to give them to. The faire was crowded. I was a little worried that someone might try something there, but everything went fine. Lucy's crowd may have finally given up for a while when her goons disappeared. I didn't see any goths at all.

Josh and the pirates were on the stage, so I led Michael over to watch. I had a strange sense of deja-vu. I'd been standing here like this when I'd been psychically attacked before. The crowd was just as good as it had been that day, but I couldn't get into it. We left before the show was over. We'd come back and find my friends later.

We had a great time annoying the guy running the knife throwing booth. We kept getting perfect hits with our thrown knives. Unlike with a big amusement park, you don't get anything if you win at the games at the faire. It kind of sucked. I'd have to go with Michael to a state fair or something; I wanted a big stuffed animal for my guest bed.

Sometimes it really scares me when I find myself thinking like that.

Domestic, I mean.

Since we'd had only a light lunch, we got something to eat at the faire. To my great disgust, Michael actually liked fried turkey legs. I think the things are hideous. They're greasy, and I've never liked the idea of gnawing meat directly off the bone. I had a rye-bread bowl full of beef stew, and a soda. I'd have to find the pretzel guy before the end of the day; I love soft pretzels.

We had to go by the leather shop, of course, since we had met again there. It seemed strange to say we had met *again*, but I'd accepted what happened when we were younger. Michael had to drag me out of the shop before I could buy a targe, a tooled-leather round shield with a Celtic knot of three hounds carved into it. I loved it. It was expensive, but it would have looked great on the wall at home. I let Michael talk me out of it... for then. I'd be back for it later, or get it from the guy's website.

I did go and buy a few small items later. I didn't want Michael to think that I was too easily talked into not spending money on the things that I want. We were growing closer, and I wanted him to like me for everything that I am. That includes leather armor and renfaires. He genuinely seemed to be enjoying himself. I asked him if he thought he would like to dress up and play along some time. He just laughed and said maybe next year. I took that as a good sign: he still expected us to be friends next year. I hoped we would be more than that, though.

We caught up with Josh and the other pirates in the tavern, and I introduced Michael. Everyone seemed pleased to see me with him. I think even Josh was happy about it. Maybe he was glad that he could pursue Rachael without me moping around after him. I'd tended to think of Josh as being after me, but that may have been an illusion. We all got along great. Michael had a good sense of humor, and joked and bantered along with my other friends. He took the jokes and harassment with great poise.

He left to go to the privies later. While he was gone, my friends teased me about my relationship with him. I took it with good grace. Okay, actually, I gave them all kinds of hell right back. Josh and I were still firing one-liners back and forth when Michael returned. He sat down closer to me than he had been before he left. He seemed a little bit possessive toward me. I grinned inside.

Rachael and Josh invited us out to dinner. We made plans and parted. We were going to meet them just after the faire at the Old Spaghetti Factory. I guess I wasn't going to get my pretzel today. I told Michael he owed me one. We left the faire, and I stopped to get gas for my Jeep. Prices were high. I filled up anyway. I was beginning to think I should have gotten something more fuel-efficient, but the Jeep fit my personality.

We met Josh and Rachael at seven o'clock. I was hungry. That soup I had earlier hadn't stayed with me. They'd changed into mundane clothes; their renfaire costumes would have been a bit out of place in a restaurant. We were seated quickly. I ordered the five-cheese spaghetti and meatballs dinner. I got ribbed about that. I ignored my friends and munched on garlic bread. I'd need to remember to get some gum or breath-mints on the way home.

"So what do you do for a living, Michael?" asked Rachael. I glanced at Josh. I'd have assumed he'd told her.

"I'm a deputy U.S. marshal," Michael said.

"Oh, so that must be how you met Michelle. Are the two of you working on a case?"

"We met because of a case. Today, we're just relaxing." He smiled over at me.

"Really? What's the case about?" Rachael seemed really interested. She was a natural gossip. Anything we told her, everyone would know next week. I nudged Michael with my foot and shook my head slightly.

"I'm quite sorry, Rachael; we can't talk about it." He sounded very natural at that sort of thing.

There was an uncomfortable pause. "So," I said, breaking it. "Rachael, when are you going to give Josh a better part in the show? Not that he doesn't make a good buffoon, but he should have a bigger part, I think."

Josh glared at me, and I smiled sweetly.

We sat and talked and ate for hours. It felt good. It had been a long time since I had a normal date, which was how I was starting to think of the day's outing. From the looks Michael kept giving me, he was, too. I was happy. Josh and Rachael kept us entertained with impressions and jokes. We had spumoni and coffee for desert. It was perfect.

We parted from Josh and Rachael with a promise that we would do this again sometime soon. When we got back to my house, Michael thanked me for a great day. He came close and put his hands on my arms.

I was almost shaking.

Just do it, I kept telling myself.

We were so close. Why didn't he kiss me?

Why didn't I kiss him? I don't know.

The moment was broken. He let go and stepped back.

"I think," he said, "that now is not the best time for this." He met my eyes. I understood what he meant.

I nodded.

"Michelle?"

I looked up and met his eyes again.

"How about after all this is over, you and I have a nice dinner and see where it goes from there?" He looked like I felt. He didn't want to wait, either, but it was for the best. I knew that. I just didn't want to admit it.

"Okay," I said. "We wait. Don't wait too long." I went to my room to take a long hot bath. I suddenly found myself quite tense.

CHAPTER SIXTY-ONE

Michael woke me up.

He didn't do it intentionally. He was yelling in the other room. From what I could hear of what he was saying, he was on the phone. I got dressed quickly and went to see what was going on. Michael was quiet and pacing in the living room when I came.

I got up my nerve. "What's wrong?"

He spun on his heel, facing me suddenly. "That dumb-ass," he said in a remarkably calm tone. "That *agent* from Homeland Security has been withholding information from me." He paused and evened out his breathing. "Julia killed twice more this weekend. Henderson has it smothered under so thick a layer of bureaucratic confidentiality that my office only just found out about it."

"Oh," I said. I sat down by the desk, out of his way.

"I have a meeting with his superior in an hour. I've got my director coming along for extra firepower. This is going to get ugly."

He got a strange look on his face.

"Michelle, is there someplace safe you can go? You can't come with me today. It would hurt my cause. Sorry."

I nodded. "I'll figure something out. Go get ready. I'll see if Lawrence is busy. He has a shit-load of security at his place. Guards, too." Michael nodded and went to chance into a suit. I'd started down the hall to go into my bedroom take a shower and change when the phone rang. I picked up the extension in my bedroom. It was Christopher. He started off with a question.

"What happened Saturday?" he asked.

I decided to be honest; he would've heard only the official story. "Michael was waiting in the hall like we'd agreed. He was attacked. Stabbed and then shot at. The gunfire we heard was theirs, from a service corridor."

"I see. Was it related to…?" He sounded anxious. "Her?"

"No, it was related to another case Michael had worked on. Two guys looking for a little payback." I'd decided to lie *that* much, anyway; I was afraid the truth would scare Christopher off.

"Thank God. I was so worried that one of us had been tracked there. I need to see you again. I never got a chance to tell you everything. Will you meet me again?"

"Yes. I'd like to know more." What a stupid question. I had been angry and worried when he took off Saturday. I hadn't thought I'd get another chance to talk to him.

"Same time and place? Today?" he said with urgency.

I wondered why the sudden rush. "Sounds good. I'll see you there."

I got cleaned up and changed in a hurry. I put on a hat to cover my hair; I didn't have time for a shower right then. Michael was in the living room tying his shoes. I told him about the call. He looked stricken.

"That's not exactly what I had in mind when I said *safe*, Michelle."

I smiled. "I know, but I like to take risks." I countered his look. "Seriously, this is our best chance to get Christopher into protective custody. I'll talk him into it. You be sure to get things set up so we can put him somewhere safe until we can use him to get Julia."

"Okay, you have a point. I'll be out of my meeting by four o'clock. Call me then on my cell, and we'll get him someplace safe." He gripped my arm. "Be careful, and good luck." He picked up his jacket and left. I saw him to the door. I felt odd about seeing him go. I realized I was going to miss his company.

I watched as he pulled away, my emotions somewhat in turmoil.

A little later, a man from the marshal service dropped off the papers for me to give to Christopher if I could convince him to come into protective custody. I hoped he would agree; it would make catching Julia much easier.

I left early for my meeting. I wanted to be able to double back a lot and make sure I wasn't being followed. I didn't see anyone following me, but then, I hadn't seen anyone on Saturday, either.

It was a typical crowded day at the mall; just about any weekend is. It seems that people begin to shop for Christmas earlier every year.

I had to park much farther out in the parking lot than I'd wanted to. I was nervous all the way into the mall. I kept expecting someone to drive by and gun me down. I was armed, of course, but that didn't always help.

A guy started following me when I passed the computer game store. I quickened my pace. So did he. I worked my way over to the part of the mall being renovated; they're always working on some part of it. I ducked around the escalators and waited, hidden by the information kiosk. He came jogging into view, and I stepped out, grabbed him, and slammed him against the wall.

He was young, maybe in his early twenties. He squeaked as he hit the wall.

"Why are you following me?" I asked. I kept my expression hard, but I already suspected that this guy was just an innocent kid.

"I thought you were cute. I just wanted your number. Honest. I'm sorry." He sounded sincere... and scared. I realized I had him pinned half a foot off the ground. He was a short one, not even my height. I let him go.

"Don't follow me again," I said. He was shaking his head as he raced off. I couldn't keep it in any longer; I laughed.

Okay, so I'm paranoid. No wonder I don't date much.

I went upstairs to the food court. Christopher wasn't there yet, but

I was still early. I got myself a soft pretzel with cheddar while I waited; I'd been craving one for several days. I was just sitting back down when I saw Christopher. He was alone, and he kept looking around to make sure he stayed that way. I began to eat my pretzel.

He sat down. I met his eyes.

"Doctor," I said to get his attention. "The best way to be noticed is to act furtive. If you don't want anyone to notice you, you need to act obvious. No one walks into the food court without pausing by most of the food vendors. Go get something to drink, at least. I'll be here."

I went back to work on my food. He got up and left. I was playing a dangerous game, but I needed him to believe I knew what I was doing. He needed to trust me, or I would never get him into protective custody. He came back a couple of minutes later with a chai latté; he hadn't looked the type.

CHAPTER SIXTY-TWO

It took Christopher a couple of tries to open the lid on his latté.

"I'm sorry," he started. "I've been retired for several years. I haven't had a lot of interaction with other people. You'll excuse me if I make what to you must seem like obvious mistakes."

I ignored his comment and smiled. "No problem. I sorry we were interrupted last time. I was worried that you wouldn't get back in touch with me. We really want to stop Julia, you know."

"I know," he said. "That's one reason why I want you to know all of this."

"Did you really know my father?"

"Yes." He nodded. "He was a good man. You look a bit like him, you know."

"I don't remember him; I have a couple of photos, but that's all."

"Michelle," he said, suddenly changing the subject, "Julia has to be stopped. I understand where the anger comes from. I couldn't believe what they did to you children in there, but what she is doing is *not* justice."

"No, it's revenge." I paused for a moment. "I don't condone what she's doing, Christopher. I went with Michael to one of the crime scenes and almost got sick. I'm not a monster like she is. Neither is

Michael. We both work to stop monsters like her."

"I just know what was done to all of you." He took a drink of his latté and made a face. Maybe he wasn't the type, after all. "I know you have the same potential for violence."

"Christopher, everyone has that potential. We're all animals. It's what we do that makes us what we are, not what was done to us. Look at the people who did this. Were they tortured as children? Probably not, but they still did those things to us. I made a decision to be a normal person. I don't give in to those animal impulses when I feel them. Even when I have gotten into fights, I've felt sick afterward. I'm just like anyone else."

He didn't look convinced, so I went on quickly.

"Look," I said, "Julia had a lot of bad stuff happen to her, but she was the one who decided that she wanted revenge. She makes her choices in life, just like anyone else. It's tragic that someone with so much potential would choose to do what she does, but that's life. I won't lie to you. You know that I've killed. I've killed five men this month." He started at that. I put my hand on his arm to restrain him. "They were men Julia sent to kill me, and they fired at me first."

I knew when I touched Christopher's arm that he'd had more to do with the project than he admitted. He'd helped implement many of the medical experiments. I tried to keep my emotions from showing on my face, and moved my hand back quickly. I had to fight down the wave of hatred and nausea welling up within me. It took all of my control not to kill him where he sat.

He nodded slowly. I think I was starting to get through to him. "I've spent the last twenty-five years worrying that one of you kids would decide you needed revenge. I should have known that it would be Julia. She was always cruel, even then. She used to say things to the other kids... They'd tell me about what she was doing. Dr. Green never cared what was done, as long his project wasn't disrupted." He met my eyes. "You never wanted revenge, Michelle?"

I forced myself to smile, it was difficult. It's difficult to want revenge when you've had your memory erased. "No, I never did.

Once I knew more about what happened, I wanted justice to be done. I'd like to see those responsible prosecuted and behind bars. Not because I want revenge, but because I don't want them to hurt anyone else. Do you understand that?"

"I do. I think I even believe you. Michael feels as you do?"

"He does. That's why he became a federal marshal: so he could stop people from doing things like that. I didn't remember a lot of what happened, but he did. He doesn't kill people unless he has to, either."

Christopher nodded again, looking at his hands.

It was time to get down to business. "I've been authorized to make a deal with you," I said.

He looked up at me.

"We want you to go into protective custody," I said. "The state police will handle the details. You will be held unaccountable for any acts you may have committed while working for the project if you are willing to give your testimony in court. You will then have the option of going into the witness protection program. Michael will make sure the details of your location and identity are destroyed, so that no one from the government can track you down."

I slowly pulled some papers out of my pocket.

"These are the official papers. You can see for yourself that they're all in order." I slid the papers across the table to him.

He took them with trembling hands. This case had the potential to burn a lot of people in government. This was going to blow the whole project wide open. It needed to be opened up, though. It had been covered up for far too long.

He licked his lips lightly. "What do I need to do?"

I took out my cell phone. It was after four o'clock. I called Michael. He sounded gloomy until I told him about Christopher; then he got excited. He told me to hold on for half an hour, not to go anywhere.

"Christopher," I said, "Saturday you were going to tell me about Julia. We were interrupted. Would you tell me now what special skills made her so valuable to the project?"

"She had a talent for psychokinetics, in particular telekinesis," he said after chewing his lip for a minute.

"Telekinesis? You mean she can move objects with her mind?" I didn't want that to be true. It would make Julia much more dangerous. I'd never met anyone who could do that, but I was willing to believe just about anything.

He shook his head. "Not exactly. She didn't have any real control, although she seemed to have an ability to push slightly. Are you familiar with the concept of chi?"

"Certainly. I even practice Tai chi," I said.

"Good, then you know that certain forces can be produced to enhance injuries or to escape damage." He said it as a statement.

"I suppose," I said. "I've never thought about it from a practical standpoint. I mostly concentrate on the flow of energy and cleansing the body."

"Yes. Julia has something more than normal chi, but less than full telekinesis." He was becoming fidgety again, looking around more.

"So what good does it do her?"

"She can kill with a hit that would normally only cripple. She can cripple with a strike that would normally be only a light touch. Be careful if you have to touch her. She can hurt you badly without any apparent effort"

I thought I might be able to make her work for it, but I didn't want to argue with him.

Michael came in alone about twenty minutes later. We both stood as he walked up. He shook Christopher's hand. "Doctor," he said, and smiled at me. I could tell he was proud of me.

It felt good.

CHAPTER SIXTY-THREE

We began to walk to the entrance. Michael explained that the police were waiting just outside. He described the system of safe houses as we walked. Christopher would be held at the state police headquarters until a house was available, probably in the morning. He would then be moved to the house, under guard 24/7.

Michael didn't tell him that we would both be with him. We knew that if he knew Julia would be coming after him, he would never do it. I felt a little bit of guilt at using him as bait, but after what I had gotten off of him when I touched him, that guilty feeling was fading fast. He was just as guilty as the rest of the people who had worked on the project. They had let a medical atrocity be committed and not one of them had ever tried to make it right.

The two state troopers took Christopher when we got outside. They would keep him safe. Michael and I walked out to my car. I told him about the conversation. Then I told him about what I had detected when I touched Christopher. His expression hardened at this, but he shrugged. We needed to catch Julia; that was all that mattered right then.

I drove him over to where he had left his car, and he followed me home. I was dying to know what had been said at his meeting, but knew better than to call and ask him while on the road. We still needed to be careful, maybe now more than ever.

We were so close to getting her.

Once we got inside, we sat in the living room and talked. Samson crawled into Michael's lap and I openly called him a traitor. We both a laugh out of it. Michael needed a few minutes to get his thoughts together. Then he began.

"I met with Agent Henderson's director. It went as badly as we might have guessed. Their office just has too much political power these days. They wouldn't budge on their policy. They really don't want us involved in this case. They had put forth a motion to have me reassigned. I'm beginning to wonder if they know more than they are letting on," he said.

"You think that they know about the project and are trying to cover it up?" I asked.

"I don't know," he said. "They are covering something up. I just don't know what. I guess the project makes as much sense as anything else. I'm almost certain that Henderson knows."

"Do they think that you and I still don't remember anything?"

"I don't know." He laughed. "They really aren't going to like the fact that we have the doctor."

"Do you think they are going to try to take him away from you?" I asked.

"They can't. I don't have him. There seems to have been an oversight in the reporting of the matter." He winked.

I shook my head. "They are going to nail you to the wall for that."

"I doubt it. They don't want to call any more attention to this than they have to. That was part of the reason for going with the State Police for the protection," he said.

"Clever. I'm going to have to watch out for you. You're sneaky."

He just smiled and me an innocent look that said 'who, me?'

"So what is the plan?" I asked.

"We'll be in the safe house when they bring him in. I think Julia has someone on the inside. She has too much information. If she finds out about Christopher, she will strike within twenty-four to forty-eight hours. We will be ready," he said earnestly.

"I hope so. I don't feel ready. I can go armed? Right?" I asked anxiously.

"Yes. I don't want you to ever be unarmed from this point forward. You are a big target also," he said.

"Oh, of course I am," I said. "That's the only reason you keep me around."

"Michelle…," he began.

I placed a finger over his lips to shush him. I didn't want him to say what I thought he was going to, not right then. "I was kidding you, Michael. When do we have to get up in the morning?"

"Very early. Our ride will call when everything is in position, say around four in the morning," he said.

"Then I guess we had better get some sleep," I said, getting up.

He nodded. "I'll knock on your door at three a.m. Good night."

"'Night." I quickly moved into the bedroom. The next few days would be hectic. I needed to sleep when I could. I tossed and turned most of the night.

CHAPTER SIXTY-FOUR

We left my house early in the morning, before sunrise. We didn't drive. We snuck out and walked quietly but quickly to the next street over. There was an unmarked police car waiting for us. We got in, and the officer took us to the bungalow the Marshal's Service would be using as a safe house for Christopher. The idea was to get us into the house before Julia set up surveillance on it. Once inside, we would have to be careful not to talk loudly or walk by any of the windows. The house was designed to make modern surveillance techniques difficult, but it paid to be careful.

It was going to be a long wait.

Once there, we were assigned rooms. I'd brought my notebook computer so I could work on my notes and play games, mostly the latter. Michael produced a deck of cards from a deep pocket. We talked quietly about the case. We didn't want the two officers, stationed by the two doors, to hear us. The windows in the house were bulletproof, as were the walls. The house was a sturdy little piece of work, strong as a fortress.

What the house had in security, it lacked in comfort. The walls and carpet were drab and institutional. The furniture looked second-hand; much of it had been repaired several times. There were old clothes in the closet smelling of mothballs and cedar chips. There was only the one old tube television in the living room.

With Christopher in protective custody, there wasn't a lot for Michael and me to do. We sat and talked or played a few hands of cards. While we played, we discussed again what we knew about Julia. We still didn't know a lot about her. She had a lot of resources; that was certain. That suggested well-laid plans of some kind, but the attacks against the personnel from the project seemed almost at random. Before we'd met, Michael had found two houses that he suspected belonged to people from the project. They'd come home to find that their houses had been wrecked. It was the same kind of destruction found in the homes of those Julia had murdered. It suggested that she'd gone to their homes not knowing they weren't there. Her actions were an odd mixture of careful planning and unplanned chaos.

The people she had working for her all seemed to be ex-military. Some might even be ex-CIA. Michael was having trouble getting a clear answer from the FBI or the CIA about the fingerprints from the dead men in the van accident. Even years later, there seemed to be a lot of distrust between the branches of government after all the finger-pointing in the fallout from 9/11.

It almost seemed that Julia had formed some kind of private military company. We didn't know what she planned to do with her forces, but none of our ideas sounded good. Since she didn't use many of her available resources for any given mission, it was assumed that they were for something besides her private revenge against the project.

Michael thought it was most likely that she'd simply formed a mercenary company from people she knew and had worked with. They might even be performing other assignments while she took her revenge here. It was like the two sets of guys in the white van. They'd talked about pick-up teams and surveillance. They may be doing corporate work. That made me think of Lawrence. I hoped he wasn't mixed up in anything like that. I'd have to call him later and see how he was doing. He might also know about any major players in the game.

Christopher found me while I was making notes on what I knew of Julia and her crowd. I figured anything I could remember might come in handy. He came in and carefully sat down on the floor. He waited until I put the notebook down before he spoke.

"I wanted to say that I was sorry about having been involved in what happened to you." He worked his hands nervously.

"I'm not sure I can absolve you of your part in everything. I thank you for coming to me and telling me the truth. I was still missing a few parts. I suppose I should thank you for patching me up when I was shot, too."

He shrugged. "I didn't do so much. They wouldn't let me work with many tools. I suppose they were afraid of you. I know I was."

I smiled. "I may have given them some reason for that."

"Indeed. At least seven reasons, if I remember correctly."

"Christopher, what was the name of the project?"

He blinked a few times at me. "It was called the Providence Project. I thought you knew that."

"Where would I have learned that? They didn't discuss much around us, you know."

"Sorry," he said. "Is there anything else I can help with?"

"There are a lot of questions I would like to ask. I'll try not to ask all million of them at once."

He chuckled and seemed to relax a bit. "Ask away."

"How did they get us children to the project without drawing attention to it?"

"All of you were from underprivileged families. It wasn't hard to convince the parents to let their kids go to a summer camp."

"That's kind of sick. I can imagine the shock we must have felt when we first got to the project." I shook my head. My stomach was starting to hurt; I hoped I wasn't developing an ulcer.

"I know, Michelle. Many of the people in the project couldn't handle it, either," he said.

"What happened to them?"

"They were disappeared, I believe. Killed."

Something else was bothering me. "How did they explain the kids who died? How did their parents take it?"

"I'm sure you heard of school bus accidents involving drunk drivers. Not all of them were real accidents," said Christopher.

I was stunned. I had only a vague awareness of those accidents; they'd been too tragic. To think that they took advantage of the accidents to hide the bodies of the project was too much. I felt tears in my eyes.

Christopher excused himself.

I cried silently for all the children who'd been promised something good, and died in torment.

I cried because I could easily have been one of them.

CHAPTER SIXTY-FIVE

When the police changed shifts, the new ones brought food for all of us. It was mostly submarine sandwiches and chips. They had stocked the refrigerator with cold soda. They were Pepsi drinkers. They got a good laugh at my reaction when I found out I couldn't have a Coke. I had a Dr. Pepper instead. I refuse to drink Pepsi. It's not ideological; I just think Pepsi is too sweet.

I decided to call Lawrence and see what he had come up with. He answered on the first ring. I could hear industrial music in the background.

"Hello, Michelle, how are you? Still breathing, I hear."

I laughed. "Hey, Lawrence, how are you doing? I'm doing well."

"Good. How is your new boyfriend working out?" He had a slight lilt to his voice.

I just growled at him.

He laughed at me and said, "Must be going well there, too. I assume you called about the files."

"I did. Any luck?"

"No." I imagined him shaking his head. "I haven't gotten anywhere with them. Your new beau never got me any assistance, so it's going to take a while. I've got my stack working on it."

"Damn," I said. "I was hoping you would have something."

"I'm afraid not. What're you up to at the moment? We could meet and discuss it." He sounded slightly drunk.

"Sorry, I'm on a stakeout right now."

"Ugh, sounds exceedingly dull." He yawned.

"It can be, at times."

"Well," He paused. "I suppose I should let you get to that. I'll certainly let you know if I find anything."

"Thanks. Listen, Lawrence, do you know of any major players on your side of things who'd be working with a private military company or mercenaries or something?"

"Sounds more likely to be a drug thing than what I'm into, Michelle."

"Yeah. Had to ask."

"Of course. Anything else?" He sounded mildly irritated now.

"No, thanks again."

"No problem. Later." He hung up. I guess it would've been too much to hope that he'd have something for me at this point.

I was beginning to wonder if I would ever know everything that had happened. I doubted I would, and that might not be a bad thing, actually. What I did remember of the project was exceedingly unpleasant. The idea that there might be other things even worse was something I didn't want to think about.

I found Michael and told him that I'd talked to Lawrence but that he hadn't uncovered anything new. Michael just shook his head. He was working on arranging the names of the people who had been killed or attacked by Julia, and trying to correlate it with their profession. He wasn't having a lot of luck.

Since he didn't seem to be in the mood to talk, I left him alone and walked around the house. The heavy drapes were drawn against surveillance. Christopher was asleep on the couch. I don't think he'd been getting a lot of sleep until he came into protective custody. He spent all his time eating and sleeping. At least he didn't smoke. I'd feared that he might be a pipe smoker or something; I can't stand that.

The day passed slowly, and mostly in silence. By the time the night shift came on duty, I was thinking this aspect of police work had to be the most boring. I found myself almost wishing that Julia would attack or something. I was bored out of my mind. I didn't know how Michael could sit there and fill out paperwork, but at least he had something to do.

I decided to go to bed right after dinner that night. If nothing happened by the next day, I was going to leave and get back to work on finding Julia. It was hard to find a comfortable position in the cot I had been assigned. The room was empty except for it, and I felt so alone. I pulled the light cover up over my head and tried to relax.

Michael knocked lightly on the door a half-hour later. I was still awake. I got out of the cot and opened the door. He was standing there with a slight grin on face and his deck of cards in his hand.

"Care to play a few rounds?" he asked.

I laughed and gestured for him to come in. We sat across from each other on the floor.

"So," he said, "what would you like to play?"

I just shrugged, so he suggested we play rummy. I suppose strip poker would have been inappropriate. I got up and got my notebook to use to keep score. I hadn't been using it for anything else.

We played long into the night. I didn't notice it was getting late until Michael yawned for what I realized was the sixth time. I was so tired that my eyes hurt. We finished up the hand we were playing and decided the rest of the game could wait till tomorrow.

I fell asleep almost instantly.

CHAPTER SIXTY-SIX

I slept soundly.

I think I was having a really interesting dream, but nothing stuck with me when I woke up. I hate when I'm having a fantastic dream and suddenly awaken. I can never remember what I was dreaming. It was an incredibly loud crash that brought me instantly awake. I drew my gun from under my pillow and rolled from the cot. My heart was racing. I could hear my blood rushing in my ears, and my mouth went dry.

Michael called my name softly from the hall and then stepped into the room. He swept it with his gun before coming over to me. That was truly paranoid. I approved.

"Are you okay?" he asked.

"Yes. You?"

"Fine. Look, I'm not sure what's going on, but it doesn't look good. If something happens, keep close to me and keep your head down."

He used his cell phone to call in the SWAT team he had standing ready for backup. We carefully left the room and moved down the hall to find Christopher.

The lights went out.

I could just barely see Michael in the glow coming through the heavy curtains in the living room from the streetlight outside the window. I met his eyes. There was a muffled thump, and then the sound of the front of the house being blown in hit me. Part of the roof may have, too.

The next I knew, my ears were ringing. Michael was dragging me. I didn't even remember being knocked unconscious. I struggled to my feet and almost fell again. He steadied me against the side of the house. My head hurt badly. I might've had a slight concussion. He said something softly about explosives and then shoved me down between a car and a brick wall. We were outside. It was just dawn, and the air was clear and cold. There was a pale, reddish light over everything. I carefully looked around me from my hiding place.

Julia must have shown up with entire her strike force. They'd then attacked the house with a ruthlessness rarely seen outside of a war. Explosives had blown out the bulletproof glass in the windows and damaged some of the walls. The roof had caved in across the front of the house. It was a wonder we'd survived. I couldn't believe we'd underestimated her that much.

The SWAT team had arrived while Michael was dragging me outside. He'd been careful, and it had taken him at least fifteen minutes to get out through the rubble. There were already two police helicopters in the air, circling. They had their search lights directed at the ground somewhere to my left. The officers in the helicopters kept shouting over loudspeakers for everyone to lay down their weapons.

I could hear an occasional rifle shot ringing out. I think they had a sniper on one of the helicopters. I just tried to hide and stay out of the line of fire. I'm not sure how they knew whom to shoot and whom not to. I didn't want to become a statistic.

"Michelle," he whispered urgently.

"Yes?"

"You're hurt. I want you to stay here and keep your head down. If any of the SWAT comes this way, don't resist if they try to arrest you. I'll sort it out later."

I nodded, and Michael ran off to my left.

I looked over the hood of the car in that direction. It was pure chaos. I'd had no idea Julia had this many people working for her. They were making an orderly retreat toward two armored cars that looked like the kind banks use to transport money, except these were black. It seemed out of character for Julia to attack like this.

The SWAT team was moving up in a leapfrog formation, trying to get close without being shot. There were a lot of bodies on the ground. I couldn't tell if they were Julia's people or not.

A sniper from one of the helicopters found his mark in the crowd getting into the trucks. 7.62mm sniper rounds make an impression. After that, one of Julia's men raced to the front of one of the trucks and came out with a long tube over his shoulder. I realized he was going to shoot down one of the helicopters. I couldn't sit in my hiding place and not do anything.

I stood without thinking and unloaded my entire magazine into him. It was long range for a pistol, seventy yards, but he was a stationary target. I fired sixteen times; some of the bullets must have hit him. The rocket fired as he fell, jerking, to the ground in a spray of blood. There was a loud swooshing roar and then a huge explosion. I think the rocket must have hit a tree or another house or something. I dove back under the cover of the car and changed mags as large clods of dirt fell around me. A few bullets ricocheted off the brick wall behind me. I couldn't tell who was shooting.

Someone came out of the house, covered in blood. As he ran past, I realized it was Victor. He ran past the car where I was hiding. I grabbed at his foot and tripped him. He fell sprawling, his gun spinning away. I crouched and took careful aim at him with my pistol. He got slowly to his feet and drew a long, nasty knife from behind his back.

"Don't!" I said, raising the gun to point at his head.

He just smiled and began twisting the knife, showing me how he was going to make me suffer with it. "Bitch," was all he said. He suddenly ran toward me.

I shot him through the left eye.

I heard a bloodcurdling scream. Julia was struggling against the grip of two of her men over by her trucks. Blood was flowing freely from a cut on her scalp. She'd seen me shoot Victor in the head; she knew he was dead. I saw the look in her eyes. I would have fired at her, but one of her men raised his rifle toward me. I didn't wait for him to fire; I dove behind the car. Bullets pocked the brick wall beside me. I'm not stupid enough to go against an automatic rifle with a pistol.

Dawn was starting to add its light to that of the various fires. Michael found me sitting with my back against a wall. Julia and her people had left. The police were pursuing, but it looked as if they'd get away. Several other armored trucks were waiting at the nearest intersection. The trucks had first joined with the others, and then they'd split up and gone different ways. No one knew which truck Julia was in. The helicopters had been called off after the rocket was fired.

We went back into the house. Christopher was in the bathroom, dead. Victor had carved him up before he came outside and I shot him. It looked as if he took his time. He must have been inside torturing Christopher while Michael was dragging me outside. I could tell Michael was hurting, but he didn't say anything. He didn't have to; we'd lost our witness and our only real lead to Julia.

I met Michael's eyes. I had a feeling that I was now a more prominent target that the doctor had ever been. What that meant, I'd have to wait to find out.

CHAPTER SIXTY-SEVEN

I'd been sitting in the Marshal's Service office since the night before. One of the local police officers had taken us back to my house to get our cars. Michael had driven separately. I wasn't sure how to feel about that. I'd driven straight downtown after leaving my house. I hadn't seen Michael since he drove away. I spent most of the night explaining to a deputy marshal what my role had been in the events at the safe house. I could tell they weren't happy with me.

I was past giving a damn.

Michael woke me up with a cup of coffee in the late morning. He apologized that he couldn't find any tea. My back hurt, and I was stiff from sleeping in a chair. With Christopher and Victor both dead, we were in a serious bind. Why couldn't I have gotten to Victor before he killed Christopher? The old man was guilty as hell, but I'd told him he would be safe. I didn't like to think what had happened had been my fault. Michael tried to cheer me up, but I didn't want to be cheerful. He left again to go to a meeting. I wanted Julia to leave me alone and life to get back to normal.

There was a lot of heat coming from the Office of Homeland Security. Agent Henderson was someplace in the building, talking to the director. He wanted Michael off the case. It looked as if he was going to get what he wanted. The police had lost six officers; another fifteen were in the hospital. The news media were clamoring to know what had happened. The incident with Christopher had been too public. Somehow, *that* was our fault, too.

Agent Henderson came to see me sometime after noon, looking entirely too smug. He had a sheaf of papers in his hand. "You are off this case!" he announced, waving the papers under my nose.

"You'll want to take a step back out of my personal space, Agent Henderson," I said through gritted teeth. "I'd hate for there to be an incident."

He took a step back and had a strange expression on his face for a moment. Then he threw the papers down on the seat next to me and stalked out of the room. I smiled to myself. At least I had the satisfaction of knowing I'd ruined his enjoyment of kicking me off the case.

I stood up when Michael came back in. He looked angry. He paced back and forth. I walked over to him and placed my hand on his arm. He stopped.

"What's wrong?" I asked.

"They're reassigning me to desk work here at the office. I'm off field duty, pending an internal review." He punched a wall hard enough to crack the plaster.

"Michael, calm down." I could see people looking our way. "Come on, let's walk along and talk someplace private."

There was a terrace on the roof. We went there to talk. It was empty except for a couple of deputy marshals eating lunch in a far corner. We stood at the edge and looked out over the city. It was a gray and dreary day. It wasn't raining, but it looked as if it should have been. Even the birds were quiet.

"Okay," I said. "What's this about reassigning you?"

"They've assigned another marshal to the case. They said I've gotten too personally involved in the case to view it objectively. They're doing an internal review to determine if my actions warrant censure," he said, gritting his teeth to hold in his anger.

"What kind of censure?"

"They could suspend me without pay, fire me, or even prosecute me for homicide," he said.

"You have got to be joking! I thought the use of deadly force was part of your job." I couldn't believe they would do such a thing.

"I'm quite serious. It's unlikely that anything will come of it. I am off the case, though. As soon as the review says I'm fit, I'll be assigned another case. The idiots have reasoned that Julia will go to ground someplace else for a while, since her brother's death." He shook his head sadly.

"What she's going to do is come after me," I said.

"Yes, I think that's most likely. I may not be able to actually work the case, but I will keep an eye on you, rules or not."

"Thanks. Just eyes?" I teased.

He looked too serious. "There's something else."

"What is that?" I was afraid to know.

"You are no longer on the case. They want the badges destroyed, and you're to have no further contact with this office or the fugitive."

I laughed. "I know about being off the case; Henderson made sure of that. As for no contact with the fugitive, tell Julia that. Who are they trying to kid?"

"Themselves," he said. "They still think this is a normal case. The bodies must just be an error on our part, not the fact that Julia has her own army. It's crazy."

"So what're we going to do? Are we going to track Julia on the side?"

Michael stared at the wall. "I've been ordered to cease all involvement with you. My relationship with you is considered to be inappropriate."

"What are you saying?"

"Until this is all over, I can't see you, and maybe not afterward, without losing my job," he said.

"Just like that? You can't see me anymore? Don't you care about...?" I stopped myself. Neither of us needed this right now.

"I'm sorry, Michelle." Michael looked at his hands.

I turned away and walked across the terrace to the door for the elevator. I just wanted to be home with my cat. Michael made no attempt to follow me. I wasn't sure what that meant. My Jeep was in the parking garage. I got in it and left. I think I drove around Cincinnati for a while before I headed home. My thoughts were confused.

I cared for Michael a great deal. It's true that I'd known him for only a couple of weeks, but we'd been together a lot during that time. We'd been through some dangerous events and had seemed to grow closer. I was hesitant to say that I loved him; it seemed too early for that. I was certainly more interested in being with him than I had been for anyone in a long while.

I stopped and got dinner at a drive-thru. I hadn't been eating right recently. I was going to have to be careful about that. I ate on the way home. I was careful when I got there. This wasn't the time to get too relaxed. I walked through the house with my gun, checking every room.

Samson was meowing piteously at his food bowl, which was empty. I keep the food bag open next to it, and I could tell he'd been eating from the bag, but he likes to make me think he's always on the edge of starvation. From the size of his cat butt, I'd say that it would take more than one missed meal for him to waste away.

I checked my mail and paid some of my bills. There was some paperwork from my insurance agent I needed to fill out. I took care of all that before going to bed. Sometimes you need a mundane distraction.

Samson curled up under my chin, and I fell asleep listening to him purr.

CHAPTER SIXTY-EIGHT

I needed groceries.

My house felt empty. It had been a week or so since I'd been alone, without someone to talk to. I found that I didn't like it so much anymore. I kept thinking of things I wanted to talk about, but no one was there when I turned to say them. Nothing I did seemed to help. I found myself walking from room to room, looking for someone. I sat in the kitchen and remembered conversations Michael and I had. I missed his quirky smile and bright green eyes.

I hadn't heard from Michael since we had parted the day before. He was in a lot of trouble over Christopher's death. I think the Justice Department just wanted a scapegoat for what happened at the safe house. They looked around and said, *Tag! You're it!* Michael was probably still filling out paperwork. Hopefully, once things settled down, he'd come by, and we could talk. I needed to know how he felt about me, about us.

I ached for him. But I was also a bit afraid of him. He was a link to a past I wasn't so sure I wanted to remember. The longer I was around him, the stronger the memories became. It was as if the two of us formed a gestalt that facilitated the failure of the memory blocks. So much of what I remembered hurt. I was worried about what I would dream next.

There wasn't anything interesting left to eat in the house. Most of the food in my refrigerator had gone bad days ago, the victim of eating out too much. I'd made tea, and it had gone cold while I wandered around the house. I discovered that Earl Grey tea is quite nasty to drink when it's cold.

Moping about the house was doing me no good whatsoever.

I needed to get out and do something. I was worried about Julia, but I couldn't live my life in constant fear of attack. I had to get on with things. If she made more trouble for me, I'd just have to deal with it as it came up. Being at home didn't make me any safer, anyway. Not when she had her own private military company.

It was raining.

It wasn't the heavy downpour of a spring shower, but rather the slow, steady drizzle of late autumn that doesn't even make an interesting sound, just a low, weeping murmur of droplets hitting the ground and leaves. The dark, turbulent sky didn't make me feel any better. But then, if the sun had been out then, I would have thought it obscene.

I was one with the weather, for once.

Let it rain.

I was in no mood to be driving far or dealing with hordes of people, so I went to a smaller, local grocery store. It was more expensive than Walmart, but I was past caring about trivial things like that. I penny-pinched out of habit; I'd been poor for too much of my life. I wasn't in a state now to care about anything. I parked in the first spot of an almost-empty row and got out of my Jeep. Something immediately felt wrong, and I turned in time to see someone running at me from behind.

I didn't have time to wonder how I'd been found so quickly.

He had a knife in his hand. He was dressed in black and had eyeliner on. I planted a kick in his stomach. That stopped him. His breath came out in a rush, his eyes widened, and his mouth made a comic O of surprise. His momentum knocked me back into my Jeep.

That was when I saw the others.

They must have followed me. Lucy's people were getting out of cars all around me. I *assumed* they were Lucy's people, anyway. They all had the same undisciplined look. I cursed my carelessness as I reached into my jacket and drew my pistol. I vowed to myself that they wouldn't get me without a fight. I wiped my wet hair out my face and stepped forward to meet the next two who were running up.

They were unarmed and slid to a stop when they saw the gun. The one I'd kicked was getting up, holding his chest. A thrown knife hit me in the leg. Luckily for me, it hit hilt first. I spun and shot the person who'd thrown it, just as she was drawing back her arm to throw another one. The shot was incredibly loud, echoing off the buildings. The blood was oddly bright in the gray, pearly light that filtered through the clouds.

I turned in a circle and shot anyone armed. This was not the time for squeamishness. My life was in danger. They screamed and cursed. I heard shouts in the parking lot and squealing tires. The tires sounded close.

I heard a car engine rev and spun just in time to see the car before it hit me. It wasn't going very fast, maybe twenty miles per hour, but I was thrown over the front. I rolled off the hood before it could carry me away from my Jeep. My legs hurt so badly that I could barely stand; the muscles began knotting as I stood. They hadn't hurt that badly when I broke them in the expressway accident, but they still fucking hurt.

The goths closed in around me.

I felt a line of fire along my left arm. I cried out. The man who cut me was reversing his grip for another slash. I slapped the knife away from him and shot him in the face. That stopped everyone for a minute. Guns are so much louder than they're made to seem on television. I fired a few shots low to hit legs and give me some space. The others just closed in as their friends fell.

There were too many of them. I had to use my pistol like a set of knuckle-dusters after I ran out of bullets. I had another mag in my pocket, but no time to do anything with it. I could hear sirens in the distance. I actually hoped they'd get here soon. I knew I'd go to jail, but at least I would be alive. I was confident that I could explain what happened. It was self-defense, after all. There had to be thirty or more goth attacking me.

Michael would surely come to my defense. Having a federal marshal vouch for me should be worth something. I was sure he would. I was beginning to think I would make it out of this alive.

I was still fighting hard for my life.

I had to make every punch and kick count.

I think it was a baseball bat that finally got me, or maybe a length of pipe. Whatever it was, something crashed into the back of my head, and there was a bright flash. I blacked out for a moment. It was long enough for my attackers. I regained my senses just before I hit the ground. My empty pistol dropped from my numb fingers.

I managed use my arm to block most of the next hit from the bat. Pain shot through me, and I blacked out again. Then I was on the ground, rolling and trying to get up. They were kicking me and beating me. There were so many; I lost count of the number of actual hits. I tried to catch the bat but just ended up with bruised and broken fingers.

I couldn't do anything but try to survive. There was just a long river of pain that flared suddenly before everything went black.

Sometimes being able to take a lot of punishment is not an asset.

CHAPTER SIXTY-NINE

I woke up in tremendous pain.

Just about every square inch of my body hurt. I felt as if I'd been kicked and beaten... which, of course, I had. I was laying on my side a small, dark room; I think it may have been a closet or a pantry. The space held a strong smell of urine, vomit, and feces. I checked myself, but it wasn't from me. That meant I wasn't the first person to be kept in there.

With that thought, a wave of terror swept over me. Then I was hit with images of pain and suffering, brutal gang rapes and torture, often combined. I struggled to regain control of myself. It was hard to do. There was so much anguish in that small room. Many people had been reduced to bleating animals by torture there. Even after I got my mental barriers up, I could feel the force of their suffering beating against me. I doubted I was going to be able to sleep in a place like this. Lucy had done that on purpose, I was sure. She knew what my specialty was. She knew the psychic traces in there would almost drive me mad.

I guess she figured it made the rest easier.

I'd been stripped, but it didn't feel like anything worse had been done to me. Not yet, anyway. I tried to keep that thought from surfacing, but I knew that sooner or later, someone there was going to try to rape me. I wondered if it would be easier to kill them or just let it happen. I decided that if they tried it, I'd fight until I was dead or unconscious again. I would never submit willingly. I would do whatever I had to do.

There was pale light coming from under the door. I didn't move to try to look out, though. I didn't want them to know I was awake. I needed to recover my strength, but every minute was a struggle not fling myself screaming against the door. I needed to get out of there. I set my broken fingers, but I didn't have anything to splint them. I'd just have to hope they healed straight.

Sometime later in the day, Lucy came in with two guards. It was hard to keep track of time, so I wasn't sure how long I'd been awake: hours, at the least. I could see the men eyeing me hungrily. I wondered how desperate a person would have to be before a dirty, bruised, and bloody woman looked appealing. I didn't want to know but was afraid I was going to find out anyway.

It was not a comforting thought. I eyed them back with a smirk on my face. I wanted them to know that I wasn't afraid of the likes of them. They were both thin and malnourished looking, probably drug addicts. That thought brought a fear of disease with it. I've been careful my whole life. If I hadn't just been beaten so badly, I would have jumped up and killed all three of them before they scream. As it was, I was lucky just to be able to sit up. It occurred to me that catching a disease was the least of my worries. They would never let me live if things progressed that far.

"Enjoying yourself?" I croaked. My throat was bruised, and I was really thirsty. I didn't think Lucy would care, so I didn't ask for water. Why give her anything else to control me with?

"Yes, actually. You're not such hot shit now, are you?" she asked me.

Lucy truly seemed to loathe me. I still didn't understand it. "Why do you hate me so much?"

She actually looked confused for a moment. Maybe she'd been

expecting me to beg for mercy or something. "You were always so good at everything. You're so good-looking, smart – you had real power. Did you use it? No, you shit it away to become an anthropologist. Then you stepped in and saved the day back in college before I could get any power for myself. You couldn't mind your own business."

"My own business?" I was angry now. "Richard was killing our friends. You were helping him!"

"You!" She kicked me. "You don't deserve to say his name." She kicked me again. I felt some ribs crack. Lucy was a big girl; she had a lot of heft. I cried out. I tried not to, but it hurt too much. She smiled cruelly and kicked me again. She was drawing back her leg for another kick when one of the guys reached over and touched her arm. He then leaned close and whispered something to her; I was too busy whimpering to hear.

"Trying to get out of it easy, are you?" Lucy hissed.

If I couldn't escape, my only hope was to make her kill me. She wouldn't think what I did to her was *easy* if I got the chance.

I managed to get control of my voice. "Heard from Victor recently, Lucy?"

I saw the guards stiffen beside her.

"What do you know about him?" she asked. "How?"

"I know that he's dead."

"Bullshit! You're just saying that to hurt me. You couldn't possibly know anything about him. He's safe. *She* would make sure of that." Lucy was barely keeping control of herself. I had to keep pushing.

"*She*? Who? You mean Julia? I know all about it, Lucy. Julia and I go way back, you know."

"You're a lying bitch."

I laughed; it hurt. "Victor is dead, Lucy. I shot him. He screamed like the bitch he was as he died, and I stood there and..." She kicked me again, in the stomach, knocking the air out of me. Then she turned away from me for a few minutes.

"You'll regret that, Michelle. It doesn't change anything, really.

We will still have everything of yours that we want. Trust me, we will have everything from you before the end. Your power will be ours, and Victor's, too."

I had no idea what Lucy was talking about, but I was afraid she was going to tell me. She must have thought I'd taken Victor's power or something. The dumb bitch didn't know that Victor didn't *have* any powers; he was just a charismatic psychopath. It hadn't occurred to me before that Lucy wanted me for my psychic powers.

She squatted down next to me. I wanted to kill her, but I was too busy gasping for breath from her kicking me. "Stay with me, sweetheart." She caressed my face, then other parts of me. I wanted to puke.

She stood and gestured to one of the guys. He left the room and came a few minutes later with a bucket. He threw it on me: ice-cold water. I shrieked, and they all had a good laugh. I lay there shaking, muscles spasming. If I could just have long enough to recover some strength, I would kill them all.

I was starting to lose my mind, I realized suddenly.

I've never thought like that, seriously planning to kill.

"I just want you to be able to follow along. Are you listening to me?" Lucy demanded. She slapped me hard.

I met her eyes. I was thinking of what I would like to do to her. She paled slightly but continued in a rush. Not so tough after all. I would have chuckled if I could have.

"Tomorrow, we're going to have some fun together. All of us together." She waited for a reaction from me. I just stared.

"We are going to tie you to my altar and use you. All of us." She ran a hand down across her breast and belly. "Then I'm going to cut you slowly into a thousand pieces. I'm going to burn you and use electricity and anything else I can think of to get every last bit of suffering from your flesh before you die. You're not my first, Michelle. I know how to keep you screaming all day long. I'm going to make it last. Then, at the end, I might let you die, or maybe just leave you to be a plaything for my boys." She laughed, and there was a hysterical note of madness to it.

It was different from the madness I'd felt from Julia. Julia was consumed with hatred for those who had hurt her; Lucy was mad with envy.

I wondered what had happened to turn her into this creature before me. I vowed to fight hard enough that they had to kill me. I'd not submit to that fate. Lucy had made a mistake. She thought she was feeding my fear, but she was just fueling my hatred.

I smiled at her.

That scared her. She took a step back.

"I just want you to know something, Lucy," I said calmly. I wasn't in control anymore; my rage had taken over completely. "I will have no mercy when I break out of here. I've escaped worse. You know what I am. You know what I can do. You think your childish torture comes even close to what I've endured?" I sat back against the wall and smiled with my cracked, bleeding lips, and then I carefully licked the blood from them.

I could feel their terror, and that fueled my rage.

CHAPTER SEVENTY

They backed out of the room and slammed the door.

That should buy me a little time. I could feel a part of me already screaming inside. I'd felt each thing Lucy had said; she'd done those things before to other women.

I'm not ashamed to say that I got sick. I didn't have anything in my stomach, but the dry heaves were bad enough. A little stomach acid came out. I didn't have anything to wash my mouth with afterward. The pain in my ribs flared again, but it helped me focus.

I don't know how I managed to fall asleep, but I must have. I was awakened by the door opening. I kept my eyes almost closed. I could just make out a single figure, who came in and carefully closed the door behind him. I waited for him to get close before I gathered myself. I heard him unzip his fly, and then I struck.

I uncoiled like a cat and launched myself into him. I still hurt everywhere, but I could move quickly again. I must have gotten *some* rest earlier, because I felt almost like myself. Actually, I felt like the girl in the dream; I may have felt more like myself *then* than I ever have.

I sank my fist into his chest at the solar plexus. He was already dead; he just didn't know it yet. I felt a weird, superimposed consciousness, and I realized the blocks the government project had placed on me all those years ago were finally gone. I was free to be what they had made me to be.

I was nobody's plaything.

I was a killer.

Lucy and her cult thought they could keep me in here and hurt me. They would find out just what they'd locked themselves in with. I was going to tear them apart.

The man stumbled back as the air left him, and I grabbed his throat with one hand and pinned him to the wall. I grabbed his crotch with the other hand and twisted. I cut off his shriek by clamping down harder on his throat. I held him there and enjoyed his pain. No, more than that: I took his energy from him. I needed it. I just held him and drained his life away. I'd never done anything like that before. I don't know what would've happened if I'd continued.

I was hit from behind.

I fell but rolled to my feet almost instantly, crouching and ready. The man I'd been inflicting pain on was crumpled on the floor, crying. Two of the cultists pulled him out of the room, while the others stood guard over me. Then they left me alone again. They didn't say anything to me. I could feel their fear.

They'd never faced anything like me before.

I moved over to the door. I could hear Lucy yelling at the fool who'd attacked me. She was telling him that since he had tried to despoil me before it was time, he would not be able to participate in the morning. He would have to stand guard, knowing what he was missing. The others made fun of him for being beaten up by a woman. They seemed to have forgotten how many of them I'd taken down when they attacked me before. I wouldn't have any more trouble tonight, but I'd have to save my strength for the morning.

I still needed a weapon.

I didn't even have clothes, but the cultists would have weapons. I'd just have to take one of theirs. I wasn't afraid of them. Soon, they would know that. I lay down on the damp, smelly floor and immediately fell asleep. I would dream of killing them all.

INTERLUDE FIVE

I am alone.

This is new for me.

The grass is cold and wet. It feels so good to be outside. I've been running for hours. I'm lost in the woods, but at least I'm not inside. I can hear the baying of the hounds, but they sound far away.

I miss the boy so badly, it hurts. Why couldn't he be here with me? Because I left him behind.

Why didn't I help him? I keep seeing shapes in the fog that look like him.

The boy and I had been running. Running the way we seem to always be in these damn dreams. We'd made it through the keypad-locked door. We thought we were safe. We were running, and suddenly there was a tranquilizer dart sticking out of his neck.

He screamed and fell. I knew I couldn't carry him. I should have tried. I stood and stared at the dart sticking out of his neck. His lips were moving, but no words came out. I think he was telling me to go.

I turned and ran. I heard voices behind me. I kept running.

I'm running down a corridor. My footsteps echo loudly. There is light ahead, a window looking out on a grassy field. Outside. I hardly even remember what outside is. I run past it to the emergency door. Please let it open. Please.

The door sets off an alarm as it opens. I don't care. I think I've been shot for a moment, but it is just the sound of the door slamming against the wall as I burst through it. I'm outside and running across the field. The boy was so close. Maybe I could have dragged him. I should have tried.

I can't stop running.

I just run and run and run.

I can hear a roaring ahead.

I'm at a river now. I slide down a steep bank, scraping my legs. The water is high and cold. There is a small waterfall here. I try to cross, but the stones are slippery, and I fall in. The dark water takes me and sweeps over me.

I'm falling, tumbling in the water.

Then I plunge into a deep pool. I'm struggling to get back up to the light. The water is swift and powerful. I'm so cold. I can feel my overworked muscles beginning to knot and my lungs aching for breath.

I wonder if I'm going to die here.

I'm not sure I care.

If I make it out of the water, I know I'll just keep running.

It's all I ever seem to do.

CHAPTER SEVENTY-ONE

There is a certain calm that comes over people who are going to die.

At least that's what they say. I didn't believe it. This was the day that Lucy was going to kill me, and there was nothing I could do about it. I was so scared that I was shaking.

The feeling of power that had come over me the night before was gone. I hadn't slept as well as I'd hoped. My short periods of unconsciousness were punctuated by terrible dreams. At least those were mostly of the regular nightmare type, brought on by my situation and environment. The room was freezing cold, and the fact that I was still wet from having water thrown on me didn't help.

The room was getting lighter; it must be dawn.

It was almost time for it to begin.

The dream that *hadn't* been a regular nightmare was going to haunt me for me for a long time. I'd betrayed Michael, back in the project. I had run and left him behind. He would have carried me out. If he couldn't have carried me, he would have stayed and fought the cultists over my body. I know that. I know I should have done that, too. I don't know why I didn't.

All I could feel from the dream was an overwhelming sense of sorrow and fear. I wondered if Michael remembered what had happened. I had a feeling that he did. Would he abandon me now, when I needed him most? I couldn't think about it. I needed to think about what I was going to do to help myself. I couldn't rely on anyone else.

I tried to make a plan for escape, but nothing came to mind. There had to be some way I could get free. I knew I would fight when Lucy and her goons came in to get me. I also knew there were too many of them for it to do me any good. If I could've out-fought them, I wouldn't be locked in a closet in their house.

It was eerily silent throughout the house.

The cultists had stayed up late into the night, partying and drinking; I guessed it must be early morning now. They'd talked loudly about the fun they were going to have. I don't think they even thought of me as a person. I was a *thing* to them: a thing to be used.

They would be coming for me soon.

There was a loud popping noise outside the room. I jerked upright. I knew that sound. There was another, louder, and then a short scream. I listened closely. I could now hear low voices as someone moved through the house. There was a short stutter of automatic gunfire. I heard a man cursing, then a scuffle. I think it was in the kitchen. I heard what sounded like a pot hit the floor.

After that, I think the rest of Lucy's people were awake. I could hear a lot of screams and an occasional gunshot. The screams became ragged, as if someone was being tortured. After a while, the screams ended. I wondered what had happened. Part of me suspected a trick.

I wasn't sure if I should call out or not. Something told me not to. I held back in the corner of my cell and waited. I could hear doors opening and closing throughout the house, as if someone was searching for something... or someone. Had Michael found me?

The door opened to my cell.

No, not Michael. Julia.

She just stood there, shining a flashlight at me, and then she laughed. It was not a pleasant sound. She gestured, and four of her men came into the cell with me. I was suddenly very afraid of what was going to happen. They told me to stand up and then cuffed my hands behind my back. A black gag went into my mouth. I didn't resist. They were armed, and it wasn't the time to try to resist. Julia would almost certainly kill me, but she'd do it quickly. I knew that. She had no love for the things she'd done. She'd just wanted justice.

They led me out of the room. Julia and her team had killed everyone. It looked as if none of her people had even been wounded. I wondered, as we walked, what exactly Julia was trying to do. Why were these people working for her? Surely they hadn't all been part of any project. Most of them were too young to have been in the same one as we were. They were mostly in their twenties. They looked and moved with military precision.

I hadn't seen Lucy yet. I wondered if she had somehow escaped. Then Julia's people led me through the living room. The vamps had set up the altar near the fireplace. Lucy's head had been torn off and placed on it. Several of the dead were arranged to look like they were praying to it.

We paused in the room so I could have a good, long look.

Julia asked me how I liked her handiwork, and then she started laughing. I thought it a bit in poor taste, even for her. Her laugh had more than a little madness in it. I couldn't reply, of course; that damn gag was the type with the black rubber ball, and my jaw was starting to ache.

I didn't hear anyone else laughing. We moved on toward the door. Just before we went out, they put a black sack over my head. Someone wrapped a blanket around me. At least I'd be warm.

The rest of the trip was in darkness. I was put into a vehicle and driven for about half an hour. There were a lot of turns and sudden stops. We might have been in a city. When we finally stopped for good, a few minutes passed before I was led out and into a building. I could hear my footsteps echoing. I was cold.

Julia took the sack off of my head and uncuffed me. She then walked out of the room. Two guards came, took me into a white-tiled room, and hosed me down with lukewarm water. I was glad of that, even though it hurt.

I'd gotten some really nasty stuff on me in Lucy's cell. The water washed away more than just the filth from the floor. Water carries away all our sins.

I still couldn't believe Lucy was dead. I knew I should feel something. Anger, regret, even happiness would have been good. I felt nothing. At least I wouldn't have to worry about her attacking me anymore. I had known Lucy for over ten years. I think I'd had trouble believing that she'd really been involved in the murder of our friends in college. I hadn't wanted to believe it. After what she had said to me while I was in her captivity, I knew she had been the motivating force in those attacks. That was hard to deal with.

They toweled me off quickly and led me to another room where Julia was waiting. She had a large syringe in her hand. I was not going to let her put that in me. As weak as I was, they still had to call in more guards to hold me down while she sank the needle into my neck. The room began to spin, and my awareness washed away on the tide of euphoric sleep.

CHAPTER SEVENTY-TWO

There is an old saying about frying pans and fire. I couldn't help but think of it as I was brought before Julia the next day. Julia's soldiers had given me a plain gray shirt and pants to wear. It was better than nothing; at least I wasn't naked. I didn't sense any strong emotions from the guards. I was just a prisoner to them.

I must have a real knack for pissing people off. I expected Julia to be angry with me for the death of her brother. She was, but not angry enough, though. She just sat and looked at me as I stood before her.

"Are you going to kill me, Julia?" I finally asked. "If so, just do it."

She sighed. "No. As much as I would like to, you are too valuable for that."

I'd hoped she would just shoot me and get it over with.

"I'm afraid you've got the wrong person. I'm not worth much. I doubt anyone I know could come up with much money." I fleetingly thought of Lawrence. He might have the resources to do something, but I'd keep that for an ace in the hole.

But Julia had other plans for me. "No, Michelle. You misunderstand me. I have no intentions of asking for money for you. Not directly, anyway. I want the use of your skills. Your combat training, reflexes, and strength would be highly useful."

"Sorry, not interested. I never saw myself as the mercenary type."

"You think I'm a merc?" she said with a laugh. "Oh, you've going to be fun to have around."

"Okay, what do you call all of this, then?"

"A black-bag operation."

I must have looked incredulous.

"Do you think all of these resources just sprang out of my ass? This is a government-sponsored operation. Look, I've been tasked with cleaning up after the project, and with bringing you in. I need to know I can trust you."

I laughed bitterly. "You can trust me to put a bullet in your head if I get the chance."

"Michelle..." She paused for a moment. "Let me tell you a story."

She settled back in her chair and then began.

"When I was in federal prison, my life was hell. I was kept mostly in solitary, sometimes for weeks without seeing the light of day. It got to me. One day, they took me out of my hole in the basement of the prison to see a psychiatrist. I went prepared to give the guy hell."

She paused to see how I was taking this.

"Why were you in prison?" I asked.

"It doesn't matter. Anyway, when I got up there, I just sat and looked out the window. The doc didn't say anything. Just watched. After a while, I got bored and tried to needle him a little. It didn't work. He gave me the creeps. He reminded me of the doctors at the project. Right before the guards came back in, he asked me a single question."

"What was that?" I asked. She seemed to want a reply.

"He asked me if I wanted revenge for the Providence Project."

"You said *yes*, of course."

She smiled predatorily.

"He told me to be ready when the time came. That I'd know what to do. Then the government shoved my ass back into solitary for a month. I was going bug-nuts. One day the guards came in and put me in chains. Then they escorted me out to a prison transport. I was being transferred out west to an underground facility. I lost hope of ever being free again."

"So what happened?" I was curious in spite of myself. She seemed sane just then. I wanted her to stay that way until I could escape.

"There was a key to my cuffs taped under the edge of the seat. I escaped; I had to kill to do it. The agency the psychiatrist was from must have had agents in the towns around there. They found me quickly. I was assigned to command this unit. On paper, it's just another PMC. The reality is much different."

She leaned forward. "I'd like you to join us. My assignment now is to take out those responsible for what happened to us. Isn't that something you want?"

"Of course it is," I snapped. "But what's the price, Julia?"

"We have to work for the government that allowed this to happen."

"I won't do it."

"You may not have a choice, Michelle."

"Kiss my ass."

She shook her head, frowning. "If you'll not join voluntarily, I've been ordered to force you. We'll have to reprogram you. You're far too flippant now. You used to understand the power of a command structure."

"We can't seem to get away from what we learned in the project, can we?" I said.

"Maybe not, but it did give us useful skills, don't you think?"

"I've never been all that interested in using them. I like my life the way it is."

"You can't escape them, Michelle. Someone would have come for you eventually."

"Fuck you."

She sighed. "I guess we can start the reprogramming process in the morning. I think you need today to rest. You've been through a lot recently. I'll have the medic come by later."

"I hope that's a painless process. I'm kind of delicate," I said sarcastically.

"I'm afraid not. It's not as easy to reprogram a human as it is a DVR. There's an established procedure developed just after the Second World War for this sort of thing."

"I don't suppose you'd just hire me freelance. I'd give you good rates, since we're such great friends." My mouth seemed to have a mind of its own.

She smiled, though. "I can't trust you, or I would take you up on your offer. As much as I would like to kill you for what you did to Victor, I won't. He knew the risks when he volunteered to go on that operation. At least you made it quick. This has nothing to do with that."

"He was going to kill me, Julia. One of us had to die. I chose him. You saw what he was into. What Lucy was into."

"Of course; I would have done the same. I just wanted you to know that this isn't about revenge. I save that for the doctors of the project."

"So is this reprogramming a quick thing?" I asked. "If so, let's get it over with." I didn't really want to know about it, and I was trying to think of a way to escape.

She shook her head. "No, Michelle. There is no quick way to destroy a stable human mind. You're already tougher than most people. It will take weeks of treatment before you are ready for the hypnotic implant personality we have prepared."

"Treatment?" I asked, hating myself. I could feel the room starting to spin.

"It is mostly psychotropic drugs, extreme electroshock, and torture," Julia said emotionlessly. "That is most effective in cases like this, where the subject needs to be physically functional afterward."

"I can see this is really getting to you," I said.

"I'm not a monster, Michelle."

I tried not to laugh. "No, you're a fucking psychopathic bitch. You always were Dr. Green's little pet." That was hitting below the belt.

She grew deathly pale, then flushed. I saw her hands clench. "Get her out of here," she said to the guards.

I'd been saving that little gem, hoping to make her angry enough to kill me.

She was in too much control for that, though.

Her plan might already have been working on me. I was so scared I couldn't think. I had long since given up any hope of rescue. Even if Michael had wanted to help me, there was no way for him to find me now. I didn't even know if anyone had noticed I was missing.

The guards led me back to my cell. I wasn't bound or cuffed or even drugged. There didn't seem to be any reason to do that now. Julia knew I wouldn't kill myself; not yet, anyway. I had a feeling that I wouldn't have another chance. I just couldn't do it. Not while there was the slightest chance of getting out of this.

I wondered if that was part of the torture.

They didn't give me any food, but they did bring me some water. There was a hole in corner that could only be a toilet, from the smell. I stayed away from that except when I absolutely had to. I was so hungry my stomach felt like it was eating itself. I knew that it was my body's fast metabolism. I could heal quickly; I also had to eat a lot or it didn't do me any good. Again, Julia knew all about it. I'm sure she was trying to make sure I was too weak to resist.

I decided that my one chance would be in the morning. Maybe they would only send one guard. If I was lucky, I could take him out and have a weapon. Then I'd have a fighting chance. I laughed. I was starting to daydream, but I needed to do something or I was going to lose it.

I paced around my cell. I was cold, but not dangerously so. I worked through my thoughts. Much of that odd disassociation was fading. I felt more like myself again mentally. I also had something else. That knot of rage I used to carry locked up inside me was now free in my mind. It was more diffuse now. Maybe confronting all of this in the way I had been was really good for me. I used to think it was the rage that allowed me to fight so well when I needed to. I knew better now. I knew that from then on I would be able to do whatever I needed to do.

I hoped.

I practiced Tai chi until I couldn't move anymore. I curled up on the floor and thought about Michael. I hoped that he was looking for me. I needed to believe that he was. I don't know if the Tai chi helped my body heal, but at least I fell asleep quickly.

CHAPTER SEVENTY-THREE

They were going to start my reprogramming that morning.

I was determined to fight to the death. I knew that Julia knew it, and I was worried. She would have made plans for my resistance. I tried my best to figure out how to take out the guard or guards when they came for me.

It did me no good whatsoever.

Two guards came in the cell while a third stood back with a rifle and covered them. They asked me quite politely to get up.

I sat up and gave the guard who had spoken a look. "You're planning to torture me for the next six weeks. Why be polite?"

He looked uncomfortable. "We're professionals. We do what we're told. It's going to be bad enough for you. Why make it worse?"

I nodded and stood. I think I understood that. I was thankful anyway. I decided to act coy. I was covered with bruises and scabs from the fights I'd been in so recently. I was hoping they might underestimate me a little. The guards looked uncomfortable. I wondered if I could use that.

"Do you have orders not to talk to me?" I asked innocently.

The two in the room exchanged glances. "No, not as such. As long as you don't resist and come along and do as you are told, there is no reason to restrain you or not talk to you. What do you want to talk about?"

"You've seen Julia fight? You know what she is?"

"We know about the Providence Project. Mostly, anyway. Colonel Owens' abilities are known to us. This way, please." He pointed out the door.

I smiled and walked out the door. The guard in the hall looked even more nervous. "You know about me, then," I said as I walked.

"I'm sorry, I don't understand," he said. The others were silent.

I turned and met his eyes. "You know I'm from the same project, don't you?"

He swallowed nervously and said, "Maybe we should just walk."

I smiled and followed the lead guard. I had a slight psychological advantage now. I needed to figure out how to use it. I felt something that made me stop in my tracks. I could sense Michael at the edge of my awareness. He was nearby.

Suddenly there was the sound of gunfire and helicopters, screams and curses. The guard with the rifle told me to stand with my face to the wall and my palms flat against it. He pressed the barrel of the rifle into my back between my shoulder blades. That was a mistake. Now I knew where the gun was. The other two guards ran off to see what was going on.

As soon as they were out of sight, I spun and sank my right thumb into the guard's left eye up to the second knuckle. He screamed and dropped the gun, clutching his ravaged socket. I walked behind him as he fell to his knees, weeping, and broke his neck. It was almost too easy.

I was glad he hadn't voided himself when he died. I stripped the outer layer of clothes off him and dressed. The uniform was too big, but I felt better with a uniform and boots on, even if the boots did feel like clown shoes. I hoped I'd be mistaken at first glance for one of the regular guards in the area. He had a pistol along with the rifle; I took both.

Outside my holding cell, the place looked as if it had been

converted from a large warehouse. Most of the walls were prefabs. The room I had been in was along one wall and looked to have been part of the original construction, maybe administrative offices or something. I briefly wondered if there were any other prisoners.

There were florescent light fixtures every few meters.

I encountered the first guards in the second hallway I entered. They slid to a stop when they saw me and started to shout. My rifle stitched lines of bright red holes across their chests. I didn't stop to check them. I ran to get out of the area.

I emptied the rifle on the way out of the building. It's amazing how quickly ammunition can run out. I wounded or killed half a dozen men, though. I finally found a door to the outside after maybe ten minutes. I drew my confiscated pistol and worked my way through the crates outside the building. Seen from the outside, I could tell it was definitely a warehouse of some kind. It looked a bit familiar, but I couldn't place it.

It wasn't quite cold outside, but not warm either. The sky was cloudy and threatening rain. I could hear traffic noise from the surrounding city. It looked as if we were somewhere in Newport. That wasn't my favorite part of town, but I'd still be happy to be there. A chain link fence surrounded the property, with those little strips of plastic woven through it to discourage prying eyes.

I was nearing the edge of the warehouse when the pistol was knocked out of my hand. I lashed out with my left and caught Julia in the jaw as she stepped around the corner of the building. She staggered back, looking surprised, and I went after her with a kick. I was too weak for that, and fell. I rolled to my feet, ready to be hit. Julia was gone. I saw her running. I could hear shouts from behind me. The police must be getting close. I couldn't just let her get away. I looked futilely for the gun for a second and then gave chase.

The fighting had been bloody and brutal at the edge of the compound. Everywhere lay dead or wounded policemen, and Julia's people, too. The ground was slick with blood. Many of the bodies still twitched or moaned; one of them off to my right was screaming raggedly.

I ignored everything and focused on Julia.

I needed this to end.

CHAPTER SEVENTY-FOUR

Julia went through a small, unobtrusive gate, and I followed warily, suspecting another ambush. She wasn't there. I caught a glimpse of her running through a wooded area to my right, and took off after her. I was getting winded. I'd been through too much. My ribs hurt. I was tired, hungry, and bruised.

I was also really pissed off.

I caught up with Julia on the small pedestrian bridge that spans the Licking River. We were both unarmed and about the same build, but she was in much better shape than I was. I'd had a rough weekend.

She smiled as I neared.

"Looking for revenge, Michelle?" she asked. She leaned against the railing and looked at the swift water, catching her breath.

I shook my head. "You know better than that."

She cocked her head. "Do I?"

"I just want it to be over. The project was a long time ago. You need to move on." I edged closer. "Let it go, Julia."

"I can't. It wasn't so long ago for *me*. I never truly got away from it." She looked tired.

"You *are* away from it. Just drop it and move on," I said

desperately.

"I can't do that. You know I can't. They made me too well. They will never let me just quit." She straightened.

"It doesn't have to end like this."

"You think you can take me?" she asked.

"If you won't leave me alone, what choice do I have?" I stood to bar her path.

She nodded, looked away, and then lashed out with a foot to my head.

I ducked under her kick, wincing, and punched at her thigh. I missed, and she hit me along the side of my head with her forearm. I stumbled, and she barely missed my head with another kick. I darted back. I hated giving ground, but she was too good, and I was in no condition for a fight. I don't know what the hell I'd been thinking. Julia was a trained and skilled killer; I was just a consultant for the police.

I blocked a kick and stepped in to deliver two solid strikes to her sides. She head-butted me and tried for my throat, but I tucked my chin and planted an elbow in her solar plexus. Unfortunately not hard enough to kill, but her air whooshed out, and I was able to step back again.

I would have kicked her at that point, normally, but my legs were too wobbly. I hadn't eaten in days, and I was quite battered and bruised. I delivered another combo of punches to her body and stepped back. I kept circling her, trying to dart in and deliver punches without getting hit.

On my next pass, she got a strike through my guard. I felt ribs crack under her fist and knew I couldn't afford to let her hit me again. I got a rabbit punch into the nerve bundle under her right arm, and she swept my legs out from under me. Her kick knocked me into the rail on the other side.

She lifted me up and bent me over the steel rail. I could feel my spine protesting. I had one hand on her wrist to keep her from crushing my throat. I was getting dizzy. She could have thrown me in the river, but she wanted me dead by her own hand. I wrapped my legs around her and threw my weight to the side. We fell to the pavement. She landed on top of me, and I felt a sudden sharp pricking from my broken ribs, making me cry out. I popped her in the face with my elbow and rolled to my feet.

She stood, wiping her bloody nose, and smiled again. That smile was really starting to get on my nerves. I thought about my chances of getting off the bridge alive, but the odds didn't seem in my favor, so I concentrated on the fight. We fought; neither of us could get a solid hit in. Then she rushed me again. I tried to pivot, but my body was too worn out. I just didn't have anything left. She caught my throat again, and this time I knew I was going to die.

Something wet slapped my face. I saw Julia's eyes widen. Then I heard the report from the shot. It was her blood on my face. I could see it pulsing from the large hole in her chest. I saw past her to Michael, at the end of the bridge. He had a rough bandage around his leg, and his gun was pointed at Julia, ready to shoot again if her had to.

Julia let go of me. Our eyes met, and I suddenly caught a glimpse, as her shield collapsed under the pain of being shot, of what it had been like for her: all those years of fear and torment in the project. She stumbled back and fell over the rail.

I cried out and reached for her, but I was too late. She was gone. The river had taken her into its embrace, and she was gone. I fell to my knees and wept. I was too exhausted to move. I hurt so badly, and not just my body. My very soul ached for her. I knew how falling into water like that felt, to be so cold and scared and weak. They worked on us too well at the project; the urge to survive was too strong in us.

It's no wonder we're all insane.

I felt Michael holding me. I wanted to tell him I was okay, but I didn't have any words right then. I just sobbed and looked at the swift water. As my sobs quieted, he helped me to my feet. I could see understanding in his eyes. I realized that he must have known much of what I felt, without me saying anything.

I nodded to him.

As we turned to walk back, we saw Agent Henderson walking out to us. His team was at the end of the bridge. Their guns were held off to the side, alert, but not aggressively. He approached us and leaned on the rail. He'd seen what happened. I had to fight the urge to snap his neck.

"I'm not the villain you'd both like me to be, you know," he said quietly.

We just looked at him.

He smiled sadly. "It's actually funny, you know. They were so afraid that you would find out what Julia was doing." He shook his head and looked out over the river.

I tried to speak, but Michael beat me to it. "What? What are you talking about?"

Henderson met my eyes, then Michael's. "Michelle knows. I'm not from the Office of Homeland Security. Julia was working for a rogue element in our government. They had her taking out all the people who knew about the project. Her orders were to recruit all of the children of the project that she could. Julia, however, was too overcome by her desire for revenge."

"You knew about it?" I gasped.

He nodded. "My job was to keep this from going public, at any cost."

"*You*," Michael suddenly said. "You were the one who leaked the information about Christopher's location to Julia." I heard Michael's knuckles crack as he clenched his fist.

"I did. I leaked the information to her through an agent I had on the inside of her organization. That agent was shot during the raid on the safe house." Henderson met my eyes. "We dug six silver bullets out of him. Witnesses said the shot was made at seventy-six yards with a pistol. Congratulations."

"He was the one with the rocket launcher. You son of a bitch..." I started toward him. Michael placed his hand lightly on my shoulder. I stopped.

"Yes, but he knew the risks. I'm not concerned about that. The reason I'm here is that we have a serious problem."

"We? What's that?" Michael asked.

"You both know too much," he said.

CHAPTER SEVENTY-FIVE

I suddenly felt even weaker. Henderson was going to have us killed, or worse. I would not go back to some damn project. I eyed the river.

Michael must have been thinking the same thing. I felt him shift his weight in that direction. "What in the hell do you mean by that?"

"None of you project kids were ever supposed to meet each other. You never should have been assigned to the case with Julia. I think someone wanted to see how much you could remember. You've made some mistakes in the past and inquired about things that you shouldn't have."

Michael nodded. "I needed to understand what happened to me. You have to know that you'll never take me alive, right?"

"I'm not interested in taking you anywhere. I have certain orders. I also have a certain leeway when it comes to fulfilling those orders."

"How is that?" I asked.

Henderson smiled. "I'm known in the agency as a man who gets the job done, no matter what. Do you plan to go public?"

I laughed. "We'd be considered lunatics, at best. We lost our only credible witness."

"Yes, I made sure of that. I couldn't have this going public. Surely you understand the unrest that would produce. Our nation needs to believe our government would never do anything like that, especially to children. Keep quiet, and my report will state that as far as I could ascertain, you both know absolutely nothing about the project and are likely to remain ignorant into the foreseeable future."

"First," Michael said, "why would you do that? Second, why would they buy it?"

"I couldn't believe what I read in those reports about the project. I thought it was a nightmare fantasy on paper, until I saw you both fight. We got CCTV footage of Michelle fighting Lucy's people in the parking lot when they picked her up." He shook his head. Then he met my eyes. "It was amazing. You took damage that would have anyone else curled in a ball, whimpering; you laughed it off and kept fighting. I envy that, but I don't envy what they did to you to make you that way. I wouldn't survive it. To do it to anyone was inexcusable, much less to children. Hell, I've got two kids myself. Do you think I want *them* in some fucked-up project? I think about it, and I get sick inside. I'll give you both all the breaks I can. Don't make me regret it."

"We won't. So that covers the first question," I said. "What about your report?"

Henderson looked out over the river. "One thing I've learned in my years with the government is that they like to think they're infallible. They'll want to believe the memory erasure technique worked on both of you. They'll accept it when I say it's true. They need to, for their own peace of mind. Yours was not the only project out there."

We stood and watched the river.

"What about Julia?" I asked suddenly. I think I was surprised that Henderson didn't have men looking for her along the banks. Maybe he wanted her to escape. Maybe he *was* telling the truth.

"We'll dredge the river. I doubt we'd find the body, even if she's dead. Do you think she is still alive?" His eyes told me he wanted me to lie to him. I glanced at Michael. He shook his head slightly.

"No," I lied. "I don't think she could have lived after being shot by Michael and then falling into the river. The Licking River is known to have a deadly current. She must have drowned."

Henderson looked into my eyes. I could tell he didn't believe me, and didn't care. He straitened up and smiled. "Good. Then this case is closed. I'm sorry about the death of your fugitive, marshal. Excuse me." He walked back across the bridge, gesturing. His men began to disperse.

The regular police and ambulances were starting to show up.

It was all over.

It had to be over, right?

Michael met my eyes and smiled down at me. "Shall we?"

I just nodded and looked out at the river again. I didn't know if I wanted Julia to be dead or alive. I knew I should be hoping she was dead, but she was too tragic a figure for me not feel something for her. I could have *been* her, easily enough.

I hoped that if she was dead, she'd found peace somewhere. Julia was right about me. I would have betrayed Michael again. I would've let her go in peace if she'd told me she would leave me alone. I had a feeling Michael knew that, too.

What I couldn't tell was whether he cared or not.

I was able to walk a little bit with Michael's help. I made it off the bridge before the darkness came, grabbed my hair, and pulled me back down into the deep, cold current that always flows just under the surface of my mind.

CHAPTER SEVENTY-SIX

The sunlight streaming through the windows was pale and thin. It seemed almost as diminished as I felt. I'd awakened in a hospital bed earlier in the day. At least it was a private room. There's nothing quite like sharing a room with another miserable person. I hate hospitals, but I had to admit that I needed to be in one. Even *my* body can't take so much extreme punishment day after day without eventually failing.

I was worn too thin.

Literally. I had lost nine pounds. I know that most women would be rejoicing, but I'd been happy at the weight I was. I'm normally fit and athletic; I felt weak, fragile, and light as a feather. That was probably just the painkillers. Not only had I been badly hurt many times, but I hadn't eaten in days. My body had been in a high metabolic state, trying to heal and continue to function. What the hospital had brought me that morning hadn't quite counted as food.

Michael was sitting by the bed, reading a novel. He didn't look too good, either, but he told me he'd refused medical treatment. The injury to his leg had been only a flesh wound. I'd been unconscious and didn't get a choice about the hospital. I didn't mind. I had no desire to do anything for a while but recover.

I mentioned to him that I was hungry.

"That's good. I'm sure they'll bring you lunch soon. Do you want me to go and ask?"

I shuddered at the thought of hospital food.

"No," I said. "I think I can wait. That's not really food, you know."

He nodded. "Just like the military. SOS: shit on a shingle."

"Thank you so much for that lovely image." I'd been hoping he would go get me something good to eat. Maybe he didn't like me that much after all.

We were quiet for a while.

I thought about my feelings concerning Julia. It felt as if the weeks had flown by since all this had started. I didn't think she was dead. I could almost sense her out there somewhere. I hoped she was okay. I think maybe what we had talked about might have helped her, too. As long as she never came around me again, I would be happy enough. If I saw her again, I would kill her if I had the chance, but that was just survival, not revenge or insanity. Or so I told myself.

I thought about that cold, swift water and shuddered. I could feel myself in that water. I felt as if I was drowning, and knew that it was the rush of so many new emotions causing me so much discomfort. That, and the memories of what that cold water was like.

I knew more about myself now than I'd ever wanted to. I could kill without thought. That was scary. At least I knew that I could always take care of myself. I doubted I would have the nightmares anymore. I knew what caused them. Now they could just be memories, and those fade with time. I would do whatever I had to do to survive. I looked at Michael and wondered what the cost of that survival would be.

"What are you reading?" I asked suddenly.

He looked confused for a moment, and then looked at the cover. "Some sci-fi thing I found in the gift shop. It's all right." He looked like he was just now noticing that he'd been reading.

"Do you think it's finally over, Michael?"

He looked out the window. "For now, yes, I think it's over."

I studied his profile. "You think Julia is still alive, don't you?"

He sighed. "Yes, I do. I think about her wound and her falling into the river, and I wonder if I could have survived. I *think* I could survive. I'm sure you would have. Therefore, Julia is still alive."

"Don't sell yourself short; you'd survive," I said. "Any of the children of Providence would have."

"I know." He held my eyes with his. "They dredged the river this morning."

I nodded. "They didn't find anything, of course."

"Of course." He smiled sadly and sat looking out the window.

"Do you think she'll come back after me?" I asked.

"I don't know. What do you think?"

I hated having my questions turned back on me. That's why I wouldn't go to see a fucking therapist. I could play that game in my own head, thank you very much.

"I don't think she will," I replied. "We talked on the bridge before we fought. It was odd. She was so sad." I felt tears welling up in my eyes and turned away. She and I were alike. She was what I might have become under worse circumstances. I didn't turn back until I was under control again.

Michael looked concerned.

"I'm okay, really. I just get sad, thinking of her growing up in that place. We had it bad, but we were just there in the summers. She was there all the time..." I shook my head. "I just want it to be over, but I want her to be okay, as well."

"I know, but she's still dangerous, Michelle. Don't let your feelings get in the way if you have to do something about her. You know she won't let hers."

"I never let my feelings get in the way," I lied.

He just shook his head. He knew I was lying but didn't call me on it.

"Oh god, I forgot about Lucy. Did they find her...?" I trailed off as the memories came flooding back. So much pain and hatred had been dealt out recently.

"I found her when I tracked you there. I must have just missed you. The damn bodies were still warm. I'm sorry I didn't get there sooner."

He stood and paced.

"Michael, what's bothering you? You've been holding something back on me."

"I've been reassigned," he said.

I nodded. "I remember."

"No, I mean again, a completely new assignment."

I looked at him. There was something odd about how he said that. "What's wrong?"

"I've been assigned to track another woman fugitive. She was last seen in Seattle. She might have been a project child. I leave on a flight this evening. I don't think they're done testing me."

I felt my heart falter. "You'll be back."

He just looked out the window. I could see the tension of his shoulders.

"Michael, be safe and come back to me. I'll be waiting. You still owe me dinner, you know."

He just smiled.

He knew what I meant.

About the Author

Paul B. Spence is a practicing archaeologist who hopes to one day get it right. He currently lives in New Mexico, where all the cool kids hang out, with too many cats.

Like most authors, he had an eclectic career path. He's worked as a retail gofer, a food service monkey, brute laborer, a rennie, a writer for the RPG industry, and many other rewarding jobs that didn't pay enough to feed him or his cats.